DRAGON'S HEIR

DYSTOPIAN FANTASY

ANN GIMPEL

CONTENTS

DRAGON'S HEIR

DRAGON HEIR, BOOK THREE

A Dystopian Fantasy

By
Ann Gimpel

Tumble off reality's edge into myth, magic, and dragons

Copyright Page

Edited by: Kate Richards

ISBN: 978-1-948871-56-3

BOOK DESCRIPTION, DRAGON'S HEIR

Rowan hasn't made a dent in coming to terms with her black-to-his bones dragon father when she gets pregnant. The dragon-child isn't even here yet, but everyone's already fighting over his future.

The third (and last) book in a magic-laced, fast-paced, fantasy trilogy. With dragons.

I'm being pulled nine ways at once. Brand new mating. Brand new pregnancy. Stronger magic than I'm used to. The Nine Worlds are failing. Rot that began on Earth has spread to Vanaheim. Odin knows more than he's telling us, and no one has any interest in working together.

The only thing everybody has in common is a sudden, weird fascination with my baby. The dragons want him raised on Fire Mountain. The Celts want us in Inverlochy Castle with them. Hel hasn't weighed in, but I bet she'd like to see her grandson in Niflheim where she can dandle him on her knees every day.

If it weren't for the catastrophe looming over our heads, Bjorn and I would escape to a distant borderworld and never look back. It's always an option. Good to preserve as many of those as possible

Keep your fingers crossed for me. And my son. See you on the other side.

BOOKS IN THE DRAGON HEIR SERIES

Dragon's Call, Book One
Dragon's Blood, Book Two
Dragon's Heir, Book Three

AUTHOR'S NOTE

If I seem to be on a dragon kick here, it began long ago. My first runaway bestselling trilogy, Earth Reclaimed, had dragons in it. So did my almost-as-successful Dragon Lore series. Dragons have made cameo appearances in other books as well.

Well, maybe slightly more than cameos in the Ice Dragon series.

Beyond dragons, I've had a lifelong love affair with both the Celtic and Norse pantheons. While writing one long-ago book, I swore no Celtic gods. Nope. Nary a one. Well, along about Chapter Five, who should come strolling out of the wasteland but Fionn MacCumhaill, Celtic god of creation, protection, knowledge, and divination.

I gave up to my muse thereafter. She hasn't led me astray yet.

Welcome to another series that blends the Celtic and

Norse pantheons. In my imagination, the deities all know one another. It was a pretty intimate circle filled with petty—and not so petty—squabbling. Add enough acts of unbelievable valor to keep things on an even keel, and the foundations of a story magically appear.

CHAPTER ONE, ROWAN

Odin's gallery in Valhalla was filled to overflowing with delegates from eight of the Nine Norse Worlds. Hel was there representing her realms of the dead and Niflheim. An outraged contingent of frost giants had also staked a claim to Niflheim as their domain. A predictable scuffle ensued that had shifted from curses to the ring of steel on steel. One of Hel's serpents was with her. Its forked tongue lashed in and out, spraying poison at the giants.

Odin crashed a fist down on the scarred wooden table that ran the length of the messy hall. The place had clearly seen better days, and it didn't appear anyone ever cleaned it.

"'Tis not why we are here," he thundered and skewered Hel and three frost giants with his single fog-colored eye. Dark hair spilled down his back in many small plaits tied off with colorful bits of leather.

I'd never seen frost giants before, but I understood why

they'd been named. Icicles clung to their whiskers and dripped down their chests. They wore skins, carried clubs and flails in addition to swords, and looked rather like my idea of caveman warriors. Big ones, though. Humanity's predecessors had been tiny by Norse standards.

The remainder of the room's occupants were interesting as well. I'd never laid eyes on a living dwarf, either, but I had seen the occasional elf.

Hel bowed in Odin's direction. "I hear and obey, my liege." Her huge, black cobra-esque snake slithered to her side and wound around her ankles much like a cat would have.

"Better." Odin still sounded grumpy. "I'll bring the Hunt in to establish order if I have to."

"We doona want them here," an elf shouted. Raspberry hair fell to his feet, and his gossamer wings were decorated with glittery patterns.

"No one does," Hel told the elf, "which is precisely why Odin threatened us with their presence."

"Ye concede Niflheim to us?" one of the frost giants boomed.

"Nay, I doona." Hel's response was acid enough to curdle milk.

Both of Odin's ravens took to the air, cawing as they circled the giants. "I said this topic is closed." Odin's voice was level and even—for once. "If ye canna comply, ye must leave. If ye do, ye will still be bound by today's decisions even though ye had no say in them."

Amid grumbling, the frost giants sheathed their weapons and lumbered to the edges of the hall. Its ceiling was at least four meters tall and supported by rough-hewn beams and upright posts.

Odin took a slug from one of the twin drinking horns draped around his neck. Thor sat to his left, his fair hair spilling down his chest in two thick plaits. Unlike his father, his eyes were more blue than gray. In contrast to his hair, his beard was flame red. Other Norse gods were arrayed around the table. No one had bothered with introductions after learning my name, probably because I was the only one here who didn't know everyone.

Zelli, the copper-scaled dragon I'm bonded to—my right as a Dragon Heir—stood behind me. Dewi, the Celtic dragon god, was next to her, red scales shining like burnished fire. I felt the occasional flare of magic between them and was certain they were chatting up a storm about me and my unexpected turn of events.

I quashed a mental wince. Even within my thoughts, I was so conflicted I was having a hell of a hard time saying the word pregnant. I'd done what I usually do when I felt overwhelmed: pushed the whole mess aside with promises to think about it later.

Not that I didn't have some time. At least I figured I did. I'm part Celtic god and part dragon. Bjorn Nighthorse is sitting next to me. He's my mate. Delight and pride and determination have practically oozed from him since the dragons sensed a hatchling within me. Bjorn carries Norse and dragon blood. I have no flipping idea what this baby will be. I mean, it will look human—probably—but the little creature will be magic incarnate.

We'll probably have to ward the nursery to keep him contained.

I should be paying attention to the meeting, but Odin hadn't said much after censuring Hel and the frost giants. Or maybe he had. I wasn't exactly at the top of my game. How could I be? I had so many questions. How long would I be pregnant? Would it be the normal nine months? Or some other variable? Dragons laid eggs. If I remembered right, it took them something like two years to hatch.

Sooooo, splitting the difference meant I had roughly sixteen months before the birth. Or maybe I only had nine. Or perhaps even less. Magical children have their own timetables. I chewed on my lower lip. Less was unacceptable. I had so much to do even eating and sleeping felt like luxuries.

Speaking of dragons, Quade is bonded to Bjorn. I neglected to mention him, but he's huge and black and part of the dragon gabfest unfolding behind me. Probably, they didn't see any reason to focus on Odin, either. So far, all he'd done was act as a referee. After a couple more transits of the hall, the ravens returned to his shoulders.

Huginn and Muninn, Thought and Memory, were beautiful birds. Twice as large as normal ravens, their black feathers glistened, and their dark eyes shone with sharp intelligence. If legends were true, they flew the length and breadth of the Nine Worlds acting as Odin's spies and feeding him knowledge as they gleaned it.

"Why is no one from Midgard here?" one of the Norse women asked. Golden hair swept back from her high forehead and cascaded to the floor around her chair. Her eyes were the color of polished amethyst.

Thor shot her an annoyed look, but she faced off against him and turned her hands palms up. "Midgard is the focal point of the current attack. It's turned into a wasteland. I assumed mortals would care about their fate, but apparently not." An eloquent shrug held a "let them stew in their own shit" flavor.

It annoyed me enough, I spoke up. "Humans didn't believe in magic. Now they're scared shitless of it. Do you blame them? From where they sit—or cower in ruins, more accurately—magic broke their world. Nothing is left of their old way of life."

"Aye?" The unknown Norsewoman raised a golden brow. "Ye'd still think they might show the slightest interest in their destiny."

An idea flashed through me. "I can secure a representative from Midgard. Probably two or three. They're not mortals, but witches. Would that be good enough?"

Breath whistled through the woman's teeth. "I suppose 'tis better than naught."

I stood, preparing to leave, when Bjorn jumped to his feet. "You're not going alone," he said.

I twisted to stare at him. "Don't be silly. I'll return before you know it."

He stared back. "How were you planning to transport the witches?"

It was a decent question. One I should have an answer for, except I didn't. While I can teleport, witches can't. "Uh, Bifrost?"

"Which is why you need me. The rainbow bridge barely tolerates your presence."

I bristled. Granted, my first encounter with the bridge hadn't been pretty, but it had been resolved courtesy of Zelli's intervention.

"No one leaves," Odin bellowed. "Not until we have crafted first steps to deal with the dark magic flowing unimpeded into Midgard. I've taken care of the witch problem. 'Tis well in hand."

The back of the meeting hall grew indistinct, fluid, and shiny with reds and golds. When they cleared, Nidhogg stepped through a portal. The Norse dragon is pure gold with silvery green whirling eyes. A smaller blue dragon named Ysien followed him into Odin's halls.

The gigantic room was beginning to feel crowded with five dragons and a bevy of Norse gods.

"I heard that last part," Nidhogg rumbled. "I agree with including a witch or two. Eyes on the ground and all that."

Speaking of eyes, I resisted rolling mine. It always slays me when ancient creatures who've been around since the dawn of time spout modern jargon.

I expected the portal to wink out. Instead, it glowed brighter. Patrick and Hilda tumbled through looking frightened out of their wits. I was already on my feet, and I sprinted to them. "It's all right," I shouted to punch through their obvious panic at being shanghaied.

Both witches zeroed in on me. Patrick's harsh expression softened, and the taut set to Hilda's shoulders relaxed a bit. "You brought us here?" he asked.

"Nope. It was Nidhogg. I don't command that kind of

power." Reaching out a hand, I hauled Hilda to her feet, and then Patrick. He was short with thinning blond hair and blue eyes. Patched breeks came to knee level, and he wore a plaid woolen shirt. His feet were bare and dirty, which suggested he'd been working in the garden when Nidhogg's magic caught him up.

Hilda was even smaller than Patrick with steel-gray hair she kept cut short. Her blue eyes held a violet cast that has always reminded me of a field of lupines. A navy-blue denim skirt covered her legs, and she wore a sleeveless red sweatshirt. Like Patrick's, her bare feet were covered with dirt.

"Crap." I shook my head. "The others will be frantic. They must have seen you disappear." The spell I'd started jumped to my call. I'd teleport to the ruins of Inverlochy Castle and reassure everyone.

"I'll take care of it," Ysien said and vanished.

Eyeing the spot he'd stood, I muttered, "Maybe not the best idea." Ysien was far from diplomatic, and I could see him scaring the witches worse than they already were.

"It will be fine." Nidhogg turned his swirling gaze my way. "I instructed him to be gentle."

Gentle and Ysien didn't belong in the same sentence, but I kept my mouth shut and rode herd on my need to control everything. It's always been one of my stumbling blocks.

"Why are we here?" Patrick asked.

"Ye have become the official representatives for Midgard." Odin sounded as friendly as a cornered wolf. "And now that the Nine Worlds are complete within these halls, we can begin. And we shall."

"Official representatives to do what?" Hilda tipped her chin up.

I was proud of her. She had to be stunned by the sheer volume of power humming around the room.

"Why, speak with Midgard's inhabitants. What else?" the blonde goddess replied. "Tell them they must help."

"We'll figure it out," I told Hilda and Patrick. Mostly, I wanted Odin to get on with things. In the grand scheme of how badly Midgard—Earth—was broken, I didn't see mortals playing any role at all.

Ysien shimmered back into view, and the gateway swooshed shut behind him. I wanted to grill him, demand a blow-by-blow account of his time with the witches, but I'd never get it.

I was used to the way the Celtic gods did things. Most of them hated meetings of any kind, so when they all gathered, it was always short and sweet. Didn't take me long to figure out the Norse pantheon loved to hear themselves talk. The blonde goddess turned out to be Freya. I listened through a long-winded rendition of her last few scrying episodes that damn near put me to sleep.

Thor and the giants were reminiscing about a hunting expedition for some mythical beast whose name I couldn't pronounce when Odin's shrill whistle brought their discussion to a halt. It must have signaled someone in the wings because platters of food materialized, carried in by dead warriors.

Many of them stayed and broke bread with us.

I admit I was hungry—feeding two and all that—but I was also frustrated. Not trusting telepathy not to be intercepted, I placed my mouth near Bjorn's ear and murmured, "How much longer?"

A slight shrug told me he had no idea.

Patrick and Hilda sat at a small table off to one side, eating. So far, other than Odin's statement about all the worlds being represented, I couldn't see any reason to have disturbed their day.

Time passed. Quite a bit as the platters emptied.

"We have come to consensus," Odin bellowed.

My eyes widened. We had? I didn't recall any discussion at all—not about anything relevant.

"We will begin with the outer borderworlds and repair the damage to the barrier that keeps them separate from all other worlds."

Talk about a long-game approach. I nudged Bjorn. He shook his head very slightly, which was a warning for me to hold my tongue. Meh. I've never been good with warnings or instructions.

I shot to my feet, unsure if I should raise my hand, or wait for Odin to acknowledge me, or just start talking. He didn't so much as look my way as he rattled off assignments for a couple of groups to assess what needed shoring up. The away teams—for want of a better label—were heavy on dwarves and elves.

I was done being quiet. "Excuse me," I began. "Before you deploy dwarves anywhere, the last batch of evil we battled on Midgard included dwarves. There were also dead sprites, a dead worm-like monster, and huge bats."

I may as well have announced Odin's mother fucked

donkeys. Every scrap of chatter died away. Every eye skewered me.

"Not possible." A dwarf drew himself up to his full height, which wasn't much more than a meter. "Ye should be flogged for spreading lies." He was garbed in dark-brown leather pants and a leather vest. His chest was bare beneath the vest. White hair fluffed around his head, and his eyes glittered like cut sapphires.

Bjorn stood next to me and bowed to the dwarf. "Well met, Gramoli."

"Master Sorcerer." Gramoli bowed stiffly back.

Bjorn circled the table until he stood next to the dwarf. "Please," he invited, "cast a truth net."

"Ye've never given me reason to doubt you," Gramoli muttered.

"Then you will hear me when I say Rowan speaks true. I saw dead dwarves with my own eyes. At least four. They were part of the enemy who attacked witches living in the Celts' old stronghold beneath Ben Nevis."

"Has darkness invaded Svartalfheim?" Odin cried.

Gramoli turned to face Odin and bowed so low, his white beard touched the ground. When he straightened he said, "Not that we ken, my liege."

Bjorn inclined his head toward Odin. "As you well know, much of the surface of Svartalfheim is uninhabited, sire. The dwarves dwell in caves."

"I see the problem," Odin muttered. He extended an arm, index finger pointing at Gramoli's chest. "When ye return, ye will cease mining for however long it takes to do a thorough search for wickedness that may have invaded your world."

"Aye, sire. And if we find aught that doesna belong, we shall kill it."

The ravens must have approved because they broke into a stream of cawing. Odin batted them off his shoulders, and they flew around the room.

"We are done for today," Odin announced.

"No. We are not." I projected my voice to make certain I didn't miss anyone.

He pushed heavily to his feet. "Ye're more trouble than that slutty mother of yours. What is it this time?"

I rolled my shoulders back and stood tall, facing him. Odin didn't scare me. Maybe he should have, but he didn't. Ever since I'd outfoxed his Wild Hunt, I'd grown cocky. "While I agree with shutting off the gates at the far end so no more evil can enter Earth, uh Midgard, it will take a long time. Months, if not years. Meanwhile, Midgard may well crumple under the strain."

I stopped to take a breath. "You overfly it with your Riders. You've seen how bad things are. How mortals have barricaded themselves into rubble piles. They're starving to death, just like the witches were before we found food in Inverlochy Castle and began growing crops to take up the slack."

Odin bared his teeth at me. "Next, ye'll be asking me to provide handouts, set up a welfare system for the poor mortals who were nearly the death of Midgard even afore the Breaking."

I winced. What he said was true. Humans were a bunch

of shortsighted fuckers who'd been intent on draining Earth down to fumes if there was a buck to be made.

"That world is gone," I said. "Long gone. We have to deal with what's left."

"Deal with it, how?" He made hurry-up motions with one huge hand. Damn he was big.

"First off, we must create a permanent seal for the Breaking site. Bjorn and I worked out a stopgap—"

"It's gone by now," Bjorn cut in. "Never was meant to last." He strode back around the table until he stood next to me again.

I nodded. "Once we have a permanent fix that will shutter the Breaking site, we can deal with whatever has already beaten its way through."

I was on a roll, and I kept going, afraid if I stopped, Odin might order me from his halls. "The way I see it," I went on, "this must be a three-pronged approach. Your outer borderworlds barricade plus plugging the Breaking site and doing a search and destroy for remaining evil."

Dusting my hands together, I smiled at him to forestall the predictable: him calling me an upstart bitch and ignoring everything I'd lined out. He narrowed his eye at me. One of the ravens circled back, chittering double speed.

Odin's expression shifted, developed an appraising aspect. Magic prickled as the smell of the sea thickened around me. Too late to ward myself. What the fuck was Odin about? I wasn't especially worried. If he'd wanted to hurt me, he'd had plenty of opportunity, but Bjorn apparently didn't share my sanguine assessment.

He raised a hand. Power shot from it forming a noose

around the flow of Odin's magic. "Leave her be. She is mine."

I wanted to drop my head in my hands. "For the love of all that's holy," I shouted. "Both of you, stop. Odin's not going to hurt me, and I don't require a knight protector."

"Smart wench." Odin offered as close to a smile as he ever came. "Pregnant wench. May I offer my congratulations."

Nidhogg lumbered close; magic probed me again. Different this time. Dragon magic. Buckets of steam followed until I was blanketed in mist. Realization socked me in the guts. I carried his grandson. Batting mist aside, I took a couple of steps back.

"Do not even think about ordering me to sequester myself in a tower—" I began.

The Norse dragon bugled laughter. "Wouldna dream of it. Young dragons can fight by the time they're a few weeks old."

I reflexively splayed a hand over my concave belly. "Not my son," I hissed. "He's going to have a normal childhood, goddammit." Protectiveness enveloped me like an out-of-control fire. I would fight for my child, offer him everything I'd been deprived of. Even if it meant raising him on a borderworld with only him, me, and Bjorn.

Nope. That wouldn't work. He'd need other children to play with. There weren't any. Not on Fire Mountain, nor anywhere else, either. I battled a deeply sinking feeling. Why have a baby at all if his existence was marked by strife from his birth?

I felt more than saw Zelli move close with Dewi right

behind her. Being encircled by dragons is claustrophobic as hell. Bjorn and I stood at the bottom of an abyss surrounded by scales and coated in steam.

"His upbringing will be normal—for a young dragon," Nidhogg said.

His words did not make me feel better, but I've never been one to shy away from conflict. "I get it that he has dragon blood from both sides, but he also has Norse and Celtic genes," I pointed out.

Nidhogg's jaws lolled into a dragon grin. "Aye, child. All of the above. He will carry unimaginable power."

"We must raise him on Fire Mountain," Dewi said, "to ensure he has everything he requires."

"No." Bjorn's voice cut into the argument I was about to float. "This is our child. Mine and Rowan's, and we shall do what we believe best for him."

I raked my hands through my hair. Fingers snagged on my mostly undone braids. Weariness racked me. The baby was barely more than a collection of cells, and we were already haggling over his future.

Meanwhile, Patrick and Hilda had fought their way past dragon legs and flanked me. Both witches hugged me. "I'm happy for you," Hilda whispered into my ear.

Hel slithered through a gap between Zelli and Dewi. Tears shone in her eyes as she hugged first Bjorn and then me. I made a feeble attempt at diplomacy. "Thank all of you for your kind wishes. They're overwhelming. I'm certain we'll, erm, figure things out."

"Best to have the fine points tacked down ahead of time," Nidhogg said. At least he'd quit blowing steam.

"Absolutely." Hel leaned into him, proud grandmother-to-be that she was.

I thanked my lucky stars—and the not-so-lucky ones too—my own mother wasn't in a position to weigh in. Ceridwen would have had ideas of her own, but I felt certain she'd have sided with Dewi, both being Celts and all.

I'd been near the end of my tether before the topic of Dragon-baby showed up. I had to find a way out of Odin's halls before I gave up and teleported away, and the lot of them added rude to my long list of failings.

"Get on." Zelli's words were followed by a jolt of dragon magic that carried me astride her.

I didn't ask where we were going. I didn't care. Away from Valhalla would do it. *"What about the witches?"*

"Nidhogg said he would return them."

The walls of Odin's meeting chamber developed the liquid aspect I associated with teleporting. When the mists around me cleared, we were in front of Bjorn's cottage. I'd have liked nothing better than to let myself in and immerse myself in his lore collection—or fall on my face and sleep for a week. But people were lined up outside his door. I got to twenty and quit counting.

Midgard facing annihilation hadn't been a good enough reason for Odin to relieve Bjorn of his master sorcerer duties. I jumped down from Zelli and pasted a smile on my face. "Bjorn will be here soon. Meanwhile, I'm happy to offer my assistance."

Maybe I have a trustworthy face, but voices blasted me with a variety of problems. I was knee-deep working with a woman whose healing spells had gone awry when Bjorn showed up astride Quade.

"Thanks." He blew me a quick kiss before jumping down from the dragon and settling in to work. Neither of us would get to do anything else until we'd made a dent in the throng surrounding his cottage.

CHAPTER TWO, BJORN

I watched Rowan's form shimmer to nothingness as she teleported away from Valhalla. Gratitude surged she hadn't refused when Zelli told her they were leaving. I understood the wisdom of moving Rowan to a less charged situation. She'd morphed into her irritable side, squared off against Nidhogg, and told him she wasn't about to spend her pregnancy moldering in a tower.

After that, Dewi had announced our child would be raised in Fire Mountain. It's tough to say no to dragonkind. For one thing, they aren't used to it. For another, viewing dragons with reverence is almost hardwired into my makeup.

Good thing Rowan wasn't laboring under that delusion. Dealing with her dragon father, who'd been twisted by evil almost to his bones, probably contributed to her mindset.

I'd had my jaws clamped so hard during Rowan's exchange with Nidhogg, I'd fully expected to hear the crack of breaking teeth. She had no way of knowing, but her outrage had been misdirected. I was who wanted to lock her away, keep her safe while our child grew inside her. One of the deserted borderworlds would be perfect, but I was being a fool.

She couldn't leave the Nine Worlds. Not now when their future was so uncertain. Neither could I.

Quade nudged my back with his huge snout. Heat from his scales was welcome in Odin's chilly halls. He was urging me to leave, but I had something to do before we followed Rowan and Zelli.

Odin and Thor were deep in conversation, heads bent together as they stood at the far end of the room. Odin had announced the meeting was over a few minutes before, and it was clear he'd moved on after lining out a strategy—one he'd clearly come up with on his own absent involvement from anyone. I might live in the Nine Worlds, but I bide in Vanaheim. I'd steered as clear of Odin, Asgard, and the Aesir as I could, only showing up when summoned to work some strain of magic or other.

I had no idea why Odin had gone to all the trouble to summon everyone to Valhalla. There'd scarcely been any discussion about the problem at hand. If Rowan hadn't had the courage to forward her opinions, there'd have been none. Small groups formed throughout the room as representatives from the various worlds crafted plans to carry out Odin's directives.

Patrick and Hilda were presumably on their way back to Midgard, courtesy of a dragon-powered teleport spell. They lacked the magic to travel to the far reaches of the universe where the outer borderworlds were. They might be useful convincing some remaining bands of mortals magic wasn't all bad, though.

If they could get close enough. I've spent time among mortals. They had a way of glomming onto a particular belief and clinging to it no matter what. Once they took a stand, it was very difficult to get through to them. I could only imagine how they interpreted the Breaking. The years since then had turned from difficult to nearly impossible as things like canned goods and other foodstuffs first ran low and then disappeared altogether.

Humans are a clever lot. They may have a whole lot of irons in the fire the rest of us don't know about, but I doubt it. They'd need raw materials, and there weren't any.

I worked my way to where Nidhogg and Hel stood next to one another and inclined my head. There wasn't a simple way to say what I had in mind, so I grabbed the point and went for it.

"I appreciate that you will be grandparents to Rowan's and my child, but until very recently, I had no idea I was related to either one of you."

"Aye, and we're verra sorry about that—" Hel began.

"Nay, we are not," Nidhogg spoke over her.

"Everything happens in its own time," Dewi tossed in from where she still stood on Nidhogg's other side.

I considered telling her she had zero stake in this discussion. No blood ties to Rowan or me or the babe. But if I did that, she'd probably play the Celt card and claim kinship bonds with Rowan, courtesy of Ro's mother being Ceridwen.

"Regardless," I forged ahead, determined to get my message across, "these next few months will be hard enough without the bunch of you working your asses off to manipulate our baby's fate until it falls into a pattern of your liking."

"I shall consult our seers," Dewi said smugly. "They will know where your child should spend his first months."

I tilted my head back and looked up at her. "There's no way you will take this in the spirit it's offered, but I don't care what the blind seers have to say. All of you have been clear the child can't be harmed. Since that's true, it won't matter where Rowan and I choose to raise him. Or how."

I expected fire and ash to rain down on me. Instead, Nidhogg lowered his head until it was close to level with mine. "Some children merely pass through your care. They are not meant to remain by your side. This hatchling is not usual for dragons."

"Or for Norse gods, either," Hel spoke up.

"How can you tell?" I looked from the dragons to Hel and back to the dragons.

"We sense its power," Nidhogg said.

I looked askance at him. "I sense its presence," I said slowly. "It's far too soon to make any other predictions."

"Fire Mountain is by far the preferred location for Geir," Dewi said.

It took me a moment to understand she'd named my son. Annoyance soured my stomach. "Rowan and I shall choose our child's name. And where he is raised. None of this is up for discussion."

"But 'tis his true name," Dewi argued. "Much as Runa is Rowan's."

"We shall speak of this again," Nidhogg said in his best

negotiator's voice. I recognized it from when he'd assigned me spy duties in Midgard.

I shook my head. "We shall not. The topic is closed." A bevy of words jostled for freedom from the confines of my throat. I kept them contained. It wouldn't do any good to tell Hel and Nidhogg I didn't especially trust either of them because they'd been so laggardly revealing themselves as my parents.

Coiling air into a cushion I rode it to Quade's back. He understood, and the walls of Valhalla fell away replaced by an unbelievable crowd of customers outside my cottage.

"The other dragons. They're not necessarily offering bad advice." Quade's deep voice rumbled into my mind.

"This is all so new, I'm not a good judge of anything right now," I told him before I jumped down and waded into the crowd. Rowan was already hard at work. This wasn't the type of thing she normally did, but magic was magic, and hers was strong.

Every once in a while, I glanced her way but never for very long. She was so beautiful, she addled my thoughts. Long red hair fluffed around her in luxuriant curls, and her golden eyes were pinched with worry and concentration. A long black skirt hugged her slender hips and long legs, and a many-times-mended blue tunic swathed her upper body concealing the curves of her breasts. Nearly as tall as me, she was strong and well-muscled. I craved the feel of her in my arms, but we had work to do.

Hours passed before she and I finished with the last of my clients. The dragons were long gone, but I was certain they'd return if we went anywhere. My collection of magical knives and swords was right where I'd left them next to my front door. Somehow, I suspected no one could steal them. They probably wouldn't suffer another's hand without making things damned unpleasant for the would-be thief.

Gathering up the hardware, I followed Rowan and carried the blades inside. Once I'd found a temporary home for the spelled metal weapons, I fell into a chair at the table. She was already seated. "Are you always this busy?" she asked, followed by, "Do you have a Closed sign we could post?"

"No to both. It's been like this for the last fortnight."

"Any idea why?" She furled both russet brows.

"Not really. I've wondered if it has something to do with the rotten places in Midgard spreading to Vanaheim, though."

Rowan supported her head on an upraised hand. "That's my take on it, and I don't like it. Means we have even less time than I figured we did. What the hell is Odin about with his outer borderworld crap? That plan could take years to implement. And why bother to import all those people for his big-ass meeting? He didn't ask for anyone's opinion."

"I've never been part of any of his council gatherings before," I told her. "That one with the Celts was the first time I'd actually been inside Valhalla."

"Mmph. I know even less about Norse history than I do about Celtic."

I got back up and tottered over to where I keep mugs and tea herbs, intent on making us something to drink. Rowan joined me and cut cheese and rolls into bite-sized bits. "I just ate in Valhalla," she muttered. "I shouldn't be hungry again, but I am."

I put a serious lid on what I wanted to say because it was such a cliché. She was eating for two, and I had a feeling the dragon baby required a lot of nourishment. I carried our mugs back to the table; she trailed after me, plate in hand. "Do you want anything to eat?" she asked.

I shook my head. The tea would be plenty for now. Once she was settled again, I reached across the table and placed a hand over hers. Questing about for a neutral topic to give both of us a break, I said, "That necklace and ring are lovely. I noticed them before, but where'd they come from? I can sense their power from here."

She tapped the onyx amulet. "This and the ring and the circlet"—she touched her forehead with its delicate golden coronet—"were originally gifts from Mother. I never understood why she gave them to me, but one morning out of the blue she handed me a lovely Hawthorne wood box with the jewelry inside. I guess she knew I'd be gone soon." Rowan shrugged. "Maybe she felt guilty. Who knows?"

"Did you tuck them away or something?" I took a few sips from my mug. The herbal mixture, heavy on mint and anise, was soothing.

"More like threw them away." She grimaced. "When I was leaving the caves under Ben Nevis after one of my last visits, they called to me. And when I put them on, they felt different."

"They would." I thought about it. "Ceridwen's locked away in Fire Mountain, so anything crafted with her magic would either fade or change."

Rowan polished off the remaining scraps of food on her plate. "The ornaments come in handy. They concentrate my magic, and they finally feel like they belong to me." She looked right at me, and a corner of her mouth curved into a rueful smile. "Thanks for being sensitive, but you don't really care one way or another about my jewelry."

"Not sure I'd put it quite that bluntly," I replied. "I was curious about the gems. How are you doing?"

Her direct gaze skittered away. "Not sure. It's a lot to take in, and, frankly, rotten timing."

"It is a lot to take in." I agreed. "Not sure the full impact has actually hit me quite yet. We haven't had a quiet moment to ourselves until now."

She laughed and scraped her gaze up from her lap. "Oh, sweetie. I don't think the 'full impact' of a baby hits any new parents until after it arrives." She turned her hands palms up. "We have to design a bombproof nursery. Something he can't teleport out of..."

"What?" I prodded after her words trailed away.

Her nostrils flared. "Do you suppose the *de facto*, erm, grandparents, are going to give us grief? I mean it's not as if they were actually parents to you, and—"

I held up a hand. "I'm not happy about the way any of that shook out, either, but Hel did do me a good turn by making certain I had loving foster parents. She could have been selfish and tried to raise me in Hel and Niflheim."

I sat straighter; my vertebrae cracked in protest. "Somehow, I believe I'd have become a very different man under those circumstances."

Rowan dropped her head into her hands and rubbed her

eyes before looking at me again. "No shit. You might have come out harsh and bitter. Like me."

"According to the dragons, Ceridwen tried to abandon you many times," I reminded her and placed a hand over one of hers. "Who knows where she let you loose."

"Not in the midst of a nice, loving family, that's for sure. Probably at the bottom of some horrible pit," Rowan muttered, followed by, "Yeah. I guess I'd forgotten about that. The dragons found me every time and brought me back to Inverlochy Castle. And then, they must have wiped my memories because I have zero recall of any of that."

She tugged her hand from beneath mine and made a fist. "No matter what it costs me, I will see that our son is surrounded by love."

"We're an us," I reminded her.

Color splotched across her high cheekbones. "So we are. Sorry. Do you have any idea how long this pregnancy will last?"

The question caught me by surprise. "Do you have reason to suspect it won't be nine months?"

"You betcha." She drained what was left in her mug. "Thanks. That was good. So about the time thing, how long do dragon eggs incubate?"

I wasn't sure, so I sent magic zipping over to my shelves of lore materials and hovered next to a couple of candidates. They floated to where we sat.

"You must be exhausted," Rowan commented. "Those books were only about two meters from us."

"I am tired," I agreed, "and using it as an excuse for being lazy."

In the interest of expediency, I employed more magic to hunt for dragon hatchling information and skimmed until I came up with an answer for Rowan. "Twenty-six months."

"Alrighty. So why wouldn't my pregnancy be an average of nine months and twenty-six months." She smiled, but it didn't exactly reach her eyes when she said, "I like seventeen months a whole lot better than nine."

"Only because you've never been pregnant," I countered.

A snort riffled past her lips. "I suppose you have?"

"Of course not, but I've helped many a woman give birth. No matter how tough or simple the birth is, the mothers all have one thing in common."

"Wait. Don't tell me," Rowan cut in. "They're relieved it's over."

"Exactly." I reached for her hand again. "However long it lasts, you have to take good care of yourself."

"Uh-uh. You do not get to dictate how I live. No one does. Not even my—er, our—son."

"Good save."

She supported her head on an upraised hand again. "I'm sorry. Everything is hard right now, and this doesn't make it any simpler. I don't want to have to be on my guard every time Dewi shows up. I can see her hovering over the cradle and planting seeds about visiting Fire Mountain with Auntie Dewi."

I hesitated before giving voice to my thoughts. I might have remained silent, if Rowan hadn't crooked a finger my way and said, "Out with it."

"If our son has as much dragon in him as everyone seems

to think he does, he'll probably fall in love with Fire Mountain—"

"Oh no, he won't."

I didn't contradict her. She was thinking with her heart, not her head. "Before I left Valhalla, I told the dragons to butt out."

Rowan's brows crawled up her forehead. "How'd that go?"

"Predictably."

"Not well, eh? I wouldn't expect it to." She shut her eyes for a moment. When she opened them, she said, "The thing I don't get is why they're so fucking immersed in this baby. It's like it's the first dragon hatchling, ever."

"Well, it will be the first one to blend Norse, Celtic, and dragon bloodlines. The way I figure things, our son will be half dragon, a quarter Norse, and a quarter Celtic, so more dragon than anything else."

"Do you have any idea what that will mean?" she asked.

"As in, will he have wings?"

Rowan nodded and closed her teeth over her lower lip. "You and me, both of us are half dragon. Neither of us has wings. Not yet, anyway. When Nidhogg dropped the whole Dragon Heir thing on my head, he seemed to believe flight might be a possibility."

"I have no idea about wings. I'm assuming he'll have a human form—and maybe a dragon one."

"So he might be a shapeshifter?"

I splayed my hands on the table. "I don't know."

"But don't you see the problems?" she persisted. "I don't

fly. You don't fly. How are we going to control him if we can't catch him?"

"You've forgotten Zelli and Quade."

"Oh no, I haven't," she shot back. "Or Dewi or Nidhogg, either. Fuck! All I want is normal, but do I ever even come close? Oh hell, no."

"What is normal?" I gentled my voice.

"That's just it," she shrilled, "I have no bloody idea. Aw crap. How am I ever going to be a mother? No blueprint. No role models. Nada. Pushy grandparents won't help, either."

I got up and walked around to where she sat. Drawing her to her feet, I folded her into my arms and just held her. After a few moments, she threaded her arms around me. I took it as a good sign. We were both so tired, we fell into a half sleep where we stood.

Consciousness winked in and out, flirting like a shy, uncertain maiden. When I thought I heard a knock on my door, I chalked it up to being not quite sentient. The second —or perhaps it was the third—time it sounded, I cast a bleary-eyed look at my door.

"Is someone here?" Rowan sounded frail and weary. "Make them go away."

Before I could untangle myself from her and investigate, my door popped open. Gwydion, Bran, Andraste, and Arianrhod strode inside.

"Kinswoman! We have come to congratulate you," Andraste cried, loud enough to wake the shades in Niflheim.

Rowan let go of me and turned to face the Celts. "Oh, please." Breath rattled from her. "You can't just waltz back into my life as if you weren't total bastards my entire childhood."

"We feel verra badly about that," Arianrhod said.

I cringed. They were almost the same words Hel had used about me. Before I could get my brain working sufficiently to string a sentence together—one suggesting they leave—Gwydion said, "We've come to escort you to Inverlochy Castle. Arawn sends his regards. By the time we arrive, he should be done repairing the Ninth Gate, and he shall meet us at our stronghold."

"Aye, we've prepared a chamber for the two of you. And your bairn." Andraste sounded so proud, it might have been her child.

"Ye'll want for naught," Bran added.

"Stop!" Rowan screeched. "Just shut up."

"Child." Gwydion laced a soothing compulsion spell in with his words. "Ye're not thinking straight. Ye're overwrought. Allow us to help you through your—"

Rowan broke into his spell and his words. "First, the dragons want to bury me in Fire Mountain. Now you want to sequester us in Inverlochy. Goddammit it all to fuck. Why does no one understand this is my child. Mine and Bjorn's."

"Thanks for the add-on," I mumbled.

She elbowed me. "Don't mention it."

Something about the exchange seemed to calm her. "I'm certain you mean well," she told the Celts, "but I'm still finding my way. Will Bjorn and I spend time in Inverlochy? We will, to be sure. For one thing, the witches are there, and they need me."

She narrowed her eyes. "Will we spend all our time

there? No. For one thing, there's the other group of witches beneath Ben Nevis."

"We would assist with that project," Andraste said. "Frankly, I was certain I wouldna care for the witches, that I'd find them lacking, inferior. Such hasna happened. I actually like them. They are enterprising and courageous. Two qualities I value."

I expected a snarky comment from Rowan. Instead, she shook her head. "Thanks, Andraste. The witches need all the help they can get."

"How'd you find out about the baby?" I asked.

"How else?" Rowan shot a sidelong glance my way. "Dewi told them."

"Of course she did," I muttered. "She went looking for allies for her Fire Mountain nursery plan."

"Aye, we shot it down," Gwydion said.

My eyes may have widened. Were the Celts about to turn into unlikely allies?

"The child will be a Celtic deity," Arianrhod said somberly. "As such, 'tisn't seemly for him to spend too much time around dragonkind. Doona tell Dewi I said that, though."

It appeared the four Celts were settling in for a long chat. I was so beat, remaining upright required an infusion of magic. "How about this?" I suggested. "We will rest a while, and then we'll teleport to Inverlochy."

Magic flickered from Celt to Celt as they conversed in shielded telepathy. I didn't even bother to try to listen in, mostly because I didn't care what passed among them.

"I shall remain without," Gwydion said. "The others will return to Inverlochy."

A blast of anger scorched me. "What? You don't believe me? When I give my word on something—"

"Stand down, Master Sorcerer—and now quite a bit more than that," Gwydion said. "I shall ensure no one disturbs your sleep. Nothing more nor less."

"Fine," Rowan said. "We agree since it's the only way to get the rest of you out of here." She made shooing motions with both hands.

"When ye get to know us better, ye'll like us." Andraste smiled.

Ro made a sour face.

It was hard not to warm to Andraste. She didn't have a shred of artifice. What you saw was what you got. All the Celts walked back out my still-open door, pulling it shut behind them. When I turned around, Rowan lay facedown on my bed. I unlaced her boots and took them off. After removing my own, I joined her.

As exhausted as I was, I figured I'd pass out, but sleep took its sweet time coming. Between Odin, the Celts, the dragons, and the baby, I had a lot on my mind.

CHAPTER THREE, ROWAN

Daylight was spilling through Bjorn's window when I dragged my gritty eyes open and rubbed sleep from them, At least I wasn't so groggy I had to flounder about figuring out where I was. Bjorn slept next to me, his breathing even. A quick scan with as subtle a thread of magic as I could command told me Gwydion remained without.

I didn't know the warrior magician slash master enchanter well. He'd always struck me as being immersed in his own importance. Perhaps I'd been wrong about that since he'd volunteered to act as our protector while we slept. It wasn't something I would ever have imagined him doing.

Gwydion obviously believed we required a guardian in Vanaheim, and it worried me. I felt certain he wasn't in the habit of going out of his way to do things he didn't believe were necessary. Or maybe it wasn't us he was concerned about but the child within me.

I hated to disturb Bjorn, but the bed was so narrow me

moving might wake him. Even if I managed to get up, the creaky pump handle and water splashing into the sink would be impossible to sleep through.

No help for it. I kissed his forehead, his cheeks, and his lips. He stirred beneath my touch and wrapped me in his arms. It felt good in the circle of his arms with his hands straying up and down my back.

Too good.

I nuzzled his neck and wriggled out of his embrace. "Nope. We are not going to get frisky. Not with Gwydion sitting on the far side of that wall." I jerked my chin at the front door.

"Frisky, is it?" Bjorn grinned, slow and lazy, making it much harder for me to get off the bed.

I did, anyway, with a regretful backward glance. No one should be as gorgeous as Bjorn with his ice-blond hair and ocean eyes. This morning, silvery flecks glimmered around his irises. His strong, square chin was covered with pale stubble. A high forehead and eyes widely spaced over sharp cheekbones reminded me of Hollywood actors I'd lusted after before the Breaking. His nose was generous with a bit of a hawk's beak to it. Harsh and masculine, it was the only break from his unrelenting beauty.

Neither of us had undressed. Probably a wise move, since it would have been far harder to leave the bed if he'd been naked.

The cabin door swooshed open. Gwydion glided inside and actually smiled. "Morning. Any chance of breakfast?"

I leveled my gaze at him. "What? You were waiting until the first hint we were awake to pounce?"

His grin broadened, and he laughed. "Not exactly, but I smelled the beginnings of sex. No time for such pursuits. They're not on today's menu, so I decided to intervene afore things became awkward."

Bjorn was on his feet. "I don't know whether to toss you out or laugh. No one has told me what I can—or can't—do within my home for hundreds of years. You're not going to be the first."

What happened next more than shocked me. Gwydion bowed, a low, sweeping affair, and said, "Apologies, Master Sorcerer. Many tasks lay ahead of us, and—"

"Enough," Bjorn muttered. "I'll make tea." That pronouncement was followed by, "Aw shit. More customers. This isn't good."

"I'll take care of them." Gwydion spun to face the open door and bellowed, "Off. Begone with you."

"You can't just shoo them away. Hold on." Bjorn stalked around him and stood in the doorway, facing outward. "It's all right," he yelled.

How could there possibly be more supplicants or customers or patrons or whatever the fuck Bjorn called those who showed up for aid? We'd treated what felt like the entire population of Vanaheim last night. I made my way to his side and had hell's own time keeping my mouth from falling open. The clearing in front of Bjorn's cottage was filling rapidly.

Double the number of people we'd treated last night stood in rough lines waiting for Bjorn's services. Elves, dwarves, and giants were mixed in with the crowd. Bjorn walked outside and started sorting the people into groups.

Gwydion moved next to me and spoke low next to my ear. "What is all this?"

I turned to him. "We fear rot from Earth is spreading. Magic isn't behaving as it should. Bjorn's aid is available without cost to any inhabitant of the Nine Worlds. He's usually busy, but nothing like this, according to him."

"I shall see if I can help. Get something together for us to eat, so we can be gone from here once we're done."

Normally, I'd have told Gwydion to go to hell. He didn't get to order me about, but there'd been no malice in his request. He was going for efficiency, and he was used to issuing instructions.

I bit back an argument and hustled into my boots. My memory from the previous night was Bjorn's larder was running low, but I'd do the best I could. While magic bounced from one side of the courtyard to the other as Gwydion and Bjorn combined their power to fix broken spells, broken bodies, and malfunctioning magical accoutrements, I brewed a large pot of tea.

That done, I hunted until I found eggs tucked in a basket. I was just done scrambling them and slicing what remained of the bread when the men came inside.

"Appreciate the help." Bjorn nodded Gwydion's way. "We need to get moving before more folks show up."

"Aye, but Odin should assign another to this particular task."

"Who?" Bjorn furled his brows and bent to stuff his feet into his socks and boots.

Gwydion shrugged. Magic flashed from him, and I recognized a sealing spell.

"You're locking us in?" I inquired caustically, confident I could break through anything he built.

"Nay. Locking them out." He snatched up a mug and poured himself a cup of tea. "Thanks."

"Oh my goodness, you're so welcome, esteemed—"

"Rowan!" Gwydion thundered.

Bjorn stepped between us. "You will not raise your voice to my mate."

"Ye're absolutely correct, but she's a thick-headed wench. Stubborn just like her mother."

"Oh yeah? And you're an ass," I shot back.

"This buys us naught," Gwydion said in a more or less normal tone. "I canna apologize more than I already have for my failings while ye lived amongst us. I am sorry. Had I paid better attention, not been diverted by Ceridwen's spells, your early life might have been better."

"None of that matters now," Bjorn said and poured himself a mug of tea. He sounded tired. It would take more than a few hours to bring us back up to full strength.

"Nay, it doesna," Gwydion agreed. "We face an unknown enemy. They are strong enough to corrupt the binding between the Nine Worlds. I fear they stretch far beyond Odin's realm as well. We were feeling...oddities afore we left our borderworld."

He addressed his next words to me. "We go to war, child. 'Tis everyone's war, and we canna afford to be sidetracked by petty squabbles and leftover hurt feelings."

I started to protest I was far from a child, but it wasn't the point. I dished the eggs into three bowls and slapped the plate with sliced bread on the table. Why was it so bloody hard for me to let go of my leftover hurt feelings? His assessment had been accurate. The only realistic path was for me to admit the truth and move on. Nothing to be gained by being sulky and bitchy.

Except it was kind of my go-to place. If I let go of the anger I'd swathed myself in, what would be left? We ate in silence. When I was done, I set my spoon down and said, "You're right, Gwydion. I will try to do better. Mother poisoned a lot of wells, including me. I've been erecting walls to hide behind my entire life. The only thing that saved me from turning into something like the Morrigan was the witches."

"Och, ye'd never have been like her." He rolled his blue eyes. Blond hair had been braided into a Celtic warrior pattern with many small plaits, and he wore his customary robes. Pale-green today and sashed in black. His intricately carved wooden staff sat near the door, glowing with a light of its own.

"Did ye even know her?" he went on. "Seems to me, we'd sent her away afore ye were born."

"You did, but the rest of you talked about her so much, I got quite a feel for her less savory personality traits." Holding up a hand, I counted off on my fingers. "Arrogant. Bitter. Ran roughshod over everyone. No loyalty, except to herself—"

A brisk bugle from outside made me smile. Zelli was here. Presumably, Quade as well. Gwydion's eyes shone with enthusiasm—or maybe it was relief to leave the topic of the Morrigan behind. Far as I knew, she was the only Celt who'd ever been exiled.

"Always wanted a dragon of my own, but they dinna react well to my requests," Gwydion was saying.

"It's because they read minds," Bjorn said. "Any dragon worth his salt who got a whiff of 'dragon of my own' would die before he'd take you on his back."

"I'll keep it in mind." Gwydion finished what was left in his bowl. I wondered if I should apologize for my lack of culinary skills. A cook, I am not, but everyone had eaten what I made, and apologies have never been my style. I got up, grabbed the dishes, and ferried them to the sink.

"At least the dragons should keep the crowds away until we leave," Bjorn muttered. "I'm extremely concerned about this turn of events."

"Does Odin know?" Gwydion asked.

Bjorn shook his head. "Complaining about something never makes much of a difference to him. I already made a bid for him to assign someone else in my stead."

"I take it he refused?"

"Nidhogg did. Said something like my talents were underutilized."

"Regardless, Odin needs to understand—"

"Things are going to hell fast?" I broke in. Gwydion screwed his features into a scowl, but he didn't rebuke me as I'd expected.

"I'm certain Odin knows what's happening," Bjorn said. "His magic is linked to the Nine Worlds. There's some type of loop that includes Yggdrasil." He looked at me. "You'd asked why Odin convened delegates from each world. I believe he did so because he sees what lies ahead far more clearly than we do. The gathering yesterday was more about him reassuring himself his kingdom was still whole than listening to what anyone else thought."

"That's not particularly encouraging," I muttered and addressed my next words to Gwydion. "What are all these tasks that require our attention today?"

"Why, settling in at Inverlochy Castle. What else? Once ye're all moved it, we'd planned an all-Celt meeting to plot out our next steps."

I glanced at Bjorn in time to see him shoot a pointed look my way. If I was reading him right, he was telling me Gwydion was my kinsman and to handle this.

I shuffled through various approaches. If I came off too strong or sounded angry, Gwydion would write me off as pregnant or hysterical or some other not-to-be-paid-attention-to label. Sucking in a breath, I blew it out and said, "Thank you for your offer. It's very kind, but Bjorn and I are not moving in. We have two homes already. His and the chamber I maintain beneath Ben Nevis."

The beginnings of a spell shimmered around Gwydion. Before he could open his mouth and try to convince me of the error of my ways, I plowed ahead. "Next point is, you're correct about this being everyone's war. What that means to me is you should be meeting with Odin and his merry band. They just held an assembly without you, so they're equally negligent."

"What was the outcome of this Norse conclave?" Gwydion asked.

I offered him points for focusing on the most important element. That decisions had been made absent Celtic input.

Decisions that might alter the outcome of dealing with our unidentified enemies.

"I'll cover it," Bjorn said.

"Thanks." I pumped water over the dirty dishes while he outlined Odin's plan of attack with the outer borderworlds, and mine to close off the Breaking place once and for all before we engaged in an all-out search-and-destroy for whomever was stuck on our side of the broken barricade.

I've mentioned that one of Gwydion's titles is warrior magician. He has strengths on the battlefield and is known to be a shrewd tactician. I shut off the water in time to hear him say, "What was Odin thinking? I understand why we'd want to amputate the flow of whatever is attacking us at its source, but only after we've taken care of breaches in our own borders."

"Which is precisely why you should all be in the same room for important decisions," I said and dried my hands on a scrap of towel. "Dragons too."

"Our plan," Bjorn said, "was to return to the Breaking site and explore it more thoroughly. Last time, we slapped a temporary fix together, but then we ran into a trapdoor. It sucked us into a strange spot I didn't recognize before I redirected us to Niflheim. I have no idea if that spell is still active or if, once tripped, it won't bother us again."

"If I'm right and Ceridwen laid that snare, she did it to fuck with me," I told them. "Presumably, her absence means the spell is dead."

"Not necessarily," Gwydion said, followed by, "I shall accompany you."

"We do not require a babysitter." I grimaced. Damn it.

My caustic side was plenty close to the surface, near enough to slither through if I didn't watch it.

"I thought we had moved past your distrust of me," Gwydion said. "Bjorn and I work well together. Ye and I would as well. If ye'd been able, ye'd have disabled the Breaking place when ye tackled it last time."

He got to his feet. "Which dragon shall I ride?"

"Neither," Bjorn and I said almost in unison.

I have to hand it to Gwydion. He laughed. "And here ye chided me for hoping for a dragon of my own. It appears ye've staked ownership claims to the duo outside."

"It's not the same," I said stiffly. "Zelli volunteered to bond with me. And Quade picked Bjorn."

Zelli bugled again. It sounded different, urgent, and sent me bounding out the door with the men right behind me. She and Quade stood over a lengthening laceration spreading through the dirt.

I readied magic, intent on shutting it before something hideous could emerge. My experience lately with holes in the ground hasn't been good. Granted, they'd all been on Earth, but Vanaheim appeared to be next on the hit list.

"Hold," Quade rumbled.

"Why?" I shouted back. "We need to shut that fissure." Power crackled, arcing between my hands.

Bjorn ran in front of me and knelt on the ground, placing his hands on either side of the widening gap.

"Don't let it get any bigger," I yelled.

Gwydion looped a hand under my arm. "I doona recognize the energy, but 'tisn't evil."

I wasn't at all certain of that, so I didn't defuse the

destructive power I'd summoned. Not yet. A gnarled length of what looked like wood poked through the opening, followed by another. As far afield from the power I held as possible, calming energy flowed from Bjorn. One of the wood-things crept across his knees. The other followed suit.

More of the shoots, this time with a greenish tinge, joined the first two, winding around Bjorn as if he were a Maypole.

"What is it?" I didn't want to get any closer. In case I had to bail Bjorn out, distance would be my friend. No point in both of us becoming trapped. Holy hell, had something mesmerized him?

Bjorn raised his head, the look on his face a mixture of wonder and horror. "Yggdrasil," he answered me. "This is the One Tree."

Gwydion hurried forward and knelt on the other side of the fissure. "Would it mind if I touched it?"

"Be still," Bjorn counseled. "If the One Tree wants your energy, it will let you know."

I felt like an ass with power arcing between my hands, so I reluctantly let it disperse. A shower of sparks fell to the ground around me. "What do you think?" I asked Zelli and sidled nearer the dragon.

"Yggdrasil seeks untainted soil to nurture its roots," she replied.

"When the ground first opened, we weren't certain what was happening," Quade said. "We feared a repeat of the abominations from Midgard, but neither of us sensed evil."

"If we had," Zelli added, "we'd have showered the gash with our own magic."

I twisted my mouth into a sour expression. "You and I, we went to the same school."

"What do ye mean?" Zelli asked.

"We've both learned that bad shit comes out of holes in the ground."

"'Twasn't always true until verra recently," she corrected me.

"Well it still isn't a hundred percent." I jerked my head toward where the men sat in the midst of a veritable garden of tree roots. They were beautiful and frightening.

I trotted until I stood behind Bjorn. "Do you believe Yggdrasil sought you out, or was this random?"

He glanced up at me. "Not random. The tree is drawn to my energy, but at least now it makes more sense. It discerns my direct link with Odin."

"Aye, and your dragon blood," Quade said.

Gwydion looked humble and awestruck, two descriptors I'd never have associated with him before today. He patted a root, and it wound around his little finger.

"Should we, uh, water it or something?" I asked. Vague memories of houseplants and landscaping from before the Breaking ran through my head.

"Nay," Gwydion replied. "The One Tree needed a break is all. A place where the air isna tainted."

I struggled with a visual of the Nine Worlds. Before, I'd assumed they were sort of a metaphorical construct, but it appeared Yggdrasil was a physical reality that strung the worlds together.

"Does this mean the bottom of the Nine Worlds has been compromised?" I asked.

"Probably." Worry laced into Bjorn's answer.

"Is there a way we can go there and look for ourselves?" Gwydion asked.

"We can," Bjorn said, "but Bifrost will like as not eject you."

"Mmph. That bridge thing, eh?" At Bjorn's nod, he continued. "Aye, when we arrived in Asgard, Odin and them stuck pretty close."

"Did you take the bridge?" Bjorn asked.

"Nay. Teleported, but we came out near Bifrost's entry point. Odin was quite clear we had to give it a wide berth, but he dinna elaborate as to why."

"If ye wish a better view"—smoke oozed from Quade's jaws—"Zelli and I can fly into the void beneath the Nine Worlds. We canna remain long, though."

As gently as if he were handling fragile artifacts, Bjorn untangled the roots that had coiled around him, and stood.

"I will watch over the tree's roots whilst ye're gone," Gwydion said.

My head snapped around, and I stared at him. I'd fully expected him to head back to Inverlochy Castle, but his tone had been tender, paternal even. As if the tree had hypnotized him into ensuring its survival.

"It's good at taking care of itself," Bjorn spoke into my mind.

"If we're gone too long for your taste," I told Gwydion, "feel free to take a look at the Breaking site."

"I'll wait until ye return," he said in the same dreamy voice.

It worried me, but I didn't say anything. What would I

have said? Christ, Gwydion, get a grip? If I told him he'd been suckered, he'd have ignored me. That's the thing about being a bit player. None of the Celts have ever paid the slightest attention to me. It might be changing, but not when something had one of them caught up in thrall.

Dragon magic snagged me and somersaulted me onto Zelli's back. "This will be like travel between worlds," she warned me.

"No air, huh?"

She puffed ash and smoke. "Worse than that. 'Tis rather like a vacuum."

Bjorn vaulted to Quade's back and asked, "Will it be safe for Rowan?"

"What you really want to know is if it's safe for our baby," I growled. "We already know nothing can hurt it, and—"

"Rowan." Bjorn's tone cut like a bullwhip. "You're my mate. My wife. I will do everything in my power to protect you, keep you safe. If that's a crime, you'd better cut me loose now because it won't improve with time."

Shame swamped me, followed by its kissing cousin, guilt. Bjorn was a good man, better than I deserved. Sarcastic twit that I was. "Sorry," I mumbled. "Let's get moving. I have a feeling we won't be gone long."

"We can't be." Bjorn angled his gaze at Gwydion.

I switched to telepathy. *"Tree has him in thrall, huh?"*

"Yeah, Yggdrasil can be very persuasive."

I readied myself as much as I could by taking huge lungfuls of air and gripping my amulet. Breathing through its prismed surface helped. Bjorn's courtyard dropped away, replaced by blackness.

I've never been scared of the void between worlds. I don't like it much, but it doesn't frighten me. I kept trying to reassure myself this would be like a hundred other journeys, but every instinct I had urged me to teleport off the damned dragon and make a run for it.

CHAPTER FOUR, BJORN

I was plenty worried about Gwydion. The One Tree had snapped him up like low-hanging fruit. He'd opened his magic to it as he explored its rich inner life and plethora of memories, but the tree had taken advantage of his trust and goodwill. By the time it became obvious I should have warned him, it was too late to intervene.

Maybe too late. In truth, I knew less than nothing about the Celtic gods and their abilities. I'd deal with Gwydion after we returned. I vaulted onto Quade, not wanting to hold everyone up. Almost before I was seated, the baked-clay scent I associated with dragon power surrounded me. We'd leave as soon as Quade's spell reached sufficient velocity.

I was worried about Rowan too. She was skittish and snappish as a starving wolf, and it took almost nothing to set her off. We needed time alone with each other, but stolen moments would be progressively harder to come by. We hadn't exactly been alone during what had been left of last night. Gwydion had been there.

Something had worried him enough to compel him to remain. If I hadn't been dead on my feet, I'd have mined for his reasons. I suppose I could have floated the topic over breakfast, but I hadn't. After dealing with what felt like hundreds of magical emergencies between last night and this morning, I hadn't wanted to think about any other problems.

A common thread was emerging amid all the magic-gone-astray complaints. Several people had voiced the same progression of events. They'd summoned power, often for something rather trivial. As soon as the channel to their magic was open, they'd sensed something ominous take over. The transition was subtle, and it happened fast. Once it was done, their magic was polluted and uncooperative.

After fixing the same issue multiple times, I'd begun counseling people not to call upon their power unless they were in dire straits. Predictably, my suggestion wasn't well-received. Those who live within the Nine Worlds—except Midgard—are mostly all magical beings. They cut their teeth on employing magic for everything from hunting food to cooking to repairing garments and boots.

"But my music store," an elf had complained. "All the instruments will sound sour unless I hand tune them every day."

I'd just looked at him and asked if what he and I had just done, which amounted to an exorcism and hadn't been especially pleasant on his end, was preferable. With a great deal of grumbling, he'd shambled out of the clearing in front of my cottage. No teleporting from now on. Everyone had to use Bifrost.

Was it only a matter of time before evil penetrated Rowan and me? And if it hassled Ro, what would it do to our son? The urgency I'd felt earlier to scoop her up and lock her away somewhere safe returned with a fury.

I tried to gather as much air in my lungs as I could. It was thinning out, and soon there'd be none at all. Sequestering Rowan somewhere was out of the question. She'd even taken exception when I'd inquired if this trip to the bottom of the Nine Worlds would be safe for her.

"Hang on," Quade told me.

I grabbed one of the horns that grew from the junction where his neck and body met up. Usually, the dragon was chattier. He may have intuited I needed to be alone with my thoughts, or else he was worried about where we were going. Or he might have other reasons for his silence I couldn't guess at.

Regardless, I've come to respect the dragon beneath me. He's wise and thinks things through. The unexpected news about Nidhogg being my father hadn't changed our relationship, and I was grateful. It would have been awful if Quade had begun pussyfooting around me for fear of Nidhogg's wrath.

I haven't exactly sorted things out, but Nidhogg appears to play two very different roles. In the Nine Worlds, he is *the* Norse dragon, emphasis on *the*. He commands dragons who inhabit the Nine Worlds, and they defer to his directives. His other role is on Fire Mountain, the dragons' ancestral home world. There he is one of twelve elders who manage dragonkind via a council structure.

Quade hit what felt like air pockets. They tossed us up many meters and then we were sucked down. Nothing left to breathe, and for once the absence of an atmosphere tugged at me. It wasn't only an issue of no air. Whatever remained had a negative gravitational pull and felt as if it was trying to suck every last molecule of oxygen out my pores. Sort of like traveling from sea level to ten thousand meters in one fell swoop.

I wasn't at all certain how long I'd remain conscious. My lungs burned, and my throat and nose felt like they'd been lined with sandpaper. The blackness around us was absolute. No form. No substance. Not a hint of shading.

"Look dead ahead." Quade had shifted to telepathy. The rough suction couldn't be easy on him, either.

What had been impenetrable gloom blew up in front of us. I expected shockwaves, but nothing traveled anywhere in this negative atmosphere. The rounded bottom of what I assumed was the Nine Worlds flashed into view. It was enormous, and I only saw the part right in front of me.

Yggdrasil's roots were a tangled mess as they coiled around the bottom of what might be a sphere or an ellipse. Quade flew lower and then horizontally. Stretching my neck, I stared upward. The One Tree's roots had blackened in places, but it looked more like they'd caught fire than rotted. The black spots had spread, though, until entire patches of roots were clearly dead.

Perhaps fire had weakened them? And then rot had set in?

I caught flashes of green and knobby wood around the black circles.

"Doesn't look good." Rowan's voice slithered into my mind.

"No, it doesn't. We have to talk about it."

"Later. When we can breathe."

I didn't bother answering. My energy was fading fast.

I had no idea how the One Tree's roots usually looked. I'd never been here before. I also couldn't estimate how long ago the damage had occurred, or if Yggdrasil was in the midst of repairing it or had jettisoned the ravaged spots.

I blinked a few times and forced myself to absorb what was spread above me. My head pounded, and my vision was hazing around the edges. We were a long way from transiting the bottom of the Nine Worlds. It loomed over us, extending endlessly. Some of Yggdrasil's roots wriggled like oversized snakes. It might have been a trick of my air-starved brain, but I thought I saw grayish conduits surfing through the void, heading right for the One Tree. When I tried to count how many, they danced around, shifting position.

Where had they come from?

Floating, bumping into one another, and moving on, they held a hallucinogenic quality, so maybe they weren't real after all.

"We are done here," Quade said without preamble. It clearly wasn't up for discussion, and I was fine with leaving. Before I passed out and fell off the dragon into goddess only knew where. The tubular crawly things gave me the creeps. I didn't smell anything foul, but I sensed it.

Quade spread his wings and flew back the way we'd

come. It took forever to reach the edges of the One Tree's roots. The dragon was definitely flying slower. I felt the strain on him and offered up power of my own. I looked around for Zelli and Rowan but didn't see them.

Probably didn't mean anything. I hadn't seen them since we left my cottage. Quade extended his great wings and took advantage of the lack of gravity to move upward. We passed through the same bumpy spot we had on the way in. Well, perhaps not the precise place, but it felt similar. Zero air yielded to a spot where I could breathe. Finally, my reflexive breaths did something other than make my lungs hurt.

We crashed out of the blackness and into the clearing next to my cottage. Quade pulled things out at the last minute, so we didn't quite splat onto the dirt. Gwydion was where we'd left him, with still more roots twining about his body.

"Sorry." Smoke and fiery ash rained from Quade as he caught his breath. "I wanted to remain longer, and so I waited almost too long."

I scrambled down from his black-scaled hide, catching my trousers on rough areas in the process. "Have you been there before?"

"Aye."

I waited, but he didn't say anything more. Maybe he was still regaining his composure. "Almost too long" sounded bad, as if we might not have made it out of there. "Did it look different?" I prodded after a glance Gwydion's way.

"Very. Dealing with the enemy will be difficult in that location. They appear to have figured out a way to maneuver in the void. We have yet to accomplish such a thing."

My brain wasn't exactly firing on all burners. "Those gray things. Those were the enemy?" I couldn't think of what else he might be referring to.

The dragon nodded to the accompaniment of clanking scales. "Did ye not feel their wickedness?"

"No. I couldn't feel anything. Uh, shouldn't Zelli and Rowan be back by now?"

"They should. Let me see if I can reach Zelli."

I was recovered enough, worry gnawed at my belly like a cancer as dragon magic ebbed and flowed around Quade. If it was taking this long, he must have reached Zelli. Or had he failed and was trying over and over? I wanted to grip his forelegs and shake him to hurry things along.

What I did instead was dash inside and grab Gwydion's staff. I'd had an idea, and saw no reason not to test it. If Rowan was in trouble, I needed Gwydion far more than Yggdrasil did. The magical accessory felt unpleasant in my hand, cold and prickly.

"Stop that," I told the staff. "Your master needs you."

The carved length of wood must have understood because the harsh sensations ceased. Back outside, I hustled to where Gwydion sat and uncurled one of his hands from around a beefy root. In its place, I positioned the staff. It began to glow with a clean white light immediately.

So far, so good. It recognized its owner, and like as not the one who'd carved it. Gwydion shook his head. When he looked at me, the hazy, unfocused expression left his blue eyes. Eyes that he narrowed as understanding crashed over him.

Without a word, he began uncoiling the roots from

around himself. He was gentle, almost as if he understood hasty movements would encourage the sentient wood to cling tighter. Yggdrasil has always been slow responding to anything. It's why I was able to escape its clutches when it made a bid to absorb me.

Gwydion was down to two roots, big thick ones that didn't wish to yield. He touched his staff to one, and it drew back as if he'd injured it. I moved the last one aside, and Gwydion sprang to his feet shaking himself from head to toe much as a dog might have.

"Thanks, mate," he gritted out. "I have no bloody idea how it conned me into feeding power into it."

"One note at a time," I suggested. "It sang to you, right?"

"It did indeed." He cast a speculative glance my way. "It's tried the same thing with you."

"Rather recently," I replied, followed by, "Freeing you wasn't as altruistic as all that. Rowan and Zelli aren't back yet."

"What's he doing?" Gwydion looked Quade's way.

"Hunting for them." If anything, the magic around the dragon had thickened. It didn't make me feel any better.

"What are we waiting for?" Gwydion said firmly. "We must go after them."

"Not as simple as all that. Quade and I barely escaped the airless gorge around the bottom of the Nine Worlds."

"There should be air and light farther up," Gwydion said. "Or Yggdrasil would have foundered long since."

It made sense. "Mmph. What we saw must have been the largest of the tree's root systems, the one that drinks from Hvergelmir."

"A pool in Niflheim, right?" Gwydion asked.

I nodded. "More like a rushing cascade. Pool is too tame a word. The other primary root systems drink from Mimir, a well in Jotunheim, and from the well of Urd in Asgard."

Gwydion tapped his staff on the ground and spoke a power word. It made my ears hurt, but the roots that had been writhing once he extricated himself quieted and began a gradual retreat. I'd run out of patience and was about to break into Quade's trance or conversation or whatever he was involved in when the magic swirling around the dragon broke into silvery streamers and dissipated.

He focused his spinning gaze my way. "They are in Asgard. We shall meet them there."

"What happened?" I asked.

"Not certain, but they ran into trouble. Hel was close and assisted them."

Breath rattled from me. If I knew anything about Hel, she'd be a lot pushier about sticking Rowan in a safe spot until our son was born. More insistent than she'd been before.

"See you there," Gwydion said. "I know the way." He paused for a beat. "I am in your debt, Master Sorcerer."

"We're allies," I told him. "Means we help each other without expecting tit for tat."

"That may be, but I still owe you." Celtic magic, green and gold and smelling of mint, thickened around him before he vanished.

Twining my own magic into a ramp, I returned to Quade's back. Gwydion was gone, and the dragon and I may as well travel together. Only a few roots remained above ground in my courtyard. I wasn't fooled, though. Yggdrasil had located safe harbor in front of my cottage. More roots were probably slinking beneath the dirt, ready to emerge when their need was great.

I should tell the One Tree I wasn't always here, but it wouldn't understand. In its arboreal mind, its needs were primary. It wasn't so different from Odin in that regard. Speaking of which, "Will Nidhogg be in Asgard?" I asked Quade.

"I doona know."

We bounced through a choppy spot, and the golden streets of the Aesir formed around us. Quade flew to the enormous stone-lined enclosure inside Valhalla's gates. The howls of the dead reached me immediately. Something had riled them up.

"See you within," Quade told me as I climbed down from my perch. He took to the air again, clearly having a way into Odin's main hall that didn't involve stairs.

Rowan ran down Valhalla's broad stone risers and into my arms. I held onto her, breathing her in. Mint, vanilla, amber with something unique to Rowan. "Sorry if I scared you," she murmured.

Gwydion shimmered into being next to us.

Rowan's eyes widened. "You got free."

"Thanks to Bjorn." Gwydion shook his head. "Perhaps we might not mention that little incident to the others."

Rowan's generous mouth stretched into a grin. "I'll hold your secret forever."

"Thanks, lass." The warrior magician bounded up the steps, staff clutched in his hand as if he'd never let it go again.

"It wasn't me," I told Rowan, "but his staff that turned the tides. Once I placed it in his hands, he broke out of thrall."

"Smart of you." She moved a hand between us and wrapped it around her onyx amulet. "Celts often use external implements to enhance their power. Gwydion carved that staff and infused it with enchantments. It's not the first he's owned. They break in battle, and he makes another."

I stepped back and dropped my hands onto her shoulders. "What happened?"

"We flew a bit too close. One of the root things uncoiled and grabbed my arm." A shadow crossed her features. "Nothing to breathe, which made fighting back doubly hard. Zelli tried fire, but fire requires air to burn. I stabbed at the root with my dirk, but it was too small to do much good."

My face must have given me away, shown her the anguish and helplessness roiling through me. It was also clear I'd mislabeled the black places in the One Tree's roots. They couldn't be the result of fire, so they had to be extensive rot.

"Since we weren't going to escape downward," Rowan went on doggedly, "Zelli blasted a path through the snarl of roots. I guess we surprised Yggdrasil because it let go of me to guard itself from us breaking through its perimeter."

"Too late," I muttered.

"It was," Rowan agreed. "We were already through, but damn, what a fucking nightmare of a labyrinth in there. At least there was air, though. Between the dragon blasting fire and me shrieking power words, I'm shocked all the dead in Hel didn't come to investigate."

"They might have, but I beat them to it," a deep, smooth voice spoke from behind me. I'd recognize Hel's inflection anywhere.

I spun to face her. Much like the last meeting in Odin's halls, she hadn't bothered with a glamour. Swathed in a leather skirt and woolen vest, Hel's bones were visible all down one side of her body. Long black hair hit her at knee level, and her dark eyes glittered with a cross between anger and relief.

"Thank you for intervening." I kept my tone formal.

"About that—" she began.

I chopped a hand downward. "We are in your debt, but it doesn't mean we're obliged to follow your suggestions."

Hel raised a sharply arched dark brow. "Och, and just what suggestions do ye expect to hear from me?"

"Never mind." Rowan smiled warmly. "You showing up when you did was welcome. Meant we didn't have to fight our way out of any more of those roots."

"They used to be thicker. The One Tree is languishing," Hel said and motioned to us. "Come within. Odin needs to understand what has happened, although he may have already heard about it from Nidhogg."

I took Ro's hand, and we trooped up the stairs after Hel. Perhaps I'd misjudged her. Or maybe she was waiting until we weren't so emotional to remind us of the baby's wellbeing. Several flights later, we trotted down the broad hall I remembered with its dust bunnies and battered coats of armor. The doors to the meeting hall had been propped open.

Nidhogg stood near Zelli and Quade beneath a bank of dirty windows. Gwydion sat next to Odin and Thor, chatting quietly.

Before I lost the train of thought that had occurred to me beneath the Nine Worlds, I herded Rowan toward the dragons. Once we were close, I said, "Nidhogg, may I ask a question?"

"Of course, but I might not answer it."

I felt like making a face at him, but didn't. "Legends say you drink from Hvergelmir."

Nidhogg snorted laughter, along with steam and smoke. "Och, they do say as much. They also credit me with gnawing Yggdrasil's roots from that pool."

When it became clear he wasn't going to say anything else, I risked adding, "Are they true?"

His eyes spun faster, turning from silver to green and back again. "Mayhap once, long ago, but not for millennia. Why is it important?"

"I'm trying to figure out if things have changed beneath the Nine Worlds," I answered.

"She is more likely to know than me." Nidhogg extended a talon toward Hel, who stood a meter away. "She is far closer to Niflheim than me these days."

Odin's ravens flew so close, feathers brushed my back. Cawing, they herded us, dragons and all, to the table. In a few words, I sketched out the events behind today, beginning with Yggdrasil's roots invading my courtyard. Then Rowan described her dilemma.

"Why did ye not call for me?" Nidhogg asked.

"Ye're joking, aye?" Zelli pushed herself taller. "If I'd quit fighting, the roots would have yanked Rowan right off my back."

"Do you know what the gray tubes are?" I asked Odin point-blank. May as well cut to the meat of things so long as we were here. "Are they why you deployed teams to the boundary near the outer borderworlds?"

Thor jabbed his father with an elbow. Odin punched Thor in the side. "Gwydion and I made a pact to work more closely together."

"Aye, I heard as much and chalked it up to political maneuvering," Thor said, his voice so deep it reverberated in the pit of my stomach.

"Best chalk it up to truth," Odin retorted.

"The gray things," I prodded.

Odin took a long slug from one of his drinking horns. The pungent reek of mead wafted my way, and I wished I had my own horn to slurp from. "I know they are there," Odin said. "They are some type of conduit carrying malevolent energy. 'Tis been eating away at Yggdrasil's roots for some time now."

"It appears the darkness has moved beyond the tree and is attacking your subjects," Gwydion said.

Odin focused his fog-colored eye at me. "Why was I not told?"

"I tried. I said I needed help."

He frowned. "Aye, but I assumed ye were being lazy."

Anger flared, quick and hot. I started to tell him off. He'd never had reason to believe me slothful. Getting into a shouting match with Odin wouldn't help anyone, though. I set my jaw in a solid line and said, "It was only today I saw a pattern emerging."

He spun one hand in a circular pattern, ordering me to continue.

"When people call on their magic, something dark jumps in, takes over, and perverts their ability."

"Is it fixable?" Nidhogg asked.

I nodded. "With a fair amount of effort. I've told everyone not to levy magic, but you know how effective that will be."

"I shall issue an edict," Odin said. "Meanwhile, three parties have departed for the outer borderworld boundary." He skewered Rowan with his implacable gaze. "What progress have ye made on the Breaking site?"

"None," she said. "Haven't been back to Midgard since my last trip through here."

I blew out a breath. I'd been afraid she was going to remind him dealing with the Breaking spot had been her idea. Turned out my relief was premature.

"That was my idea," she went on with scarcely a pause. "As was killing off what doesn't belong on Midgard."

"Aye, well kill them on the rest of my worlds too," he growled and flapped his hands at us in obvious dismissal.

We never had sat down. Leaving was as close as a teleport spell, but I wasn't quite ready to go. "Rowan and I will tend to the Breaking and see what we can do."

"I shall help, along with my kinsmen if they are needed," Gwydion said.

The ravens cawed. Leaving Odin's shoulders, they flew around the room making an infernal racket. Maybe they were trying to dissuade me from what came next. It was probably ill-advised, but I plowed ahead anyway. "What will you do next?"

"Are ye addressing me?" Odin roared.

Tempting as it was to vanish in a cloud of magic, I said, "Aye. We're playing on the same team. Means we should know what everyone's doing."

Something that sounded suspiciously like a cackle emerged from Thor. He stood and strode from the room.

"We should leave." Rowan nudged me.

My stubborn side wanted to wait Odin out, but it was misguided. Even if I won the current petty battle of wills, he'd make me pay somewhere down the line. He and Loki had that in common.

The gray tubes weren't going anywhere. We'd deal with the Breaking site first. "Your spell or mine?" I asked Rowan.

"Ours," Zelli and Quade said in unison. A blast of dragon magic somersaulted me through the air and onto the dragon. Rowan sat astride Zelli. Valhalla wavered around us.

"That was a mistake," Quade said once our travel spell was underway.

I didn't have to ask what "that" referred to. *"Yeah, but a satisfying one."*

"Really?" The dragon's tone was threaded with sarcasm. *"His realm is dying. He is linked to it, so he feels every grunt. Every groan. Every bit of slippage."*

"I get that. But my point was to ferret out what he was doing about it other than feeling sorry for himself."

Midgard formed around us. When Quade spoke next, he'd shelved telepathy. "Evil is draining Odin too. What if he's doing everything he can to keep from sinking?"

That possibility hadn't occurred to me, mostly because I viewed Odin as invincible. Feeling about two centimeters tall, I jumped off the dragon and sprinted across cracked and broken dirt to the Breaking site. The dikes I'd built were gone, the stench of death and rot much stronger than the last time I'd been here.

A flash of copper wing told me Zelli and Rowan had arrived. Gwydion strode from behind a pillar that had recently been a troll, its features still visible. Together we waited for Rowan to dismount once Zelli landed.

I felt a jolt as she married her power with mine. "Why is it worse?" she mumbled.

"Worse than?" Gwydion arched his brows.

"Our last jaunt through here," she said.

The fine hairs on the back of my neck prickled unpleasantly, followed by a chilly sensation tracking down my spine.

The vertical gash that had hosted Ceridwen's Breaking spell pulsed ominously. "Strike!" I shouted.

"But we doona know what it is," Gwydion shouted back.

"We don't have to," Rowan told him. "Nothing good ever comes out of that hole." Power blasted from her upraised hands, courtesy of our joined magic.

CHAPTER FIVE, ROWAN

Somehow, we'd escaped Valhalla before anyone brought up the baby. Maybe it meant I could slide by not thinking about it for a little while. Gwydion's brush with Yggdrasil had diverted his attention away from me. After Hel had shepherded Zelli and me to Niflheim, I'd been certain she'd insist I remain glued to her side, but she hadn't said a word.

Zelli thumped down about ten meters from the Breaking site, and I hustled off her back. She felt responsible for the roots snagging me because she'd been so close to them. After her third apology, I'd told her not to worry about it, but she'd been uncharacteristically quiet since then.

Everywhere Bjorn and I went, trouble found us. I'd assumed the Breaking place would have gone back to what it was before he constructed crafty little braces to contain what was left of its wickedness. Not only were the L-shaped catchalls gone, but the opening was half again as big and rimmed with slimy-feeling gunk.

All I had to do was look at it, and the slime came alive, almost as if it was breathing. My power joined Bjorn's, rather like an overzealous homing pigeon. We're stronger together than individually, much stronger.

I needed strong right about now. After my fight with the One Tree, my reserves hovered far lower than I would have liked. That's the thing about slinging power words about. They really suck all the juice out of you.

Gwydion just showed up with his own opinions, reminding me of the adage about too many cooks. He wanted to slice and dice and examine the foulness. I didn't give a jolly fuck what it was. I wanted to annihilate it. We could dissect it later.

Without waiting for him to agree, I lobbed as much destruction as I could muster at the damned thing, cursing my mother all the while. I thought I'd moved beyond wasting energy blaming Ceridwen. Guess I was wrong.

Bjorn's magic had a steadying effect. I zoomed in on it rather than Mother's treachery. If I had my way, she'd rot in a cell forever.

The dragons worked in tandem too. Without exchanging words, they took the top third of the Breaking. Bjorn and I targeted the middle section, and Gwydion worked the lowest part. I hadn't been at all certain he'd do anything besides argue, so having him deal with the bottom segment made a certain amount of sense.

If he slacked off, we'd get there eventually anyway.

Maybe.

This wasn't going well. "What are we doing wrong?" I shouted as I watched one more short section we'd just shut peel open again.

"Something's undoing it. From the inside." Bjorn sounded short of breath. I got it. I was working way harder than I wanted to be.

"Told you we needed to evaluate what we're fighting," Gwydion muttered just loud enough to make certain I heard him.

"Alrighty, Mr. Last Word," I yelled his direction. "What do you think we should do?"

"Not certain. If I was, I'd have said something," he replied.

Meanwhile, the dragons had painted their section with so much fire, rocks were melting into goo, but the breach just pulsed harder. As if what we were doing was feeding it... Shit. Crap. Fuck.

"Stop!" I shouted.

"But we'll lose ground," Bjorn protested.

"Can't see as we've gained any," Gwydion observed.

Much as I hated to admit he was right, he was. "I have no idea how," I said, "but that thing is borrowing our magic and using it to nourish the breach."

"Och. I dinna ken until I quit," Zelli snarled, "but the reason it took more and more effort was exactly that. Something within is siphoning our power."

"And turning it back on us," I said. "Not directly, but it dispatched our destructive spell to wreck more of the breach. We'd shut a portion, and someone boomeranged the magic back at us to open it again."

"Perhaps not someone but something." Gwydion sounded thoughtful.

"Not many can twist dragon, Norse, and Celtic power to their bidding," Quade said.

It did narrow the field. Put that way, I couldn't think of anything powerful enough, or savvy enough, to manage it. Standing and staring at the suppurating hole in the ether was counterproductive. Even if we hadn't made any headway, I'd felt better while we were fighting it.

"Any idea where it leads?" Gwydion had cocked his head to one side. Magic arced from his upraised staff as he did what he'd wanted to do to begin with. Assess the damned thing.

"Might have been a good question for Mother," I growled.

"Nay, she wouldna have any idea. I feel her energy, but 'tis minor compared with everything else it's mixed with."

"Loki claimed the spell originated with him," Bjorn said. "He crafted it and then passed it to Ceridwen's dragon lover, Cadir."

"I canna believe Ceridwen was that stupid." Gwydion banged the butt of his staff on the ground. Sparks flew every which way.

"You weren't there," I told him, "but our best guess was Cadir lured her with inducements he still loved her. All she had to do was cast this spell, and they could be together forever."

"Doesna sound like the goddess I knew," Gwydion muttered. "She used men. Never knew her to be obsessed by them."

Fire flew from Zelli and Quade, a sure sign how furious —and ashamed—they still were with Cadir. I wasn't enamored of him, either. He might have donated the sperm that made me, but after that his dad contributions had jumped off a cliff. The one and only time I'd met him, he'd tried to kidnap me and then turned it around to make it my fault.

He was dead. I'd cut out his heart, and Dewi had cast it into the volcanoes on Fire Mountain...

"Rowan?" Bjorn's tone held that solicitous note that had crept in ever since he found out I was pregnant. He meant well, but I wanted to strangle him and scream at him to leave me alone.

"Yeah." I tossed my head back. "Sorry. Wasn't paying attention."

"Someone needs to go inside." Gwydion looked at me as if he expected me to volunteer.

"Inside there?" I stared at the suppurating gash. He nodded, and I said, "If you're so all-fired interested, be my guest."

"I'm considering it."

"What are you expecting to find?" I asked him.

He shrugged, reminding me of a physics professor I'd had in a long ago college class. Dr. McGovey had been more interested in whether something was theoretically possible than in whether it was a good idea or not.

"Probably related to those gray things we saw wriggling through the void under the Nine Worlds," Quade spoke up.

Bjorn turned to the dragon. "If that's true, I should talk with Yggdrasil. I'd thought the black places in its roots were burned spots until Rowan pointed out fire wouldn't ignite in the absence of air. I should have figured that out on my own, but it means the darkened areas have to be rot, and it's been spreading for a while now."

"Talking with the One Tree is not a good idea," Gwydion said.

"It's not so bad, long as you keep your guard up," Bjorn told him. "The problem would be encouraging it to communicate. Mostly, the tree sings and lives in its dreams."

"Aye. I ken well enough. I was there." Gwydion set his mouth in a tense line.

I raked hair out of my face and tried to connect the dots. I'd gotten at least some sleep, but I still felt frazzled and fuzzy. "What does talking to Yddgrasil have to do with that?" I pointed at the pulsing gap. It looked about the same as it had when we showed up. At least it wasn't worse, but our efforts hadn't done a damned thing.

A creeping malaise held a wrong feel; I took a few steps back and built a ward. The change was instantaneous. "It's still draining us," I warned.

Magic flared around Bjorn and Gwydion. Apparently, the dragons had their own methods of dealing with the magical thievery. Their scales probably provided natural protection.

"Thanks," Bjorn said. "Presumably, the tubular things are some type of transfer mechanism."

"What tubular things?" Gwydion furled his brows. After Bjorn described what we'd seen, Gwydion's next question was, "If 'tis a transfer mechanism, where does it begin?"

"Odin suspects somewhere near the boundary separating the outer borderworlds," Bjorn replied.

"If that were true," I said, "why aren't they attached to anything? It seems to me they can't do much harm floating about."

"They were not attached when we were there," Zelli said.

"Mmph, so they may have been earlier." I thought about it. Had our unexpected presence interrupted something, and they'd let go abruptly? They hadn't been all that close.

"Odin may have understood more than we offered him credit for," Bjorn said. "Cutting off whatever is powering this at its roots might be the only way."

"What did ye do last time to counteract the Breaking place?" Gwydion looked at Bjorn.

"Mixed fire and earth and built a magnetic trap to defuse the residual evil clinging to this place. But then it wasn't this large, and malicious intent merely oozed from it. Now it's more like a flood."

Gwydion snapped his fingers. "Solves one part of this puzzle. Ye left magic lying about. The entity strengthened itself on the casting ye built."

"Probably so." Breath hissed from between Bjorn's clenched teeth. "So much for another go at attempting to contain it."

"Not a good idea," Gwydion agreed. "'Tis all or naught. Either we wipe it out of existence or leave it be."

"We canna leave it be," Zelli argued. "'Tis growing."

"I wonder if other gateways such as this one exist?" Quade mused.

"I really do not like that line of inquiry," I told the dragon.

"Mayhap not"—he angled his eerie gaze my way—"but we must attend to every possibility."

Thinking about it made me even more tired than I already was. "I should check on the witches," I mumbled. I wasn't concerned about the splinter group growing vegetables in Inverlochy Castle's courtyards, but most of my friends remained in caves beneath Ben Nevis.

Casting a sidelong glance at the Breaking site sent icy tendrils down my spine. "Do you suppose it's safe to leave it unattended?"

"I already answered that," Zelli said. "In a word, no."

"That much worse than afore, eh?" Gwydion asked.

"Much worse," Bjorn and I said almost in unison.

"I've kept an eye on it for years," I told the warrior magician. "Right after the Breaking, it was so bad I couldn't get within a hundred meters, but gradually the horrible, warped malice pumping out of the hole faded. It actually receded so much, it barely felt evil anymore."

He set his staff on the ground in front of him. Light glowed from within, bright and inviting. Holding up a hand, he counted off on three fingers. "Cadir is dead. Ceridwen is imprisoned on Fire Mountain. Loki is, presumably, imprisoned in Jotunheim."

Before he could say more, Bjorn jumped in. "My money's on Loki. He's almost as connected to the Nine Worlds as Odin. Perhaps more in some ways because of his giant blood and Hel's role."

"You don't think Hel has anything to do with him?" I

squawked. It had just come home to roost that Hel being Bjorn's mother meant Loki was his grandfather. I snaked a protective hand across my belly. The world would end before I'd allow Loki within spitting distance of his great-grandchild.

Bjorn turned both hands palms up. "No idea. He is her father, and she borrowed his magic to seduce Nidhogg." After casting a surreptitious glance Gwydion's way, he added, "I'm not certain we ever truly understand the gods' motivations or aims."

"Ye've joined our august ranks," Gwydion noted wryly. "Or did that escape you?"

"Being a half breed doesn't count," I reminded him.

He ignored my comment. Probably just as well. Everything about this patch of ground was making me antsy as fuck. The Breaking spot had not only grown, it held a different feel. Darker. More malevolent than before. I didn't see how the amorphous gray things could possibly be related to it. Maybe I was being too literal, but they hadn't been connected to anything—at either end.

Surely, if they served as a kind of conduit, some of them would have stretched beyond my field of vision. They hadn't. The ground heaved beneath my feet. Great. More earthquakes.

I judged the shifting, rolling landscape and picked the flattest spot. A brisk leap landed me squarely on it. Before I had a chance to congratulate myself and yell for Bjorn to join me, the inviting patch of dirt opened into a crater, sucking me into blackness. Dirt fell on me as the chasm closed over, blocking out Bjorn's outraged hollering. Unlike my last unexpected jaunt away from almost this same place, he hadn't been fast enough to reach me.

Just as well.

I'd been conned. Just because I'd been an idiot was no reason to sweep the whole world into the same trap.

Damn it. I knew better. There'd been a reason for the single flat place, and I'd played right into somebody's hands. "I'll get you," I shouted. "You're horsemeat."

My words echoed back at me. Before I ended up too far away to use telepathy, I shouted, *"Bjorn!"*

No reply. Distance couldn't be the issue. I'd only been falling for a few moments. Falling. Yeah. Need to fix that part first. I righted myself and did what I could to slow my downward trajectory. Turned out I couldn't stop myself completely, but being upright helped. Teleporting to somewhere familiar had to be my next move. The void between worlds would be an improvement, even though where I was now had air.

I should be worried. Frightened. Instead, I was angry I'd been duped. There'd be plenty of time to be scared later. If I tried—and failed—to get myself out of this mess.

I had a shit ton of questions. Had something targeted me specifically? Or would anyone landing on that particular level spot have been snapped up? Was this a variant of the same spell that had snared me the first time Bjorn and I had worked together on corralling the Breaking?

I felt for Mother's magic and didn't find it. At least it argued against this being the same casting that had given me heartburn last time. I had a feeling teleporting would be difficult, but I tested it, anyway.

What choice did I have?

Waiting around to be rescued isn't my style. Besides, it presumes someone could find me, which was scarcely a given. I took my time, grateful when each step of my process seemed relatively normal.

Magic accessible. Check. Mix fire with air. Check. Feed in more air. Check. Determine destination... I thought about the most promising spot and chose Inverlochy. Returning to the area I'd been jerked from was pointless. By now, everyone would have scattered, hunting for me. If I could get to Inverlochy, the Celts could raise Gwydion. Presumably, he was with Bjorn and the dragons.

Hell, if I made it out of this pit, I could find everyone myself.

Convinced I'd done as well as I could, I fed the destination into my teleport casting and kindled my spell. I was smooth, confident. I didn't hesitate. Ha! I should have been smarter. My spell snapped back in my face like a large-caliber rubber band. It smarted, and I rubbed my jaw.

"Think," I said out loud. And then I repeated the word a few more times.

Everything had been normal—until I'd tried to use my magic to forge a pathway out of wherever I was. Teleport spells aren't necessarily directional, not in the normal way of visualizing north-south-east-west. They're more metaphorical than linear. Kind of a "beam-me-up-Scotty" undertaking where your cells start at point A and end up at point B without a physical transition zone.

I thought of another approach that might bypass my prison— if I was on the right track. This time I worked fast, before whatever had me in its clutches caught on and stymied my efforts. In less time than it takes to tell, my astral self hovered above my body. The projection that was also me floated easily. I directed myself upward, but before I left, I examined the problem from my current aerial perspective. Sure enough, a brass-colored cage circled my body. Not solid, it glistened with eerie magic. Something about its weave had defeated my effort to teleport.

Why hadn't I noticed it from within its confines?

Not a question I was likely to come up with an answer for. Many types of magic exist, and I'm only familiar with a small portion of them.

I needed to hurry. At some point, the siren call of my body would force me back to it. I didn't relish the collision. Leaving was easy. Returning hurt like a bitch.

After traversing dirt, rocks, and mud, I popped out into the clearing around the Breaking spot. As I'd feared, everyone had left. Maybe I still had some latitude before my body grew impatient. I floated higher, hoping to discover something I could leverage to help myself.

A portal snapped open beneath me. Bjorn, Gwydion, Andraste, and a bevy of Celts poured from it. Zelli and Quade winged into view. If I'd had my body, I'd have fist pumped the air. My next task was getting someone's attention. A neat trick since no one could see me or feel me. Even if I landed square on their head.

Astral projection is phenomenal for eavesdropping. Less useful for other pursuits. Regardless, I started with Zelli. She was closest; maybe our bond could reach across my lack of a physical presence. I hovered right in front of her. She flew through me. This time, I straddled her, wrapped my spectral arms around her neck, grabbed her horns.

The dragon felt so good, I wanted to cry. But she had no idea I was there. I tried telepathy, but it was a joke. The part of me that could push words out was a gazillion miles underground.

Zelli thumped onto the ground with Quade nearby. Dewi flew through a gash in the sky and joined them. "If we find her"—the Celtic dragon goddess fisted a foreleg and shook it—"she will go to Fire Mountain. No more arguments."

Yeah, well, we'd see about that.

I waited for a chorus of disagreements, but no one voiced them.

Damn it.

Bjorn had begun an incantation I didn't recognize above the spot where I'd fallen into oblivion. Perhaps because I was a spirit, I could see his magic and the Norse enchantments weaving in with it. The mix was colorful as fuck. When the dragons added their power to the mix, a veritable rainbow formed, shaping itself into an enormous arrow that augured into the earth.

The ground parted before the onslaught of magic. More than parted. I've never known earth to move so fast. The chasm deepened until I couldn't see the tail of the arrow any longer. I felt it, though, burrowing downward. I'd have had to be dead not to sense the enormous trail it blazed deep into Earth's mantle.

Hope surged, so bright I could almost, almost taste it. Would they find my body before it moved beyond the reach of their magic? I opened eyes I didn't realize I'd squeezed shut. Hope turned into a blazing inferno. If I could do anything with my spirit form, it meant my body was moving toward me.

An unholy glow shimmered around the opening forged into the dirt, and grew brighter by the minute. I felt the pull of my body but resisted. I'd wait as long as I could—in case something went wrong.

I did not want to end up trapped again. By now, whoever was behind this surely knew I'd made a run for it. Part of me, anyway. If they'd had enough magic to counteract seven Celts, Bjorn, and three dragons, they would have.

In a deeply personal place, I was delighted some combination of magic was enough to temporarily defeat whatever was out to sabotage the Nine Worlds.

The glow took on an iridescent sheen; the tail end of the arrow backed out of the hole. My body, cage and all, was encased in it. I felt the inexorable pull to be whole again. The arrow was moving slower now. Everyone surged closer to it, urging it with renewed magic and stronger, more insistent incantations.

Halfway.

I was done waiting. I could help. Right now, my magic was missing from the group effort. I let myself slam back into my body, ready to pivot as fast as I could. No wallowing in how shitty the transition was. Not this time. The moment I was whole, I shot power outward and glommed onto Bjorn.

His shout told me everything. Harsh. Feral. Victorious. He knew we were going to make it.

Light blinded me, and then I was in his arms. Somehow,

the cage had vanished. Behind us, I heard the Celtic spell that would shut the hole and keep it closed. Hope to hell it worked better than our attempt to seal the Breaking spot.

"Rowan. Aw shit, you scared the life out of me," Bjorn murmured.

Too wiped out to talk, I leaned into him. Not much point in telling anyone about my astral separation. They'd have rescued me, anyway. And probably with somewhat less effort, if I'd been available to help sooner. Besides, this way, I wouldn't have to deal with Dewi's pronouncement about me and my baby and Fire Mountain.

Before anyone could get into that discussion, I squeaked out, "Home."

"Of course, darling. Ben Nevis?"

I nodded and felt his magic surrounding me. I wanted to sleep for a week, but I wouldn't be that lucky. Someone would show up in my little chamber. By the time its walls formed around us, I'd started to shake. I'd had a hell of a close call, and it was just beginning to sink in.

Many things are worse than death, and being buried alive is one of them.

CHAPTER SIX, BJORN

Rowan is ungodly strong. It's one of the many things I love about her. When shudders racked her body, I understood what a rough go she'd had. Fierce protectiveness shot through me. I wanted to rip whoever had done this to her from one end to the other. Flay flesh from bones—if they even possessed such things. I made a grab for level-headedness, reminded myself we'd won this round. It made absolutely no difference at all.

Fury and apprehension traded places, pummeling me with a dizzying round robin of conflicting priorities. I refused to leave Rowan's side, but I'd have to in order to hunt down and annihilate the thing that singled her out. She'd insist on coming along, which would complicate things still further. I had no right to order her to remain behind. She could thumb her nose at me and follow wherever I went.

I tightened my hold on her. We had to be equal partners. I'd been onto something with not having a right to tell her what to do. No matter how worried I was about her—about our child—she was still her own person. I was an ass to discount her magic. She might not have gotten herself out of the last trap, but she hadn't had much time to work on it, either.

Reminding myself to have faith in Rowan and her common sense and her magic and her sheer grit, I guided my travel spell toward her chamber beneath the most sacred mountain in Scotland.

It had required a mix of Celtic, Norse, and dragon magics to neutralize the mesh that wound about her. Under different circumstances, I'd have wanted to examine the webbing, find out how it was constructed so we could guard against such an occurrence again.

Under different circumstances. Not when it controlled the woman who meant everything to me. Her room formed around us. As my spell faded, I carried her to the edge of her bed and sat, still holding her in my arms.

"Can I get you anything?"

"Uh-uh. Not yet," she mumbled.

Mort dashed into the room and jumped on my back, clawing his way around my body so he could get to Rowan. Luxuriant black fur encased his feline form. He clearly couldn't decide if he was happy or furious. Yowls mixed with deep purrs; the occasional claw dug into me. I could relate to exactly how the cat felt. Tansy followed Mort carrying a welcome pot of tea. The rich scents of rosemary and wild mushrooms filled the chamber as she poured us mugs and stirred honey into them.

"Thanks," I told her as she handed me one.

"Smells divine," Rowan said. Letting go of me, she maneuvered until she sat on the floor at my feet. Mort followed her to the floor. First he plopped in her lap, but after she stroked him a few times, he crawled up her body and ended up curved around her neck. The yowls had mostly ceded to purring.

"You look like you've been through a war," Tansy said and placed a mug close enough for Rowan to reach it.

"Because I have." Rowan offered a wan smile.

Tansy patted her shoulder. Her blonde brows knitted into a thin line, and I felt witch magic flare. "Oh my," she breathed the words. "Are you—? I mean it seems like you might be..."

"It's all right." Rowan extended a hand, and Tansy grasped it. "You're correct. I am pregnant."

"How long? When will the babe be here?" Tansy's thin face blossomed into a blinding smile. She let go of Rowan's hand and clasped hers together. "This is so exciting. I was last to be born in these caverns, and..." She started over again. "Not that you'll necessarily be here for the birth, but it would be such an honor to attend you. Not by myself, of course. Hilda and Leif, they're the healers."

Color splotched her cheeks when she looked at me. "And of course, your magic far surpasses ours. If you'd prefer Norse healers to our own, I understand." She dropped an awkward curtsey. "Congratulations to you both."

Tansy was so kind and so genuine; her enthusiasm and her deep caring for Rowan touched my soul. Her green eyes moved from Rowan to me and back again. "The babe will be half dragon. Will she be able to fly?"

Rowan chuckled. "First off, it's a he. And I have no idea. About much of anything, including how long I'll be pregnant. It won't be very convenient if he can fly since neither Bjorn nor I can."

"Oh. Hadn't thought about that. I'm certain you'll figure things out. May I share the good news?"

"Of course," I told her. "The other group of witches already knows."

"Ooooh. Back with more tea in a little bit. Unless you've fallen asleep. Then I'll just tiptoe in and leave the pot." Still grinning from ear to ear, Tansy turned and bolted from the room.

Rowan picked up her mug and took a long drink from it.

"Feel like talking?" I asked.

"Not exactly, but it's probably a necessary evil." She scooted around on her butt until she sat cross-legged on the floor facing me.

I wasn't certain where to begin, so I picked the hardest part. Unpleasant, but she still needed to know. "That trap," I began, "had your name all over it."

She nodded somberly, mug clutched between her hands. "I figured as much. What kind of magic could do that? It not only nabbed me, it imprisoned my power. I could do whatever I wanted within its confines, but if I tried to direct anything outward, it snapped back and clonked me over the head."

I must have been grinding my jaws or making a face because she shook her head. "Out with it."

"Out with what?" I felt impotent, helpless. "Things happened almost too fast to follow, but what I saw was this.

You jumped to the only unmarked bit of ground left. A net sort of oozed out of the air and draped around you. Describing it makes it sound like it took a while, but the whole thing was done in less than a couple of seconds.

"I dove for you, chucked magic at the webbing. So did the dragons and Gwydion. Nothing we did made any difference. That net rebuffed me. I couldn't grab hold of it. The earth opened up, and you vanished in a flurry of clods of dirt that rained down on the broken place."

Rowan blinked a few times and closed her teeth over her lower lip. "Interesting," she murmured. "All I remember is jumping, the ground opening up, and being gone. I had no sense of a physical snare, nor did I feel it once I was underground. At first, I tumbled, but I righted myself pretty quickly. Tried to stop moving, but all I managed was to slow things down. When I cobbled a teleport spell together, things got ugly fast."

I uncurled my hands. They'd formed fists as I listened to her. "I'd have found you. No matter what it took. Gwydion was pretty spun out too. And the dragons were beside themselves, stomping about and bugling and throwing fire. They stayed to keep an eye on things while Gwydion and I raised the Celts. We gathered a small group and led them to where you'd been taken."

I stopped long enough to gather my thoughts. "I was certain if we waited too long, you'd move beyond the Nine Worlds. Would have made things more difficult."

Rowan dropped her head into her hands. When she looked up, she said, "I'm confused. I do not see the connection between Yggdrasil's rotting roots, the Breaking spot, and the gray things beneath the Nine Worlds. Is Loki still pulling puppet strings from the sidelines? How about Ceridwen? How certain are we she and the Morrigan haven't joined forces? Both of them enjoy the fuck out of a good shitstorm."

"What worries me," I forced the words out because I couldn't keep them contained, "is they painted an X on your back because of our baby."

The light in Rowan's eyes turned hard. "Your point?"

"Not sure I had one, except we are going to have to be more cautious than usual."

She shook her head slowly from one side to the other and then back again. "Cautious has never been part of who I am." Hair had fallen into her face. She shoved it behind her shoulders with an impatient gesture and curved a hand over her belly.

"I will do my best to ensure things go well. For the babe and me. Doing my best does not include sequestering myself in Fire Mountain or Niflheim or Hel or Asgard or anywhere I'm simply waiting out my pregnancy."

Rowan rolled her shoulders back. "What happens after he's born? Do I leave him with the witches while I'm out fighting to keep Earth from collapsing into dust? Do I leave off fighting until he's a years old? Two? Five? Will anything be left then?"

"None of this is easy—" I began.

"Not done," she broke in. "Not looking for sympathy, either." She drained her tea before continuing. "I'm a practical woman. I've had to be. No one ever sugarcoated anything or made things easy for me. Practical means I like to think things through, have a plan. Kind of like the plan the witches and I came up with around growing crops. It held risks, but the benefits outweighed them. Or my plan keeping an eye on the Breaking spot."

I nodded, offering encouragement. She was obviously working through something important. When she looked up at me, her eyes looked more dragon than human. They revealed her turmoil. Anguish spilled from her. "I can hardly find time to eat or sleep. What kind of mother will I be?"

"You're not alone in this," I reminded her.

"Are we going to take turns fighting? Kind of negates the benefit of how amazing our magic is when we mix it together."

I slid off the edge of the bed until I sat across from her. Taking one of her hands, I said, "Whatever we face, we have each other. Hatchling dragons can fight from a very young age. It was one reason the dragons opted to keep their young behind Fire Mountain's gates. They did not want them to become part of anyone's army."

"Define very young."

I thought about various books I'd read. "A month, or perhaps two at the most."

"I'm not sure whether to laugh or cry." She reached up and stroked the cat with her free hand. "Will he fly? Will he shapeshift? Will I need to nurse him, or will he eat whatever dragons do?" She leveled a glance my way. "I'm assuming they eat meat."

"They hunt, yes."

I caressed the back of the hand I still held. "All those things will show themselves in time. Meanwhile—"

"Meanwhile, what?" she snapped, almost immediately adding, "Sorry." Her eyes narrowed. "Crap. Dewi is outside. Tell her to go away."

A quick scan verified Rowan's words. "What did she say?" I asked.

"Ordered me to meet her outside. I'm not going."

"I'll go." I got to my feet. "I can't tell her to go away, though. Can you imagine how well that would be received? I'd piss her off, and we'd end up in a squabble that would go nowhere."

"Then tell her I'm asleep or something."

"She'll know you're not."

"You think?" Rowan grimaced. "Usually, I'd tell her to fuck off. But I don't have the energy to fight with her."

I bent and kissed the top of Rowan's head. Mort growled a warning. I understood. Rowan had been gone far too much for his taste, and he wanted her all to himself. So did I. "You and me both, mate," I murmured and walked from the room.

I felt for Ro, but she had to buck up. There are no accidents. Fate had sculpted her, made her resilient. She'd find her way. I'd planned to use these few minutes to organize my thoughts, but it would be best to see why Dewi was here.

I had my own ideas about that topic, but I wasn't going to make the mistake of inserting my expectations. The corridor flashed by, and the door swooshed shut behind me. Dewi stood a few meters away, scaled forelegs crossed over her ruby chest.

"Where's Runa?" she asked.

"Rowan"—I stressed the name she preferred—"has had quite a day. She's resting."

"Pfft. She doesn't wish to talk with me."

I walked closer. "Why would she? You ignored her through a miserable childhood. You and all the rest of your kinsmen. Now that she's pregnant, you want to imprison her."

"I do not." The dragon shot fire skyward.

"Well, it's how she's interpreting it." I inhaled sharply, nostrils flaring. "Fire Mountain may be your home, but it's not hers. How long will the pregnancy last? Will the baby be more dragon than human?"

Dewi regarding me through whirling eyes shading through the green spectrum. "Finally. Ye're asking smart questions. The pregnancy could be verra brief. And 'twould surprise me if the babe wasn't more dragon than human."

I digested the information. "How is that possible? Rowan and I are both half dragon, and our human forms are fairly entrenched."

Dewi uncoiled her forelegs and shrugged. "Aye, the child is half dragon, but not just any dragons. Nidhogg and Cadir."

"I can see where Nidhogg might add something special, but Cadir?"

"He wasn't always what ye saw." Her voice softened. "Once he showed great promise. Unfortunately, 'twasn't tempered by great wisdom. Magic can be a curse, even for dragonkind. Some were jealous of his ability; he had few associates. In the end, his isolation led to bitterness and—"

"Made him ripe for Loki's plucking," I finished her thought.

"Aye, something like that." Smoke puffed around the edges of her jaws.

"This still isn't adding up," I told her. "Nidhogg is my"—I stumbled over the word father and tried again—"male parent, and I haven't come close to sprouting wings since Hel yanked away the glamour."

"The situations are not the same." She shook a talon my way. "This baby already knows precisely what—and who—he is. You languished through centuries afore ye discovered your birthright."

The word languished annoyed me, but I pushed it aside. Something she'd said banged around in my head. "What do you mean by very brief."

"Och, the pregnancy. It might only last a few weeks."

"How is that possible? I thought your eggs incubated for over two years."

"Eggs, aye. But this baby is within Rowan's body."

"Help me out here," I said. "I'm not seeing the difference."

"Although we bathe our eggs in our power, 'tis far more intense within a body than we could ever manage in our nests. Also, the energy is different in the Nine Worlds than on Fire Mountain."

I felt Ro's magic before I saw her walk to my side. She inclined her head to Dewi. "Apologies. I was being a brat."

"Accepted, but there is more to this." Dewi lowered her head until it was nearly eye level with us.

"Figured you'd know," Rowan said. "The child is, um, talking."

"Of course, he is." Dewi sounded pleased.

"He told me you were part of his dragon ancestry, and he wished to greet you properly."

"And I shall greet him as I have every dragon who was ever hatched." Dewi scrunched lower and splayed a taloned foreleg over Rowan's belly. Where it had been flat when I'd left her room, it had developed a definite curvature. The dragon puffed steam until it billowed around us.

"You just made him very happy," Rowan said.

"He has done the same for me." Dewi straightened. "I shall leave you to rest and eat, but be quick. We leave verra soon."

"For where?" I asked.

"To clear the space beneath the Nine Worlds."

I winced, not wanting to annoy the dragon, but I had to ask, "Does Odin know?"

"Why should he?"

I planted my feet shoulder-width apart. "Because you're allies now. All that Norse-Celtic rivalry has to be laid aside. What if Odin set some kind of snares? When we left Valhalla, he was on his way to take a look at the problems we saw. Worse, what if he's still there and your magic clashes with his?"

The steam turned to ash. "I see the problem," Dewi rumbled. "We shall make adjustments. Meanwhile"—her jaws lolled into a smile—"Zelli and Quade will be by to get you in a couple of hours. Be ready."

Before Rowan or I could lodge a protest, request a bit more time, magic boiled around the dragon, and she vanished.

The cat was still curled around Rowan's neck. "I owe

you an apology too," she said to me. "I felt overwhelmed, but it's a shitty excuse."

"It's all right."

"No. It isn't. I've elevated pushing people away into an art form. It's long past time I got over it. Speaking of time, we don't have much. Feel like cleaning up?" She lifted Mort down despite his staunch protests and told him to go back inside. Of course, he ignored her and stalked around meowing like a mad thing.

The corners of my mouth twitched. "We don't have a very good track record with baths."

She chuckled, and the sound warmed me. "We're so new, being naked together should lead to...other things. If it didn't, I'd worry about us."

"Aha! You just admitted it."

"Admitted what?" Rowan glanced my way.

"You want to see me naked," I teased.

"I do. Would you prefer the pool or the cisterns in the cave?"

"Surprise me." My body's response to her suggestion was so immediate it astonished me. It ran far deeper than her beauty and her allure. Deep, primitive, savage, the most profound parts of me screamed she was mine. I wrapped my arms around her and fell into the power she wove around us. Hers and yet more. I felt her dragon nature more acutely than before as the stark flanks of Ben Nevis fell away replaced by a circle of standing stones and a glowing turquoise pool.

I'd been here before. It was a secret place not quite belonging to Midgard. Still part of the Nine Worlds, but removed by a few degrees. I still held Rowan in my arms. She fit against my body as if she'd been molded just for me. Angling my head, I crushed my mouth down on hers.

More than wanting her, I had to have her. She opened her mouth to mine and wove her hands into my hair as she held my head. Her nipples turned to peaks against my chest, and the press of her belly cradled my more-than-erect cock. Maybe someday we'd get around to elaborate foreplay, but it wouldn't be now. Urgency beat a path through me, all mixed up with heat and need and loving the woman in my arms.

She moaned and writhed as we kissed, mouths glued together, tongues sparring. She bit my lower lip. I bit back. My hands worked their way down her back, but I wasn't satisfied kneading the tight, high globes of her ass. Rucking up her skirt, I dipped a hand between her legs, seared by the heat of her.

She muffled a shriek and ground herself against my questing fingers, all fervor and magic and slick neediness. I teased and rubbed and plumbed her with fingers while pressing my palm against her vulva. I knew she was close, so I added a bit of magic, and she dissolved around me. Holding her, watching color paint her breasts and face as she came humbled me and made me feel a million meters tall.

"I promised you a hundred of those," I rasped.

"We have a few more to go," she managed, despite struggling to get her breath back.

"I'm taking that as an open invitation."

She placed a hand over mine and pressed herself into me. "It's more than an invitation. I'm yours. Prickles, bitchy moods, and all." Her mouth sought mine, and our kiss took off where the last one had left off.

My cock was so ready, keeping a noose around its randiness was out of the question. It had slipped its bonds; any illusions I had about who was in charge were pipe dreams. It pressed against the front of my trousers that had become uncomfortably snug.

I tore my mouth from hers, hating to let go for even long enough to divest ourselves of our clothes. I was breathing so hard, my words came out garbled. "Propose a contest. Who can undress faster?"

Rowan laughed. "You're on." She whipped her top over her head and unfastened her skirt and stepped out of it. All that remained were her boots.

I'd meant to undress, but I was starstruck staring at her. Her breasts were full, belly rounded. It lent her a Madonna appearance and made her all the more desirable. If that were even possible.

She glanced down at herself. "Just kind of happened," she murmured. "Is it okay? Am I still—"

"More than okay. I can't get over how incredibly lovely you are."

Rowan grinned, slow at first, but then it reached her eyes. "Could you get over it long enough to take your clothes off?"

I laughed and stripped out of my vest and shirt before kneeling to deal with my boots. Finally, I got around to my breeches. Freeing my cock was a relief, and it jutted from my body. Meanwhile, Rowan had removed her boots and was bending over the water, presumably warming it. Her ass parted, offering me an alluring view of her sex framed by red curls. In my present condition, cold water would be fine. Nothing could quench the fire roaring through me.

I walked to her and filled my hands with her breasts. They were firmer, not just fuller, and the touch of them delighted me. My cock nudged her opening as I cuddled her breasts and twirled the nipples. "Damn, woman. You have the finest ass."

"Bath first," she said. "Both of us stink."

"I'm putty in your hands."

She snorted. "You can't smell us?"

I could, but it didn't matter to me. We'd come from a battlefield. Our sweat was well-earned. I wrapped an arm around her waist, and we walked into the water.

CHAPTER SEVEN, ROWAN

The soft blue waters of the pool surrounded me, first my legs, then waist deep, and then my breasts were submerged. All the while, I was intimately aware of Bjorn next to me. The scent of his power, rich with the salt tang of the sea, invaded my nostrils. When he'd stopped dead and just stared at my heavier breasts and no-longer flat belly, I'd been afraid I wasn't pretty anymore.

Not that I've ever been invested in how I look, but I wanted so much to be pleasing to him. Gah. I sound like such a girl, but the approval radiating from him had soaked into my bones, my soul.

He grabbed handfuls of sand from the bottom and scrubbed my back and arms. I mixed magic in with sand—as a stand-in for our lack of soap—and worked on the grime and grit caking his hair and streaking down his face.

A giggle escaped me. "Damn. We're both hot messes."

"Fighting is dirty business. Turn around. I'll get your hair."

Eventually, we were more or less clean and playing in the water like a couple of kids splashing each other. "It's easy to believe we can shut out the world when we're here." I said.

"Because we can," he said solemnly. "But someone will find us, even here. Besides, you and I aren't runaway types." He tipped my chin up with an index finger. "I love you, Rowan."

My throat tightened with emotion, and I wrapped my arms around him. His mouth crashed down on mine, and we were back where we'd begun, standing on the shore among the circle of sacred stones. Lust spiraled, developed a will of its own. He scooped me up and carried me out of the water to a thick stand of marsh grass.

His kisses were sweet and hot and urgent. His mouth traveled down my neck and back up to my face, biting as he went. I hung on as he lowered us into the dense, prickly grass. He lay on his back and arranged me so I straddled him. His cock throbbed between us. Hard and thick and beautiful. I longed to worship it, take him into my mouth, but he had other ideas.

Lifting me, he pressed the tip of him against my entrance and thrust fast and sure, only stopping once he hit bottom. A slow, lazy smile etched into his face. "There. That's perfect. You're perfect." He twitched his appendage within me. I tightened around him. We did that for a while. Twitch. Tighten. Twitch. Tighten. Lust thickened until not moving became a contest of wills.

He broke first.

Hands still around my hips, he slid me up his shaft and then back down. He stretched me, touched places so deep and private, emotion rocked me as my body climbed high, surfing the crest of one wave after another. Magic brightened the air around us, turning it liquid with shades of blue and gold. Men had touched my body before, but I'd never let anyone near my essence. I'd kept my soul locked away. Before it had only been for me, but now it was Bjorn's as well. I should have been frightened of the way I'd opened myself, but it felt right. He felt right.

We felt right.

"Darling. Darling, Ro," he crooned in Old Norse. He was moving faster now, and his cock swelled bigger within me. I waited, hovered at the top of the next wave of sensation, wanting to take him with me. Wanting him to drown in heat and love and lust, right along with me.

I felt the moment when passion took him. The still, quiet spot before semen juddered from him, but when his climax was as inexorable as the tides. Tightening my muscles around his engorged cock, I urged him to spill himself within me, to join me in ecstasy.

We came for a long time, and then we held each other as breath and reason returned. One perhaps slower than the other. I must have smiled because he asked, "What?"

"You've bewitched me. Besotted me. I'm done for."

"Nay, wench. 'Tis you who've bewitched me. After all, ye passed as a witch for many a long year." He was still speaking Norse.

I smiled. He grinned back.

"I'm happy," I whispered. "So happy, it's scary."

He stroked my cheek. "I want you to be happy, darling. Tell me about our son talking with you. What was it like?"

I nodded. Of course, he'd want to know. "Odd. Mystical. Magical. Normal. All wrapped up in one. He has a small voice, a child's voice. I knew instantly it was him. He didn't say much, but he knew Dewi was close and was quite insistent about meeting her."

"Makes sense."

"Why? I couldn't figure it out."

"Dewi was the first dragon ever to hatch. She's kind of like the grande dame of dragonkind. Our son would recognize her as special, important."

I thought about it. "Do dragons have archetypal memories?"

"I'm not certain. They—er, we—all share a mind link with Nidhogg. Things have been different for me since Hel removed the cloaking. I'm still sorting it out. What about you? You may not have known about your dragon father, but has your power altered since discovering you're a Dragon Heir?"

I considered the question. Everyone—as in Nidhogg and Ysien—had intimated gates would open, angels would sing, and I'd suddenly be elevated far above where I'd been. "Hasn't happened yet," I murmured. "Frankly, I'm not expecting it to. The biggest alteration in my magic was you."

"We pack a hell of a punch working together." Bjorn traced the line of my jaw with a calloused fingertip.

"Even more than that. Words don't come close to describing what a joy it is when your power weaves with mine." I felt my face warm, but I kept on talking. "It's silly and schmaltzy, but I believe we could conquer any foe. If you'd been closer when Yggdrasil's roots grabbed me, escape would have been trivial."

Vertical lines formed between Bjorn's blond brows. "At least theoretically, Quade and I were close. Did you try telepathy?"

"Yup. Did that right off the bat, but it ricocheted back at me after our brief exchange about the One Tree's rotted-out roots."

The lines deepened, and I could almost taste his worry. "After all my fine talk about protecting you, I made a few assumptions. I didn't test them, and they weren't true."

"What assumptions?" He looked so distraught, I wove my fingers into his hair and smoothed it away from his face.

"We talked once, complained about the lack of air. I figured you were somewhere near me, even though I couldn't see you."

"It was a reasonable supposition. Damn it, Bjorn. We can't know everything." I buried my face in his shoulder. We'd have to leave soon, and I wasn't ready to jump on Zelli and head back into the airless void where it was tough to think, let alone launch a campaign to deal with the gray things.

If they were even the problem.

"Your mind is busy," Bjorn murmured.

I nodded. "Always. Even though Odin believes so, I'm still not convinced those gray tubes were malevolent."

"One of you is wrong," Bjorn said bluntly. "I thought I sensed treachery oozing from them, but the environment was so bizarre, I wasn't certain. Quade was convinced they're evil, though."

"Hmph. Interesting. We must make certain we remain together," I told him. "Which likely means traveling together and not with the dragons."

"I've already thought about that." He kissed my forehead. "We need to get back, so we have time to eat something, but tell me about our baby. What language did he speak?"

A smile curved my mouth as tenderness for my unborn child ran through me like quicksilver. "The dragon's tongue."

Bjorn reached between us and curved a hand over my belly. "I can't wait to meet him."

I felt the same way. Given the sequence of events where our baby had spoken to me and I suddenly looked pregnant, I had a feeling perhaps things would proceed rather like time-lapse photography. It about killed me to let go, but I untangled myself from Bjorn and got to my feet, scooping up clothes and boots. His as well as mine.

He joined me; sea-tinged enchantment snapped us up and deposited us in my chamber. Mort yowled at the touch of magic and raced out of the room, hackles in full bloom. He'd return soon enough. I dumped our garments on the floor and knelt to separate them.

"Everything is so dirty, I hate to put them back on," Bjorn said and dragged breeches up his long legs.

"Know what you mean," I agreed. "But they're just going to get dirty again. May as well wear them rather than polluting something else." What I didn't mention was that anything as prosaic as laundry had taken a serious backseat.

Once we were decent, we hurried to the kitchen. A pot of soup was warm, so I ladled some into two bowls and we ate quickly. I'd been fighting a creeping sense of unease from the time we returned to the caves, but its source wasn't obvious.

Finally, I gave voice to my apprehension. "Do you feel it?" I asked.

He angled his head to one side and regarded me. "Feel what?"

Crap. Maybe I was edgy, imagining things. "Never mind," I mumbled.

Bjorn set his spoon down and took one of my hands, cradling it between his. "Uh-uh. You asked for a reason."

I finished the dregs from the bottom of my bowl. "I feel like something is skulking just beyond where I can get a good grip on it. Like we're being spied on by someone who wants to remain hidden."

The bite of Bjorn's magic flared around us as he sent a seeking spell outward. Just for the hell of it, I pushed my power into his. His casting had been subtle, but it burst into a punishing glare of blue-violet light.

"Oops. Too much." I dialed back my contribution while following the tentacles of his casting, hunting for clues. "I don't get it," I said.

"Nothing's there." He corroborated my assessment.

"Must have the pregnancy jitters." I attempted to make light of things and didn't do a very good job.

"Or whatever it is was listening and made a run for it." His words held grimness. While I was grateful he believed me, we didn't need to borrow trouble.

So far, we'd had the kitchens to ourselves, but our luck was certain to run out. Not that I didn't enjoy the witches' company, but I didn't have time to burn on conversation. The creepy-crawly sensation was back. And so quickly, I felt certain it had never completely left. Whatever it was probably couldn't penetrate the Celtic magic protecting these caves, but that didn't mean it wasn't lurking nearby.

I stood and gathered the residual magic still simmering around us into a travel spell.

Bjorn understood my intent and got to his feet. Together, we teleported to the open area outside the caves. It was full dark. I blew out a breath. In and among everything, I'd lost track of the passage of time.

"Two choices," Bjorn said. "Either we go to Inverlochy and join the Celts. Or we just head for the underside of the Nine Worlds and do what we can."

"What about the dragons?"

"If we wait for them, they'll insist we pair off like we have been. Me on Quade and you on Zelli. That configuration doesn't work where we're going. You and I lose track of one another."

"Something still doesn't feel right."

"Any idea what?" he asked, sounding so concerned and so tender some of my concerns faded. A little.

"I don't know. We could wait for the dragons and tell them we're traveling separately."

"We could." He took a step back. His face was illuminated by a stray beam from Arianrhod's moon when it peeked between two thick, gray clouds. "Your call, Ro. What do you want to do?"

Why was this so hard? Normally, I didn't have trouble selecting a path and riding it until it blew up in my face. Then I chose another. I'd never been invested in waiting for companions to support me, mostly because I'd never had access to such a luxury. I'd fought alone and fought well.

Riding the coattails of past successes, I said, "Let's go. At least, we can look around. If we don't like what's there, we can always teleport back to Inverlochy."

"I agree. Never been into decisions by committee."

A snort blew past my lips. "Geez, for a second there, I was picturing you in a three-piece suit presiding over a meeting in a boardroom."

"I may know what all those things are, but I've never owned such an article of clothing, and I've steered clear of human business dealings. They're mostly so drenched in greed, they turn my stomach."

"Know what you mean." I rolled my shoulders back. "Let's get this over with. I don't like that place, and the sooner we get there, the sooner we can leave."

"We'll take Bifrost to Niflheim and teleport from there. It will take a bit longer, but it also offers us the advantage of stealth. We'll be more effective creeping up on our target than if we just pop out in the void."

I took his hand and laced my magic with his to bind us together. "Ready when you are."

We walked through darkness to a point about a kilometer away. Far enough to figure out if anyone was tracking us with magic. "Seems safe enough to punch through to the bridge," I ventured.

"Aye. Either they're slow to react to changes in our position—"

"Or nothing was there to begin with," I mumbled. "I like Door Number Two better."

"So do I." The air crackled with his power, and a gilt-edged gateway formed.

"Fancy." I trotted through.

He followed on my heels. "And unexpected. I didn't do anything differently, yet the gateway seemed to be bleeding off excess magic."

I waited for Bifrost to steal my will, but apparently the Rainbow Bridge was done fucking with me. Markers flashed by. It was tempting to stop in Vanaheim and take refuge in Bjorn's cottage with his books and scrolls. Maybe we'd have a chance to stop there on the return leg.

"Quick detour," Bjorn announced as we neared Vanaheim.

"What for?" My previous longing to take refuge in his cottage returned in force.

"A couple of blades. I had the damned things forged, and we may need them."

A gateway formed, much plainer than before. We stepped through. Power bubbled around Bjorn just before two blades—one long, the other short—materialized on the ground next to him.

"Elegant," I commented.

"Pfft. Necessary. If we went home—to my home, that is—we'd be tempted to stay for a while." He buckled the sword belt and sheath into place and rekindled his portal.

"You must have read my mind," I told him. "About wanting a respite—from everything."

"Not a good idea. Time seems to be running short."

Something about hearing the words out loud breathed life into them. Made them truer than they'd have been otherwise. I followed him back onto Bifrost.

"One. Two. Three," Bjorn counted off markers. Power arced from his fingertips, and another portal formed. The incessant chill of Niflheim blasted me even before I was fully out of the bridge's controlled environment.

"I remember this part," I said.

"Tough to forget," he agreed.

"Last time I was through here, I was with Zelli. She's kind of like a bake oven, and it was welcome."

"I bet." He made a snorting sound. "Perhaps not bringing the dragons was shortsighted."

A hasty scan told me we weren't all that far from a cave where I'd once taken refuge. "Shall we take the same route I did when Hel aided me?" I asked, wanting to get moving before I turned as frosty as the icicles and snowy ground stretching around us. Did the trees ever leaf out? Or was it perpetual winter here just like in Jotunheim?

"What a lovely surprise," Hel's rich contralto brought my head whipping around.

She was wrapped in thick skins, fur side turned in. Serpents glided by her side. Two huge, black cobra-esque snakes clung to her much like guard dogs would have except their tongues flicked in and out scenting the chilly air.

"Not a social call," Bjorn told his mother. "Please. Show us the quickest route through Yggdrasil's roots."

Hel turned her dark gaze my way and scoured me from head to toe. "The child is growing."

"They do that." I'd begun to shiver. "Would the path you led us along the other day work best?"

A corner of Hel's mouth turned downward. "Och, all business, then. Perhaps the friendlier parts can happen later. Why do ye wish to traverse the One Tree's roots?"

I was cold, my patience thin. "Everyone has a different approach to dealing with the unknown threat to the Nine Worlds," I said. "If part of the problem is the alien forms floating beneath us, we can eliminate them. Might help. Might not. Right now, we're playing a game of exclusion. Eventually, we'll kill off the right element."

"Och, child. It could take centuries." Hel's gimlet gaze was still glued to me.

"If you've a better idea, let's hear it," Bjorn urged.

Hel tossed her head back and laughed. Once she got hold of herself, she said, "Dinna take you long to seize your power."

"We don't have time for this," I spoke up. "If we tarry too long, the dragons will show up, and then we'll have another argument to address."

"I wondered where they were. Regardless, I shall come with you," Hel said.

"We didn't ask you along," Bjorn retorted.

"If I let that stop me, I'd never leave Niflheim." She shrugged. The exposed bones on one side of her body clinked together.

"Can we get moving?" Cold seeped through the frozen world into the heart of me, stripping me of the will to do much of anything. I remembered my first trip here all too well. The soothing effect of Hel's magic had eroded my determination to find a way out. It aided her keeping the dead in line, but it also made the living stop caring what the fuck happened next.

"I propose a journey to the borderworld where Cadir lived once he escaped the dragons' exile," Hel said.

"Why there?" Bjorn asked.

"'Tis a logical spot for the origins of whatever is attacking the Nine Worlds." Hel blew out a breath. "Someone had to monitor the spell. Just because Cadir is dead and Loki imprisoned, the enchantment could still be there. We willna know unless we go and see for ourselves."

Interesting she didn't refer to Loki as Father. "Have you, um, spoken with Loki?" I asked.

"Ha! I wasna speaking with him afore this mess, and I certainly am not now." She shook a bony finger my way. "He will escape, and sooner rather than later. Father is wise and shrewd. He will bribe someone or cast them into a deep sleep. The moment he no longer has eyes on him, he will be gone. If he isn't already."

"What do you think?" Bjorn asked me.

I wrapped my arms around myself and sent magic to warm my frozen feet. "How do you know where Cadir holed up?" I asked Hel and netted her in a truth spell, beyond caring if it pissed her off. I was over arrogant deities who assumed they could make their own rules.

Rather than snarling at me, she didn't miss a beat. "I shall cast a blood spell. Not too many borderworlds in that vicinity, and I'm wagering Loki only visited Cadir's."

Her reply pinged cleanly off my casting. I reeled it in and said, "I'm game."

"Me too," Bjorn agreed. "Might be a better idea than our original one."

Hel nodded solemnly. "Odin has been through here several times. He traverses the roots, examines the damage, and grumbles about how much thicker the alien magic has grown."

"What?" I took a step back. "Does that mean he can't get rid of those gray things?"

"He's tried," Hel clarified. "He wipes them out. The next day, more of them are back."

"Mmph. He might have said something when we were all assembled in Valhalla," Bjorn grumbled.

"Indeed. At least sending groups to the outer borderworlds makes more sense now," I said.

"Odin has never been particularly forthcoming. About anything. I shall transport us," Hel said.

Bjorn wrapped a hand around her upper arm. "We shall blend our power...Mother."

"Ye doona trust me."

"Why should I?" he countered. "Were our situations reversed—"

She chopped a hand downward. "Stop." Bending, she petted the snakes' heads and spoke to them in a perversion of Old Norse. They turned and glided off across the ice just as she'd instructed.

"Such darlings." She beamed after them. "They're Jormungand's sons."

It took me a moment to identify the name. He was the

World Serpent and Hel's brother. Fenrir, the wolf, had been the third child in that family. I shielded my thoughts. I hadn't grown up in the worst family in the world, after all. Having Loki for a father and a snake and a wolf for siblings couldn't have been a ball of laughs.

No wonder my brand new mother-in-law was tough as an old buffalo hide.

Enchantment blasted me from all sides. At least it held warmth. For once, I looked forward to the void between worlds. Grasping my onyx amulet, I instructed it to concentrate air, so I'd have something to breathe once the ice-shrouded gloom of Niflheim fell away.

CHAPTER EIGHT, BJORN

Hel nailed it when she accused me of not trusting her. I didn't. Not as far as I could see her, but perhaps she was on the right track with this particular decision. Her magic slotted with mine creating something stronger than the two of us working alone. It wasn't as pronounced as when Rowan and I teamed up, though.

Probably because we brought complementary power to the table, whereas Hel and I were shooting from the same pond.

I've never cared for the void between the worlds. No one in their right mind would embrace the sense of nothingness. I kept an arm firmly around Rowan and did a few spot checks of our trajectory. We were heading in the correct general direction.

Where I could maybe see Hel playing tricks on me, she wouldn't wager something that might injure her only grandchild. She was lonely. Even though she had a seat at Valhalla's table, she'd always been on the outs with the other gods. No matter what they said to her face, her appearance was unsettling enough, they didn't seek her out. She'd risked a lot getting pregnant with me. Nidhogg's undying enmity for one thing. Except by the time she got around to confessing, so much time had passed it was almost a non-issue.

Because Nidhogg liked me.

If I'd turned into an enemy, the outcome might have been quite different. At least until our half-dragon child came to light. Regardless of how he felt about me, Nidhogg was certain to welcome another dragon into the fold. And then it dawned on me that I was another dragon too. It was a big mouthful to swallow because I didn't feel any different. My magic was stronger, but everything else was pretty much the same.

We floated through darkness so absolute, not a flicker of light broke the vista. I sensed Hel and Rowan. If I dug a bit deeper, I could feel our baby's energy—and his magic. When I looked through my psychic view, I could see all of them, but my Earth eyes had checked out.

I expected this trip to last a while, but gray edges formed. At first I thought it was my mind playing tricks on me, but after I blinked a few times and they didn't go away, I figured we were closing on something.

"Goes quicker with you," I told Hel.

"Och, and ye sound surprised. I doona like it out here. Breathing is high on my list."

I wanted to ask if she'd had success tracking Loki, but I

could have finessed the same blood tracking as her. Knowing I had Loki's blood made me squirm, and more than a little. Even before I met him, I'd hated him with an instinctual loathing that popped up at the sound of his name. Hel was correct. He would escape. If history was any predictor, Odin would let him go without the fanfare of trying to track him down.

I didn't blame him. Keeping Loki corralled was more trouble than it was worth, but if the Nine Worlds ever failed my money was on Loki standing behind its collapse. And capering and laughing and being his usual dickish self.

The next time my lungs ran through their reflexive efforts to breathe, they captured some air. The gray edges were lifting.

"Almost there," Hel said, sounding tense. Did she know something she hadn't shared?

"You okay?" I asked Rowan.

She nodded. I felt the motion against my shoulder and wrapped the thickening air around us to cushion our descent. Who knew what this place would look like? I'd seen borderworlds as lush and verdant as tropical islands and others that were a lot like Fire Mountain. Every iteration in between existed too.

Hel forged a path through a forest canopy. The world smelled fresh and pure. In a bid to discover what else lived here, I sent power arcing outward.

"I already checked," Rowan said. "Birds. Small animals. Nothing much bigger than a raccoon, although they don't look the same here."

We rolled out onto soft, spongy ground. I heard the

sound of rushing water not too far away. Hel was nodding to herself. "'Tis as I expected. Loki's feel is all over this place. Cadir too."

"Of all the people to end up related to," I muttered.

She made a rude, snorting noise. "Och. Try living in the same household. Mother took the three of us and made a run for Jotunheim. 'Tis where we were raised."

"Your mother is Angrboda, right?" Rowan asked. "Sorry, my knowledge of the Norse pantheon isn't all that swift."

"Aye, 'tis Mother's name. And we were grateful the giants took us in. Loki is universally hated, but there was still a huge discussion about what to do. To hear Mother tell it, we slid under the gate by a couple of votes."

I looked around at thick forest with even denser underbrush. Birds cawed. Insects hummed. A small chipmunk-like creature with pointy ears chittered madly at us.

"No one lives here," I said.

"I sense Cadir," Rowan said in a studiedly neutral tone. "Wonder what he lived on. Dragons need more than the odd rodent."

"He probably moved about," Hel said briskly. "Three worlds lie in reasonably close proximity to this one. Shall we?" Without waiting for an answer, she strode along a faint path I hadn't noticed.

"Have you been here before?" I fell into step behind her with Rowan between us.

"Nay," Hel replied. "Blood calls to blood. Loki walked this track."

"Cadir too," Rowan muttered. "Or rather, he flew over it."

Flowering shrubbery smelled like a cross between roses and violets. A mellow sun floated overhead suspended in a pale-green sky. I was impressed by this borderworld. It was as beautiful as any I'd visited, and I had no idea why it was uninhabited. Perhaps its proximity to the outer borderworlds was a deterrent. The more I thought about it, the more convinced I was that had to be why it remained empty.

Hel doubled back and turned hard right. We walked beneath an archway fashioned from boughs twined together and into an open meadow. A small, neat cottage sat at the far end. My eyes widened. "I had no idea dragons could build houses."

"Loki made this one," Hel said. "'Tis his style of craftsmanship."

"Was that how he conned Cadir into working for him?" Rowan asked. "By building a home for Ceridwen?"

"We doona know—" Hel began, but she quit talking.

Dragons didn't live in houses. They wouldn't fit for one thing. Rowan pushed around Hel and trotted smartly to the front door. Power shone around her as she shielded herself before twisting the knob. Polished wood suspended by tarnished brass hinges swung inward.

If I'd had any doubt before about who'd inhabited this cottage, it departed fast. The place reeked of Loki and of Cadir, even though I was certain the dragon hadn't done more than poke his snout inside.

"Hold up," I called to Ro and hurried to her side.

We peered through the open doorway into a sparsely

furnished space. It looked a lot like my home with a corner bed, a kitchen area, and a small table. Hel crowded behind us. I didn't sense foul magic or any snares, so I said, "It's okay to go in."

Rowan walked to the table and tapped it with a fingertip. "Look. He was telling the truth about building a home for Ceridwen and me." Her eyes shone with unshed tears.

Someone, probably Loki, had carved names into the tabletop. Cadir. Ceridwen. Runa. "He preferred your dragon name," I said.

"Of course he did," Hel snapped. "Damn Ceridwen. She and Loki pushed Cadir over the edge."

"Did you know him before?" Rowan asked.

"Aye. Most dragons pass through the Nine Worlds. He was no exception. Always a bit of a social outcast, if I'm remembering correctly. His magic was strong, but his isolation rendered him vulnerable. 'Twas how Da got his claws into him." She shook her head until her black hair shimmered like liquid midnight and addressed her next words to Rowan. "That slut of a mother of yours had no principles, either."

"Tell me something I don't know." Rowan blew out a heavy breath. "Let's leave this place. It makes me sad."

Hel stepped next to Rowan and placed a hand over the dome of her stomach. "Know this, child," she said in the dragon's tongue, "your grandsire would have loved you."

"He understands," Rowan said after a short pause.

It was petty, but I wanted my son to talk with me too. When Ro and I had a private moment, I'd lay my hands on her belly and greet him properly. We walked slowly from the cottage and shut the door behind us. "At least we have a place to look for Loki if he escapes," I said.

"We do," Hel concurred. "And 'tisn't if, but when. I plan to make certain Odin knows about this cabin." She angled her head to one side as if she were listening. "We still need to hunt for runaway dark power. I doona sense aught. Do either of you?"

"Would Cadir have cast seriously wicked magic near where he wanted his love and child to live?" Rowan asked.

"Good point," I replied and turned to Hel. "You mentioned three other borderworlds in close proximity. Can you make a guess which of them might have served as a launching point for the invasion that followed Ceridwen's Breaking spell?"

"Follow Loki's trail." She eyed me with asperity. "I'm not the only one to share his blood."

I winced but didn't hesitate to pick up the banner she'd tossed squarely in my court. With a hand firmly tucked beneath Rowan's arm, I shepherded us along the faint track leading from the cottage.

"Almost wish I hadn't seen this little place," Rowan murmured.

I understood exactly what she meant. "Easier when you can hate cleanly, isn't it?"

She nodded. "I guess no one is 100 percent bad, but—"

"Loki is," Hel tossed out from behind us.

Ro slid from under my grip and twisted to face her. "All right. Absent Loki—and Ceridwen—most villains have at least a smattering of redeeming qualities. Cadir had enough, it's going to be hard to keep the hate flame burning."

"Probably better to let it go out," I said. My words were accompanied by blistering insight about Loki. Despite his lack of any compensatory graces, resenting him would eat me up.

Hel shot me a knowing look from under lowered brows.

"Stay out of my thoughts," I growled.

"Och, child, we've always been linked. When the glamour shielded you from who ye were, ye wouldna have sensed the connection, but if ye look for it now ye'll locate it."

"Later," I muttered, and then added, "I didn't like it when Nidhogg stuffed a spying moonstone down my craw. I also don't care for the idea of you being a permanent resident in my head, and—"

"Not the time for this," Rowan cut in. Bending, she withdrew her dirk from its thigh sheath and handed it to me.

I took the blade from her. The two I carried were major overkill for something as simple as a five-centimeter gash. A quick chop across the base of my thumb, and blood flowed freely. I shaped a few blobs into a line of willing volunteers and healed my wound. Ro took her dirk back.

The next part would be hard; my spell curdled on my tongue twice before I managed to name Loki kinsman and instructed my blood to follow the bond. Perhaps because there was no competition when it came to Loki's blood, the ruby balls stretched into an obvious line.

Hel nodded. "Would have been my first supposition."

"What would have?" Rowan asked.

"The realm that lies to the north of us. 'Tisn't as pleasant a place as this one, but it lies closest to the barrier separating the outer borderworlds from all other worlds."

"Wonder how that project is coming?" Rowan mused.

"What project?" Hel asked.

"Didn't Odin send out a few work parties to seal the rifts? The places Cadir chewed through to free himself?"

"He did," I answered her.

"Aye, they should be done by now," Hel said.

I wasn't at all certain of that. If shutting the breaches was so simple, Odin would have taken care of it long since. Rather than giving voice to my concerns about Odin viewing the teams as unimportant, and possibly collateral damage, I summoned a casting to move us in the direction indicated by my blood.

"Ward yourselves," I said and kindled the spell to track my blood. In a burst of caution, I called the crimson drops back to me and obliterated them as soon as I'd carved out a path. Blood is a funny thing, and I did not want any of mine running about loose. It was a good way to give something malevolent a free ride directly to my magical center.

"Doona hold concerns about me. I shall meet you there," Hel said and left in a cloud of Norse magic with its scent of the sea.

Rowan joined her power with mine. The edges of my spell swept us away, but the trip was exceedingly brief. Cadir's world had barely faded when another formed around us. This realm was as barren as the last place had been verdant. Pockmarked by boulders and cliffs, its cracked dirt spread around us.

A blast of wickedness so pervasive my hair stood on end

met us before my casting had fully faded. I smelled decaying flesh and the stench of too many long-unwashed bodies in close proximity. The reek twisted my stomach, but I couldn't see its source.

"Feels like the right spot for something corrupt," Rowan said briskly.

Hel joined us and wrinkled her nose. "Gah. Horrible."

"Where's it coming from?" I asked.

"Doona know." She turned in a full circle, power pulsing from her.

I had perhaps a nanosecond's notice before the nearest cliff face blew outward. The noise was horrendous, as if the very bones of the world beneath our feet were being ripped asunder. Our shared power blazed to life, and I dragged the longsword from its sheath. The blade caught fire, blazing with magic and purpose. I'd compliment Hagar on his skill—if I ever got back to Vanaheim.

"Wait!" Hel cautioned. "Let us see what emerges."

Rocks the size of my head were still shooting out of the crumbling cliff. Some blasted outward; others surged straight up in the air, reverberating when they hit the ground. Was this how it had developed all the gouges?

A deep rumble turned to a pissed-off roar. The ground shook.

"Something's coming out of there," Rowan shouted and upped the ante as our magic swirled together. White-hot jets of energy pulsed from her extended fingertips, adding still more damage to the growing chasm.

A low hissing snarl emerged from Hel. "Goddess curse

them all. 'Tis a Draugar. I thought I'd crushed them all, cleaned out their nests to make certain naught remained."

"What's that?" Rowan asked.

"Nine Worlds' version of the undead," I told her.

"But isn't everyone in Niflheim, and all those dead warriors in Valhalla, undead?" Ro persisted. "And the Wild Hunt."

"Aye, but they stay put," Hel retorted. "Draugar are the ones who escaped my bonds to prey on the living. 'Tis why the carnage at Arawn's Ninth Gate was so serious. The Celts have their own version of Draugar, and—"

The rumbling intensified, morphing into a battle cry as an enormous skeleton garbed in battle armor pelted into the open, axe at the ready. Bits of flesh clung to his skull, and fat, white maggots crawled here and there.

"As I live and breathe," the man boomed. "I never thought to lay eyes on you again."

Bands of glimmering white shot from Hel's hands and circled the Draugar. All he did was laugh. "Ye canna touch me. Your da's magic is stronger than—"

"We shall see about that, Bjarke." Hel said as her power swirled faster, kicking up dust where it contacted the ground.

"Och, ye remember my name." He aped a low bow

"I remember far more than that. Ye stand accused of many crimes. Among them the rape of female children."

He shrugged; armor clanked. "I did naught but what the Hunt does, but when I applied for a seat with them, Odin turned me down." He took a few steps closer. "Because of you."

Hel offered a smirk. "I have an odd way of doing my part to keep the Hunt pure."

Next to me, Rowan made a choking sound. I culled up a memory of her bargaining with Odin to protect Tansy from turning into fodder for the Huntsmen.

The whirling vortex around Bjarke was moving closer. Near enough to touch him. He shied away from contact with it. It didn't appear my blade was needed, so I sheathed it.

"I propose a bargain," Hel announced and strode until the leading edge of her spell was right next to her.

"I might be interested," Bjarke replied.

"Listen and listen well," she said. "'Tis my right to imprison you, hold you in the ice cells far beneath Niflheim, but my offer is this. Ye may roam free within my domain—in exchange for information."

"Ye canna force me back."

The flow streaming from Hel's outstretched hands intensified. I directed some of the power I shared with Rowan into Hel's spell. The vortex snugged around Bjarke until the edges of his tarnished armor took on an insubstantial appearance.

"Aye, I can," Hel said.

"I am not the only one here," he warned.

"How many?" I spoke up.

He laughed uproariously, but his mirth turned into groans as armor flowed into itself, clearly melting.

"How many?" I shouted.

"Too many to count," he gritted, followed by, "I accept."

Hel infused more power into her casting. I didn't blame her. Given an opportunity, Bjarke would probably make a dive for whatever subterranean nest he'd claimed for his own. Or leave entirely.

"Are all the Draugar here?" Hel asked.

"Nay."

"Most of them?" Hel persisted.

"Nay."

"I am not in the mood to drag information from you bit by bit. Do I make myself clear?" The shining nimbus of her power closed on him, and he grunted with pain. Or with something. I thought the dead had moved past the point where anything affected them.

"We are all in this region," Bjarke screeched. "But not on this world."

"Keep talking," Hel said, and then added, "Loki is imprisoned on Jotunheim. It will be a while afore he is free to sow chaos."

Bjarke may have looked surprised. Tough to tell when all I had to work with was bones. "The dragon. He opened channels between the outer borderworlds and this small group. Our job is to keep them open."

"For what purpose?" I moved to Hel's side along with Rowan.

"We were promised Midgard."

"By whom?" Hel thundered.

"Loki. He wanted allies close at hand."

"Is it just Norse dead here?" Rowan asked.

He shook his head hard enough to dislodge a few maggots. Undeterred, they slithered back onto his armor-clad form.

Hel chopped a hand downward. "Why did Loki open a

channel for evil to invade the Nine Worlds?"

"He has plans, and that is all I shall reveal." Bjarke tossed his mail-clad head back.

Fury streamed from Hel, adding a reddish mist to her spell. The whirling vapor closed around Bjarke, spinning faster and faster until nothing was left but a blur. When it cleared, the Draugar was gone.

Hel lowered her hands. "I still doona know how they escaped."

"I'm guessing Arawn's bunch from behind the Ninth Gate joined them," Rowan muttered. "Arawn was complaining about how Loki had penetrated his realm. I bet it was for the express purpose of breaking the locks on the Ninth Gate."

"How many Draugar were in your care?" I asked Hel.

She turned her dark gaze on me. "Hundreds."

Rowan's head snapped up as if she were listening intently. She took off at a dead run for the hole, shouting, "Hurry."

"What is it?" I called after her. When she didn't answer, I bolted after her with Hel right behind me. The broken cliff face led to a tunnel so low I had to crabwalk to get through it. I heard Hel cursing; my guess was she'd had to crawl.

The shaft had a downward cant and smelled of wet dirt. The rot smell was more pronounced here; the presence of so many dead had to be the source. Something about decay stuck around, even after the source had left.

The passageway opened abruptly. Rowan had kindled a mage light, and its bluish illumination cast the interior of an underground chamber in stark relief. Bodies had been scattered about like so much debris. They smelled clean by comparison.

"We were speculating about the groups Odin sent this way," Rowan said, her tone a study in controlled fury. "Well, here's one of them."

I bent closer to an elf. His throat had been hacked open with a crude blade, and his fair hair was caked with dried blood. Death had come quickly, but he'd been in agony.

Hel moved from body to body. "Odin deployed three groups. Hopefully, the other two meet with a better fate."

"It's a nice fantasy, but I bet they're just as dead as this bunch." Rowan fisted a hand. "With hundreds of undead, this was scarcely a balanced contest."

"When Odin sent them here," I spoke slowly, "he thought they'd be closing portals. He never counted on an army of shades."

"An army of shades led by Loki." Hel's nostrils flared. "No wonder my father has been in such a cheerful mood here of late. He had plans. Big ones. Monumental ones. His confinement on Jotunheim won't be more than an inconvenience."

Leaving the six dead went against the grain. They'd died doing their liege's bidding. I dragged a dwarf over by the elf. Hel and Rowan helped until the bodies were stacked together. "We should burn them," I said, "but outside."

Hel nodded. Her magic circled us all, living and dead. When it cleared, we stood close to the spot where we'd interrogated Bjarke. She began a familiar chant. The Norse ode to the dead. I joined in. Before we got to the second verse, the bodies caught fire. Hel's flames burned clean and true. Soon only ashes remained.

"Their spirits are in Valhalla," she told us.

When I looked at Rowan, her belly was bigger. Somehow, our son sensed the presence of evil and knew he was needed.

"So long as we're close," Rowan said, "Shall we hunt for the channels pumping poison to Earth and close at least one or two?"

"Aye, splendid idea," Hel replied and raised her hands. I felt her cast a seeking spell, and wove Rowan's and my enchantment with hers. The riddled labyrinth that formed before my eyes was so much more extensive than I'd imagined, apprehension gripped me.

I chucked my alarm aside, replacing it with fury for the senseless deaths of the men and women we'd just immolated. They deserved our efforts to avenge their passing. Next time I was in Valhalla, I'd make certain to find them and tell them what we'd done.

"Goddess be damned," Rowan yelled. "The maze is moving."

"Good news," Hel shouted back. "Means it's illusion."

"And bad news," I muttered. "Those are a bitch to counteract."

CHAPTER NINE, ROWAN

I'd keyed power into a particular part of the labyrinth when it slithered away from me. At first, I was convinced I was seeing things, but the second time it happened couldn't have been coincidental. That was when I shouted a warning. I was still steeped in outrage over the dead we'd transported out of the cave. Had Odin known he'd assigned his subjects to what amounted to a suicide mission?

If it had been Gwydion or Andraste, the answer could have been yes. They were warriors, immersed in battle strategy. Collateral damage meant nothing to them.

Meanwhile, the baby had grown. Something about Hel's assertion his grandfather would have loved him coupled with the bodies in the cave might be behind it. Or maybe they were totally unrelated. Hard to tell with these things, plus I'm scarcely an expert on being pregnant.

The maze had shifted once again. No way all those

channels could be real. The ground we stood upon would have collapsed forthwith. I experimented with looking through my third eye. After a couple of tries where I varied the wavelength, I could see differences in the network shooting off in all directions.

Bjorn wouldn't like my next suggestion, but I didn't see any help for it. "Look at them through your psychic vision," I said. "It shows which are real. We need to jump into one and follow it to—"

"Fuck, no, you're not doing that," Bjorn snapped.

"But how will we know where they're coming from if we don't?" I retorted.

"Ye're not putting the babe at risk," Hel told me.

"For Christ fucking sake. Dragon babies are indestructible. If Ceridwen could have rid herself of me, she would have. And I'm certain she tried—many times."

Hel curled one big hand around my upper arm. "Monsters could remove the child from your body, raise him steeped in darkness."

I grimaced, appalled by her implication. "Just what are you thinking I'd be doing? Standing by while they stole my son. No fucking way."

"As a compromise"—Bjorn stepped between us—"we have a good visual on at least one of the conduits. It may be a minor one, but I say we seal it."

"They'll just build more. It's why we have to know where they're originating from," I told him. I was tired. Arguing among ourselves was an energy drain I didn't need.

"I don't believe they can construct more channels without Loki," Bjorn answered.

"Aye, and without Cadir too," Hel said.

They raised a valid point. The two primary sorcerers were out of the picture. For now. Not that Cadir would rise from the dead, but Loki was still a player—just not right now. It was good enough for me. I borrowed liberally from Bjorn, retreated to my psychic view of the maze, and fired destructive magic into its heart. Bjorn joined me. Hel did too. Among the three of us, it didn't take long. As we nuked the real part of the labyrinth, the illusory parts went up in little puffs of noxious smelling smoke.

I was breathing hard from the effort of channeling so much power. And I'd been half expecting more of the undead to storm our position, but none showed up. Had they been linked to Bjarke and felt him disintegrate? They couldn't have felt him die. He'd already been there and done that.

About the only dead-but-not I knew much about were vampires. They've been around forever, but their ranks didn't really swell until the Breaking made their lives easier. Before that, they kept a fairly low profile. The advent of the Internet—where all someone had to do was google how to kill them—had a dampening effect on their nocturnal wanderings. Didn't take much, not really, to get rid of them. But it required proximity. Beheading was effective. Or a silver stake through the heart.

Yeah. See. Proximity. Magic from a distance wouldn't accomplish either task. Basically, I avoided them. They reek of rot, and they've always creeped me out. Meanwhile, the dirt hiding the underground channels was falling in. Bjorn grabbed my arm and tugged me briskly to one side.

He waved a hand in front of my face. "Rowan?"

"Yeah. Sorry. I got lost thinking about vampires."

Hel crooked two fingers in the universal sign against evil and hissed. "Och, they're far worse than the Draugar."

We retreated a few more meters from where the cliff had blown outward. "Explain." I circled one hand in a come-along motion.

"Explain what?" Hel drew her brows together.

I extended my fingers and counted off on them. "Lots of undead things. For one, vampires. For another Draugar. Number three are the warriors running around Valhalla. Number four, the Riders in the Wild Hunt. And then there are ghosts that got stuck where they died on Midgard. For some reason, they can't move on. Beyond those, I'm certain Arawn has a few problems in his care, or maybe more than a few."

"Had," Hel corrected me. "As I understand things, the Ninth Gate was demolished, and whoever Arawn wished to corral is long gone."

"The Hunt are handpicked warriors from the dead who ended up in Valhalla," Bjorn said.

I didn't even bother to mute the snort that ripped through me. "Really? If they're the cream that rose to the top, I'd hate to meet those who didn't make the cut."

"Ye just did," Hel pointed out. "Bjarke told us he applied and was turned down."

"But didn't he live in your domain?" I asked.

"Eventually," Hel replied. "He began in Valhalla and was such an annoyance, Odin shunted him my way."

"Moving on." Bjorn's tone was brisk. "Vampires are unique to Midgard. They don't live elsewhere, and—"

"I know about them," I broke in. "They make new vampires when they feed from humans. I'm not totally clear on the exact process, but they drain them until they're mostly dead and then offer them vamp blood to drink. It resurrects them."

"Aye, but they can feed and kill and not bother augmenting their ranks," Hel told me. "In truth, they prefer it. Less competition for food. Some of them keep a stable of humans and animals. They drink from them, but not to the point of death. It's rather akin to keeping food in a cupboard. 'Tis there at the ready, and ye doona have to hunt it down every time."

"Ewwww." A shudder ran through me. I hadn't heard about that little wrinkle.

"The Draugar were truly wicked men, right?" Bjorn angled a glance Hel's way.

She nodded. "Aye. Women too, and they doona care for being contained. I believed I had that niggling problem covered. Apparently, I haven't looked in on them in far too long."

"You're in good company," I muttered, thinking about Arawn and his Ninth Gate problem.

"'Tisn't an excuse. Eventually, I shall round them back up, but 'twill take a long while I fear."

"Mostly, those in Valhalla behave themselves," Bjorn said.

Hel laughed. "Aye because the rejects head my way."

I considered the information. "Next question. It appears

we're facing an army of the dead. What's the best approach? For vampires, I've always dealt with them one by one. We need something quicker, more efficient."

"I'm not certain that's the whole of it," Bjorn said.

"What do you mean?" I cast a questioning look his way.

"The outer borderworlds have always been a slagheap for undesirables, those who had no place in any other world. But those consigned there were still very much alive. Many are immortal."

Breath hissed from my lungs as the scope of the problem expanded exponentially. "You're suggesting that while Loki and Cadir may have been the generals, they had others more than willing to do their bidding?"

"Exactly," Bjorn said. "Others who are far more than shades. The dead can cause disruption, but their attention spans are miniscule."

"Verra true," Hel chimed in. "Without direction they lose focus."

"Direction provided by the living," I mumbled and rolled my shoulders back. "Nothing for it but to go have a look ourselves."

"'Tis a nice theory," Hel began when a burst of light caught the edges of my vision. The unmistakable scents of dragon—herbs and hot baked clay—blasted me.

Bjorn wrapped an arm around my shoulders and turned us so we faced a fire-rimmed gateway. I girded myself for two furious dragons. What I got was three. Dewi flew through, followed by Zelli and Quade.

Dewi thumped down so close the ground shook and a fine cloud of dust surrounded us. I figured she'd yell at me.

Instead, she snared Hel with her whirling eyes and said, "I expected better from you."

"What, precisely, do ye mean?" The Norse goddess of the dead stood tall. Her head reached the bottom of the dragon's jaws.

"Running off with the Dragon Mage, the Dragon Heir, and their unborn child. No one knew where ye'd gone, and—"

"Tracking us with magic was simple enough," I interrupted her diatribe, not caring about being rude.

"Aye, 'twas simple because your hatchling emits enough power to light worlds," Zelli snarled around a mouthful of teeth.

"Ye were extremely fortunate others dinna reach you afore us," Quade bellowed, sounding just as put out as the other two dragons.

I clasped both hands over my belly, shocked by how fast the baby was growing. Trapped between indignation—because no one seemed to believe in my ability to exercise common sense—and worry I was underplaying the objective dangers, words didn't jump to my command.

"We have discussed this—" Dewi began.

My tongue untied itself. "If by this, you mean my baby—"

"Our baby," Bjorn reminded me.

"Yeah. Our baby. Anyway, I refuse to be bound by any discussion that didn't involve me—and Bjorn." My gaze swept the group; I did my best to project defiance. Crap. Why did they all feel the need to treat me like I was ten years old?

Dewi tapped my chest with a bright red talon. "We have discussed this," she repeated, "and ye will hear me out."

"Depends on what you have to say," I told her.

"We shall go to Fire Mountain," she steamrolled right along.

"Nope. Not going back there. Too close to Mother for one thing, and you're harboring ideas about shackling me in some cave until the baby is born."

Zelli lowered her head until she was at eye level with me. "Ye will listen until Dewi is done. Ye wish us to treat you as an equal? Then act like one."

I cringed. I'd been a brat, but I was angry. No one had any rights over my body—except me.

"We hold concerns about your youngling," Dewi went on. "He commands strong magic, and he will be a liability until he's born. At least then 'twill be simpler to build protections around him."

I was actually biting my tongue. Once I tasted blood, I backed off, but I couldn't keep my mouth shut. "If by build protections, you mean sequestering him in Fire Mountain, I'll never agree."

"Nor will I," Bjorn said.

I cringed again. Why did I keep bypassing his role in this whole thing? "Sorry," I muttered.

"It's all right," he spoke low into my ear. "But we do need to hear their idea."

"Finally." Quade puffed a very small cloud of steam our way, letting Bjorn know that forgiveness for our moral slippage was possible.

"I get a say." Hel nodded briskly. "After all, 'tis my grandchild we're discussing."

"Aye, and ye're who crafted the harebrained scheme of running directly into danger, Grannie," Dewi shot back.

I raised my hand, palm facing out. "She may have suggested going to Cadir's lair, but it was a solid idea. Bjorn and I wouldn't have agreed, otherwise."

"Not the point," Dewi said. "Ye will come to Fire Mountain and soak in the magic of our most sacred pool. It will encourage yon hatchling to emerge. Once he is with us, we shall determine...what happens next."

The studied pause between the words *determine* and *what* bothered me. "You're not telling me—us—everything."

"What she isn't saying"—Bjorn's voice was deep, steady—"is she doesn't know if our son will be a shapeshifter. If he has a dragon form, it will provide a number of natural protections."

I shifted my gaze to the ground in front of me and did my damnedest to ward my thoughts. I'd been warming to the idea of my son in my arms, his little mouth attached to my breast. How would I cuddle a creature with scales? Would it nurse? Or would it be born with teeth and start right in on meat?

A soothing cooing filled my mind, and I got hold of my runaway emotions. The child had sensed my distress and was doing his best to comfort me. *"No, little one,"* I sent inward in the dragons' tongue. *"I am fine. Grow strong within me."*

"We shall discuss this," Bjorn told the dragons. "You will offer us privacy while we do."

He hooked an arm beneath mine. We walked a few meters away before his magic surrounded us. "What bothers you most?" he asked without preamble.

"Giving up control."

He nodded. "Aye, I'd have bet guilders on that answer." He placed a hand over my stomach, and I felt the prickle of Norse magic—briny and thick with herbs and honey—as Bjorn got to know our son. His mouth curved into a soft smile.

I wanted to ask what pleased him, but I could wait until he was done.

Fingers still splayed across the taut dome of my belly, he raised his gaze until it met mine and nodded his head. "Our son likes Dewi's proposal. He wishes to emerge—so he can fight in the war that's nearly upon us."

Alarm ratcheted through me. "But he can't. He's too young. He needs to have a childhood, like you did. Nothing like mine." I was babbling, but I couldn't seem to stop.

Bjorn moved his hand until he cupped the side of my face. "Ro. Our child is more dragon than anything else. Dragons are warriors."

"But we're half dragon," I protested.

"It's different for him. Not sure I completely understand why, but he inherited dragon blood from both of us. You and me, we had only one dragon parent. And he knows about who he is already. Ceridwen made certain you didn't. And Hel hid the truth from me."

I closed my teeth over my lower lip. "This is so hard. I want to do the right thing. He's safe where he is." I patted my stomach.

"Is he?" Bjorn asked. "Once Zelli mentioned his magic, I took a few steps back and tried to view it as an outsider might."

"And?" I crooked two fingers.

"He does shine brightly. Very brightly."

"How will him being born change that?"

"It won't," Bjorn said, "but we can teach him to cloak himself."

My shoulders had slumped. I straightened them, feeling acutely out of my element. "What do you think we should do?"

Bjorn shook his head. "That question is yours to answer. I will support you either way."

"Either way being we go Dewi's magical route, or let the pregnancy proceed as it would anyway?" When he nodded, I glanced down at myself. My breasts were swollen, so was my stomach. Every time I looked at myself, my body had changed.

The cooing, chirping noises from within me intensified again.

"What are you thinking?" Bjorn asked.

I smiled wanly. "You could find out easily enough."

"Aye, but I'd rather have you tell me."

"Not sure it's just one thing. My mind is zinging off in a whole lot of directions, but the item that keeps popping to the top is maybe my obsessive desire for our son to have a fairy-tale childhood isn't realistic. Maybe it's not something he'd want. If he's mostly dragon, he won't be interested in toy trucks or playing ball games."

"Might be a good thing," Bjorn said, "since we scarcely lead fairy-tale lives."

"Maybe someday."

"Aye, but not for a long while, I fear."

He didn't remind me about the ragtag army massing on the outer borderworlds. He didn't have to. Absent oversight from Loki and Cadir, they were sure to run off the rails, and not in good ways. Castoffs, throw-outs, the batch of human and magical trash had nothing to lose.

And a legion of dead champing at the bit to do their bidding.

"All right," I said, proud my voice was steady, "I'm ready to accede to Dewi's plan."

He brushed a thumb across my cheekbone. "I'll be with you every step of the way."

Gratitude swamped me, made me dizzy. My throat thickened and my eyes stung. "I don't deserve you."

"Funny. I feel the same way about you." He swept an arm downward, and the magical curtain dissipated. Bending forward, he kissed my forehead before stepping away. The gesture was so tender and so sweet, it made the lump in my throat worse. I swallowed around it, determined not to cry.

The dragons had moved so close they stood practically on top of us. "Good choice," Dewi purred, if something that big and imposing could be said to sound anything like a cat. I thought about Mort, and wanted to go home. Not to Fire Mountain, but home.

"We can do that once the child is here," Zelli told me, proving privacy and dragons were incompatible bedfellows. A cushion of familiar magic swept me onto her back, and the deeply fissured earth of the borderworld fell away, replaced by the filtered light of the dragons' journey tunnel.

We held silence for a while before I said, "We were never in any danger, but we found one of Odin's teams."

"Aye, all dead. I saw it in your mind. I am sorry, but I fear the other two groups fared equally badly."

"I already figured that out. Um, this immersion thing, how will it work?"

Zelli nodded solemnly. "I figured ye'd ask. The hatchling, he's growing far quicker than any of us believed he would, and—"

"Do you know why?" I cut in.

"Aye. He senses he is needed. We've had similar occurrences with some of our eggs. 'Twas how we discovered the pool hurries things along. Remember the shelf where the god of the winds found Dewi's egg?"

"Yes."

"Other eggs occupied that verra same shelf. One particular clutch edged forward until all four eggs fell into the pool. No one was watching over the nest because no one had ever needed to before. If they had, they would have fished the eggs out, and we never would have discovered the pool's intrinsic nurturing capabilities."

"That's fascinating. Go on," I urged. Somehow, I sensed my child was listening intently too.

"One day long ago, many of us were gathered outside when Dewi let out a shriek and vanished in a flood of magic. We found out later, she'd heard the squawks of young dragons, figured she'd been wrong about when the clutch would hatch, and made a run for the nursery.

"She found all four hatchlings splashing in the pool and scooping fish into their little mouths. Dewi said it was adorable. When she hunted for the shells—because we always bury them—they were at the bottom of the pool."

"So she put two and two together," I murmured.

"Aye, that she did. Those eggs had many months to go afore they would have hatched on their own, but we were in the midst of a war with the Celts—one that eventuated with them making Dewi one of their own."

I'd always wondered how that had come to pass. "Sounds like a tale in and of itself," I said.

"It is, but we shall save it for another time," Zelli replied. "We are almost to Fire Mountain. The others are as excited as I am. Ye'll have quite the greeting party."

"They know?" I squeaked, feeling shy and wondering if dragons were going to crowd around me while I labored.

"Of course they do. Your child will be welcomed, well-loved." After a pause, she added, "Ye worry too much."

"I never used to."

"Aye, well motherhood changes us."

I rubbed my hands over her scaled neck. "Do you have children?"

Her jaws lolled into a smile. "Aye, one. He is a joy."

The channel broke apart around us, and we floated gently down onto the red earth of Fire Mountain. Dewi hadn't been joking. Dragons closed from every direction, bugling, trumpeting, and blanketing me with steam.

The stream of cooing from within me turned into a miniature bugle that touched my heart and filled me with hope for the future. What kind of world was I bringing my son into? How could I teach him everything he needed to know in time? Never mind, dragons were indestructible. What if he got hurt?

What if—?

Zelli reached around and plucked me off her back, setting me on the ground. Bjorn melted through the crowd of dragons and placed a protective arm around me. "Let's do this," he murmured.

The baby was practically bouncing inside me, he was so excited by almost being free. I laughed. The independent little punk was going to be a lot like me.

"What's so funny?" Bjorn asked.

"Nothing. I can't wait to meet our son."

Bjorn tightened his grip around me, and we ducked into the caves.

CHAPTER TEN, BJORN

I hadn't expected Rowan to agree to come to Fire Mountain, not without a whole lot more fanfare than we'd blithered through. Finding the dead elves and dwarves and Norsemen had been horrific, though. Perhaps that had been part of her decision. Odin's group hadn't just died; they'd suffered. Whoever killed them had set out to exact maximum pain.

If Nidhogg was anywhere close, I'd make certain he had a full set of details he could relay to Odin. Not that I knew the ruler of the Nine Worlds well, or at all, but he'd been looking progressively more worried. All the magic in his realm ran through him, so he had to feel the rot in Yggdrasil, and the pain in Jotunheim. Had he known about the Draugars' escape?

Perhaps, although if it had eluded Hel's notice—and she was a stickler for details—it may not have been obvious to Odin, either. Thor was another story. If rumors were to be believed, Odin had tried to rope him into taking up the mantle of more responsibility many times. Thor had little interest in stretching his power beyond Asgard and Midgard, the two worlds he watched over.

I've often wondered where he was before the Breaking. Why he didn't sense the onset of trouble. While Odin is cunning, Thor is straightforward, good-natured. He wants to see the best in everyone, which could explain how he totally missed the signs Midgard was heading for a serious fall.

Or he could have been slinging thunder about or playing with his hammer, Mjollnir. Or riding herd on Loki, although I'm certain he had no stomach for that assignment. Odin must have offered quite the array of incentives to convince him to agree.

The dragons were out in force to greet us. I had no idea how many years—centuries?—had passed since a dragon was born in Fire Mountain. Any doubts I may have harbored about our son being mostly human vanished once I spoke with him. He has a dragon's heart, a dragon's curiosity, and impatience with anything standing in his way.

To his young mind, he was called for a purpose, and that purpose was to bring his will to bear on the upcoming struggle to salvage the Nine Worlds. I'd read tales of magical children who bypassed normal channels because their talents were needed.

It made me proud. And sad. I'd hoped for an infant. One who needed Rowan and me to tend to it. We might have a babe like that someday, but this one wasn't it. He'd be independent almost from the moment of birth. I considered telling Rowan, but she'd figure it out soon enough. She had plenty ahead of her. No matter how badly the child wanted out, the birth would demand all of Rowan's attention. They always did.

After the dragons divested me of my blades, reassuring me they'd be waiting when I left, Rowan and I traveled the same path we'd trod the day we'd been here for the dragons' council, the one when Nidhogg instructed all of dragonkind to aid us if we required it. The arched entry to the cavern housing the sacred pool loomed ahead.

A subtle thread of music reached my ears. Was it the cave's doing? The pool's? Or some blend of dragon magic I didn't recognize. Regardless, it was soothing. We crossed beneath the entry. Zelli, Quade, Dewi, and Hel entered the chamber as well.

Rowan ducked from beneath my arm and spun to face the doorway. "It's enough," she said in a clear, ringing voice. "My son thanks you for your caring, for your interest, but no one else shall enter until we are finished."

Steam from many throats billowed into the room. Thick and warm and smelling of dragon magic. A stout bugle was followed by the sound of shuffling feet as dragons moved aside. Nidhogg's golden snout poked past the lintel, followed by the rest of him.

"I claim kinship bonds," he announced.

Rowan folded her arms across her swollen belly. "Mother would make the same assertion. She shall not be anywhere near me—or our child."

The edges of my mouth may have twitched. Rowan had included me—finally—without me reminding her the baby hadn't been a product of immaculate conception.

"No worries on that front," Nidhogg rumbled. "I'll crush her myself if she escapes from where we put her."

I was vaguely curious where that might be, but not enough to ask. We were here for a reason, and any mention of Ceridwen was upsetting to Rowan. Zelli herded Quade and Nidhogg to a distant corner of the cavern and draped a magical veil between us and them.

The copper dragon lumbered back to where we stood and nodded at Rowan. She sat on the floor and unlaced her boots. On her feet again, she slowly stripped out of her clothing.

"May I join her in the pool?" I asked Zelli.

The dragon hesitated for a moment before she nodded.

Hel settled near the edge of the water and crossed her legs beneath her. Silvery-blue magic sluiced from her in waves, and I sensed her eagerness. Dewi trudged next to her, moving forward until her large hind feet were mostly immersed in water.

I stripped out of my clothes and boots and tucked an arm around Rowan's waist. "Do you know how beautiful you are?" I spoke low. The dragons would hear me. So would Hel, but I didn't care. Her breasts were full, ripe, and tipped with golden nipples. Her belly rose in a mound in front of her. I said a hasty prayer to Freya, goddess of fertility, asking for an easy time for Rowan.

Color bloomed on Rowan's gaunt cheeks. "Thank you."

Together, we walked into the pool. The water was cool, but not unpleasantly cold. Fish clustered around us, biting at my legs. Dewi began to chant. It spread like an echo as the three other dragons in the cavern and everyone crowded into the hall took it up.

"Walk," Zelli instructed.

Walk we did with my arm threaded around Rowan's waist. We remained in the shallow section and scribed an ellipse as we moved from one end of the pool to the other and back again. Somewhere around the third or fourth circuit, a fine silvery mist surrounded us. I could still hear Dewi's chant, but I couldn't see Hel or Zelli any longer. The water turned dreamlike. Strange creatures poked their heads and tails and wings in and out of the haze.

A faint light shimmered around us. It took me a moment to understand it was coming from the onyx gems Rowan wore. Ceridwen had fashioned them, and the fact they'd chosen this particular moment to glow worried me. Taking care so Rowan wouldn't notice, I tried to test their magic but didn't get beyond them screaming Celt in my face.

Of course they were Celtic, and they were clearly not going to give me one shred more of information.

"Where are we?" Rowan asked. Her voice was faint, as if she wandered far from me.

"In a dream," I told her.

The mist thickened; the scents of mint, vanilla, and amber surrounded us. Rowan groaned and stopped walking.

"Come on," I urged.

She shook her head. "No more. It's time."

I trusted her assessment. "We must return to the shore." I was worried about our son being able to breathe.

"No." She groaned again, followed by a muted howl.

In our shared vision, the water dropped away, leaving us

on a sandy spit. I didn't question it. Strong magic surrounded us, orchestrating what would come next. The gems glowed brighter, but they were a small part of the enchanted working that held us in thrall. I might be able to break free of the enchantment, but I didn't want to. I was exactly where I belonged, with the woman who meant everything to me.

Rowan was mewling, holding the sides of her belly with both hands. I could see it ripple as contractions buffeted her, one after the next. Pillows materialized out of nowhere in the middle of a bower lined with otherworldly white blossoms. Similar to lilies, but not, they smelled sweet. Almost like jasmine.

I scooped Rowan into my arms and carried her to the bower, laying her so her back was supported by pillows. Her legs fell open, and I bent each knee, bracing her feet on the fuzzy material beneath us. I gripped her hands. I'd delivered many a babe during my tenure as Master Sorcerer.

"Rowan. Look at me, darling."

Her face had been screwed into a mask of pain, but her eyes flicked open and latched onto my face. "Good," I crooned. "Now breathe. Nice and deep."

She puffed out a breath or two in between grunting with pain. "Water? Where did it go?"

"Don't worry about that. We're in a perfect place to welcome our son." A quick check convinced me she could push. "Next time the pain hits, push," I told her and kept a close eye on her belly. When it fluttered with the start of a contraction, I squeezed her hands. "Push, darling. You can do this."

She was panting and writhing. I wished I had herbs to

dull her pain, but I had nothing except magic. It would have to be enough. I reached between her legs and sent power within her to hasten the birth. She yelped. "Not much longer," I told her. "Come on, Ro. Push. Now."

Between her laboring and my magic, I caught a glimpse of blonde fuzz as our son's head moved lower in the birth canal.

"Felt that," she gasped.

"Aye, he's almost here." Excitement coursed through me. This wasn't a random birth I'd been called to officiate at. This was my son. My boy. Our child. The skin across Rowan's abdomen tightened again.

"Here we go," I told her. "Push hard."

A low keening shriek tore out of her, but the baby slithered from her body. I caught him, held him, and waited for the placenta as I marveled at the miracle in my hands. He was incredible. Beautiful. Perfect. Tiny nails on fingers and toes were already curved into miniature talons. His hair was fair, and his skin glowed pale gold. I turned him and rubbed his back, encouraging him to breathe.

A tiny gasp was followed by a faint bugle.

"Let me see." Rowan propped herself on her elbows and bent forward, craning her neck. "Ooooh, he has your hair."

"Well, ye dinna expect another red-headed stepchild," I teased in Old Norse. It's the language I revert to when I'm so addled by emotion, I can't recall any others.

She laughed and reached for our son. I laid him in her arms and waited for the cord to quit pulsing before I cut it. Rowan kissed the baby's forehead and murmured, "I love you."

I laid a hand on his warm back and told him he was everything I'd ever hoped for, but I said it into his mind.

He nuzzled for Rowan's breast and latched on, sucking hard. One tiny hand reached until he grasped the still-glowing onyx gemstone suspended from its golden chain. The cord had quieted, so I sliced through it with magic and gathered the placenta as it slid from Rowan's body. We'd find a safe spot to bury it, hiding it away from any who would seek to establish power over our child.

Even dragons who hatched from eggs had placental material.

"Isn't he perfect?" Rowan crooned.

I set the afterbirth material aside and lay next to her, holding both of them. My heart swelled, overcome with love and tenderness. "Indeed he is. Just like you."

"Ha! I'm a mouthy bitch."

"Only one of the things I adore about you." I was back to English.

The baby made little sucking noises, pudgy fingers still holding tight to Ro's amulet. The air surrounding him was electric, vibrant with magic. Whatever had created the illusion around us, it was holding together. Bower. Flowers. Pillows. We were probably in the bottom of the lake, but none of it mattered.

What did was our son was here. He opened his eyes and looked right at me. Golden like Rowan's, his eyes spun like dragon orbs. The power around him thickened, developed deep copper edges. I inhaled the distinctive scent of dragon magic. Hot clay baked under a Mediterranean sun.

The child in Rowan's arms shifted in the blink of an eye.

One moment, he was human, the next a small, perfect gold-scaled dragon nestled at her breast, still drinking hungrily. Tiny wings were tucked along his back, and a delicate tail wrapped around him. He still clutched the amulet, but talons had replaced fingers.

Rowan hugged him tighter. "Beautiful," she murmured. "So beautiful."

He was, indeed. Something occurred to me. I leaned near the small dragon. "Tell us your name."

"Wait. Don't we get to name him?" Rowan asked.

"Nay. Dragons name themselves."

Greedy little thing that he was, he didn't lift his mouth from Rowan's breast, but I heard his voice in my mind. *"Geir. My name is Geir."*

"Welcome, Geir," Rowan said and looked at me. "Dewi knew."

I remembered how outraged I'd been when she'd named our child. I owed her an apology. "She did, indeed," I said. "Probably because she has an archetypal link to every dragon, even those not quite born yet."

"Do you suppose he'll shift often?" Rowan raised her brows into question marks.

"I have no idea. He'll be his own person, and we'll stand by him and love him." My throat was rough, raw with all the feelings running through me. Fierce protectiveness rocked me to my core. I would stand by my boy. And Rowan. No matter what faced us.

The power around us developed an insubstantial aspect. We were about to move to another level, probably back to reality. If a special land that catered to dragons could be labeled as such.

Sure enough, the pool came into view. We were on the rocky outcropping where the god of the winds had discovered the first dragon egg. I kissed Geir's forehead, and then I kissed Rowan before gathering the placenta and cord and standing.

"I will take those." Dewi held out her forelegs.

"We must hide them well," Nidhogg said.

"I shall be the one to bury them," I told the dragons. "May I present our son, Geir."

Warm laughter rippled from Dewi. "Och, ye've warmed to his name."

"Apologies." I offered half a bow. "I had forgotten dragons name themselves."

She bent low, breathing in the dragon nestled at Rowan's breast and puffing steam over him. "Come with me," Dewi said. "It tempts fate to leave the birth matter uncovered."

Nidhogg angled his head and sent clouds of steam around Rowan and his grandson. A string of musical notes flowed from him as he welcomed Geir into the fold of dragonkind. The tune was poignant and called to my dragon half as well.

"I want to come and bury the placenta," Rowan said, "but I don't want to disturb Geir. He's hungry." She shifted him to her other breast.

"Of course he is." Nidhogg's deep voice rumbled. "We must find him tender meat. He will grow quickly."

"How about if I show you the spot later?" I asked Rowan.

"Aye. I must know too," Geir's small, melodic voice reverberated in my head.

Nidhogg puffed steam. "Definitely my blood." He sounded proud.

When I glanced at Hel, she looked ethereal with the widest smile I'd ever seen gracing her bone-riddled face.

Zelli and Quade puffed more steam. While everyone was admiring Rowan and our babe, I summoned magic to move me across the expanse of water to where I'd left my clothes. Dewi took the afterbirth while I dressed, and then the two of us quietly left the chamber.

The entire corridor was filled with dragons and steam and bugles and congratulations. Everyone wanted to greet Geir and offer Rowan their best wishes. Their goodwill warmed me. Nothing like having all of dragonkind on our side.

"You can all go in now," I told them. "Rowan and Geir will cherish your greetings."

"Not too many at once," Dewi cautioned. "Only a few, and then ye can trade off."

While we walked, I told Dewi what we'd found off-world and detailed our suspicions, filling her in about everything from Cadir's cottage to the cadre of dead on the borderworld where she'd found us.

She's a good listener and waited until it was clear I'd run out of words before saying, "Odin needs to know his people have been slaughtered. We must determine who inhabits the outer borderworlds and how they're organized."

"Why go to all that trouble?" I asked. "We could just

obliterate the worlds and be done with them."

"Ye're assuming everyone on those worlds is part of this."

I shrugged. "Does it even matter? Anyone who ended up there was evil to their bones. What difference does it make if we kill off a few who weren't directly involved..." Reason stepped in. I was still running on a high from the birth of my son.

Dewi turned down a side passageway, and we dropped lower into the cave system. When she finally stopped, she turned to me. "Ye figured it out, eh?"

"I did. We can blow the borderworlds apart with lethal magic, but it will also finish obliterating the barrier between those worlds and everything else. A fair number of those banished to the outer worlds are probably immortal. Once they're no longer trapped behind the barricade, they'll teleport to the most convenient next stop."

The dragon handed me the placenta and cord. Then she sent a bright arc of magic at the ground beneath our feet. A hole formed and grew deeper. Once it was large enough, I reverently placed Geir's birth material at the bottom. My magic jumped to the fore and pushed dirt back into place. Once I was done, I added a few swirls so the spot looked like the remainder of the cavern floor.

"Nicely done," Dewi said and turned to me. "As things stand, it appears there are holes in the barrier that keeps the outer worlds separate, but they're not large enough for more than a few creatures to penetrate it at any given time. That would explain why when ye've fought, the enemy shows up in waves."

"Easier to shore up the barrier than to deal with what

happens once it's gone?" I furled my brows.

"My take, but we must discuss this with everyone present."

"Does that mean dragons, Celts, and Norsemen?"

The dragon nodded. "Loki will not remain imprisoned long. We have a brief opportunity, and we must move quickly." Her jaws parted in a derisive smile. "Our tendency is to talk something up one side and down the other. We canna do that this time."

"Keep the meeting small," I suggested. "Odin, Thor, Gwydion, Andraste, you, and Nidhogg."

"We must include the blind seers," she said. "And Arawn. His realm got dragged into this."

"Surely, he's repaired the gate by now."

"Even if he has," she replied, "he has yet to corral those who made a run for it and are probably among the army of shades poised to wreak havoc in the Nine Worlds."

"Fine. When do we begin?" I started back the way we'd come with Dewi alongside me. Dragons take on a glowing aspect underground. Makes it simple to see, even in the dark.

"We shall bide here for a fortnight," she said. "It will offer Geir time to grow and become stronger—"

"He'll only be two weeks old," I cut in. "He will not be part of any fighting. Rowan, either, if I have anything to say about it."

Dewi rocked back on her haunches. Laughter rolled from her along with steam. "Och, proud daddy that ye are, ye'll be surprised how fast young dragons can grow. Especially younglings with as staunch a purpose as Geir's.

He made the decision to forego pleasant dreaming time within Rowan's body. He will tell us what he wants, and we will listen to him."

I didn't like it but wasn't about to argue the point. What bothered me almost as much was the uneasy feeling we were running out of time. Did we even have two weeks to muck about while my son grew stronger?

"I share your concerns." Dewi had quit laughing. "And, aye, your thoughts are crystal clear to me. We shan't be idle. By the time your child can accompany us, we will have plans firmly in place."

"Why does he have to come?" I persisted, feeling stubborn—and protective.

She bent low enough to drop a taloned foreleg on my shoulder. "This is why he is here," she told me. "Each of us has a life task. Some of us have many. His first is the coming war. It is why he was born."

"How can you be so sure?"

Her whirling eyes gleamed in the gloomy murk of the passageway. "The same way I knew his name. Ask your son. He'll tell you quick enough."

I thought back to my insight from earlier. The one about magical children coming through us but not needing parents. I'd accepted it then. What was different now?

Dewi's claws tightened across my shoulder blade. "The difference," she said, "is the hatchling is here, and every protective bone in your body has been activated."

"I guess I'm underestimating him," I muttered.

"Nay. Ye're underestimating yourself. Ye can let him spread his wings and be the dragon he was born to be."

"He has a human form. Will he use it?"

Dewi's scales clanked as she shrugged. "I have no idea. We must trust his innate wisdom."

And there it was. She'd tossed down a gauntlet. I'd either rise to the challenge or not. "Come on," I said in a voice I scarcely recognized as mine. "I want to get back to my mate and my son."

If he was only going to remain a baby for a short time, I didn't want to miss any more of it than I already had.

CHAPTER ELEVEN, ROWAN

After what felt like a million dragons had trooped through the cavern with the pool, they'd offered us a lovely room with a raised bed and comfortable chairs. Once upon a time, they must have had those like Bjorn and me stay with them or they'd not have had a room like this ready for us.

The birth high was fading, and my nether regions were sore. But the warm bundle of scales in my arms was worth everything and then some. He had teeth—plenty of them. But he was careful with my breasts, almost as if he understood biting his food source was bad form.

I dozed off and on. So did Bjorn. I have no idea if Geir slept. Every time I opened my eyes, he was nursing. He'd figured out I had two breasts, and he moved to the other after he'd drained one.

Hours passed. Perhaps as much as a couple of days. When I was awake, I ate and drank. Someone thoughtfully kept a teapot filled and biscuits and something sweet and creamy available. The next time I awoke, Bjorn wasn't there, but I wasn't worried. Geir nestled in my arms, perpetually attached to a breast.

I couldn't quit looking at him. Examining every tiny scale and his perfect little wings was more satisfying than having the finest piece of art to study. A lighter shade of gold than his scales, his wings had remained tucked against his back. Bjorn sallied through the door carrying a platter heaped with some kind of meat. It smelled divine, and my mouth started to water.

I was done living on biscuits and jam.

Geir unfolded himself from where he'd been curved against my body, gave a precious little yip, and spread his wings for the first time. They sparkled as he used them as an air foil to float to the ground.

Bjorn laughed and set the platter down. Our baby leapt square atop the stack of meat and dug into it, chewing and swallowing so quickly I almost couldn't see his jaws move. "Not so fast," I said and swung my legs off the bed. I was still sore, but I'd focused magic to work on my stretched places.

Geir didn't even lift his head; Bjorn laughed louder. "Somehow I'm not worried he's going to choke."

I laughed too, at the absurdity of everything. The youngling didn't need my motherly advice, and I felt certain we'd butt heads more than once. "Gosh, here I thought that was food for us," I said.

"So did I," Bjorn retorted. "Nidhogg disabused me of that notion after he was done putting the plate together, but he said if I returned fast enough Geir might still be eating when I got back here with more of the same for us."

On my feet, I walked a few steps in both directions and fine-tuned my healing efforts. Someone had laid a fancy cream-colored robe over the bottom of the bed. I slipped into it, enjoying the fine weave of the fabric against my body. Bjorn wrapped his arms around me, and we stood leaning into each other and watching our baby decimate enough meat to feed a full-grown man. Or two.

"Do they have kitchens here?" I asked.

"Aye. Nothing like we're used to. For one thing, they have no use for ovens. Why?"

"Once our darling is done, I say we all go there. It might be the only way you and I get anything to eat."

"Yeeesssss!" Geir screeched into both our minds, followed by, *"More!"*

"Dewi told me he'd grow fast," Bjorn said. "At the time, I didn't fully appreciate her statement. How are you feeling?"

"Not as bad as I expected." I rolled my eyes. "I got off light. I wasn't pregnant very long, and the birth was relatively quick. It doesn't appear we'll have any of the usual downsides of being new parents."

"Like waking up every couple of hours and not being able to leave the baby alone?" He arched both blond brows.

"Something like that, but it makes me a little bit sad too. I want to take care of him."

Bjorn curved a hand over my still partially swollen stomach. "Maybe the next one will need us more."

A small snort burbled past my lips. "Next one? Sheesh. We have a war to fight, worlds to salvage. There may never be time for another baby. Hell, it's a good thing Geir is an independent little cuss."

He looked up from the meat platter, golden eyes whirling. *"More food."*

"You're not quite done with what's there," Bjorn told him.

"I will be, and then I want more." Geir spoke out loud in a high, piping voice that sounded a lot like his telepathy. He angled his head to one side. "Take me hunting."

I squatted next to him and opened my arms. He jumped into them and started pulling my robe open, intent on more milk. "Hold up, little man."

He stopped yanking on the lapels of my robe and regarded me. I took it as a good sign he'd stopped what he was doing when I asked him to. "No hunting until you're bigger, and then I'm certain your grandfather and Dewi would be delighted to take you."

"Want you. And Da." Geir bent his head at an angle to look at Bjorn.

"Maybe all of us can go," Bjorn said, "but I'm with your mum. Eat and grow strong. Then we can hunt." He bent and pried Geir out of my arms, a complex array of emotion washing over his face.

I pushed upright. "Lead the way," I said since I had no idea where the dragons prepared food. In truth, I was surprised they had anything as prosaic as a kitchen since I assumed dragons consumed everything raw—once they were grown. The meat Nidhogg had selected for his grandson had been cooked, probably courtesy of dragon fire.

Gaggles of dragons lined the corridor. We stopped to chat with each one, and Geir experimented with short flights from Bjorn to several dragons and back again. He was clumsy in the air, but I was certain that phase would be short-lived.

The intense interest other dragons had in my son both delighted and surprised me. Not that I'd spent any time among dragonkind, but I'd never viewed them as particularly compassionate or loving.

"Was the corridor this crowded when you left last time?" I asked Bjorn.

"Aye, but I'm not who they were interested in. Starting to feel like I missed out."

"You? At least you had parents who gave a crap—even if they weren't dragons."

He laced his fingers in with mine. "I'm sorry. If there was anything I could do, a magic wand I could wave and make your early years better, I would."

A wave of love so profound it nearly flattened me stole both breath and words. Geir had been chattering up a storm to a red dragon, who cooed right back. Suddenly, he launched himself off her shoulder and made a beeline back to Bjorn. He grabbed Geir out of the air. "What's up, buddy?"

Geir hissed. When he opened his mouth, a tiny gout of fire emerged. The other dragons fell silent. Magic reeking of hot clay cut through the rounded passageway. If I'd had hackles, they'd have risen along my back. Something wasn't right.

"Let me through," an imperious voice demanded.

"Not a chance," a black dragon bellowed. Smoke, ash, and fire filled the tunnel.

"Fuck. Crap. Damn," I muttered between coughs. "How'd she get loose?"

"She?" Bjorn sounded confused.

I nodded as annoyance soured my mood. "It's Mother. Take us to the kitchens. Now, please. I would, but I don't know where they are."

"I demand to see my grandson." Ceridwen's unmistakable strident tone battered me.

"Bind her," a dragon shouted.

"How'd she get loose?" another asked, mirroring my thoughts exactly.

"Got her," another voice yelled, followed by an outraged howl and the stink of Celtic magic. Usually the mix of mint and vanilla and amber smells good, but not this time.

I didn't know how she'd freed herself, and I didn't care. What mattered was my son who'd gone on full alert. More fire issued from his mouth, and he trumpeted a challenge.

"Not smart," I told him. "She's bad news."

"Bad," he agreed.

"Show some respect," Ceridwen bellowed from behind a wall of dragons.

"Ha!" I yelled back. "You show some for once in your sorry immortal life."

A flurry of red scales announced Dewi's arrival. The dragons parted to let her through. Potent magic boiled around her. When it cleared, both she and Ceridwen were gone, leaving fumes of baked clay and burned mint leaves.

"I thought the dragons had her under control," Bjorn muttered.

"Control and Mother don't belong in the same sentence. Bet she cooked something up with the Morrigan, or else she fucked her dragon jailer or something. She has plenty of magic. Enough to sense Geir's birth."

"But she didn't care about you. I don't get it," he persisted.

Breath swooshed from me. I was still conflicted about Mother. My current struggle was not to feel sorry for her. All she'd requested was a look at her grandson. A grandson who clearly wanted nothing to do with her. I shook my head. I should borrow a page from Geir's book. He was obviously wiser than I was and didn't trust her at all. For all I knew, she had some nefarious magical plot close to hand, and the moment she got near Geir, she'd launch it.

"Look, Mister Voice of Reason," I told Bjorn, "she didn't want me, but it doesn't mean she didn't view me as her personal property, and Geir in the same light—by extension."

"I'm not the enemy, Ro." He tucked both arms around Geir, who seemed to be settling down.

Our son opened his small mouth and piped, "Food. Now."

"Of course." Bjorn kissed him and set off along the passageway with me trailing behind. What had Geir sensed? He'd been almost like an early warning device and had beat a path to Bjorn before any of the rest of us knew Ceridwen was nearby. Thank the goddess he had the sense to come to us for help. I could just as easily have seen him flying right into Ceridwen's not-so-tender embrace shooting fire at her.

Grandson or no, she'd have flattened him with magic. Mother has always been a temperamental bitch.

I hustled to catch up with Bjorn and Geir, wincing when my sore tissues rubbed against each other. Geir puffed steam. I wished I could puff some back. Instead, I stroked his head. "What did you notice?" I asked.

"Notice?" More steam.

"When you hurried to Daddy," I clarified.

"Wicked. Bad. Too close."

"You did the right thing," I told him. "She is bad, and she would hurt you."

"Not what she said." He trained his whirling eyes at me over Bjorn's shoulder.

Oh-oh. "She talked with you?" I tried for a gentle tone, no neat trick when outrage began in my feet and flashed through me like a tidal wave.

"Grandma," he said and reached for me with a small foreleg. I gripped it.

"She is your grandmother," I agreed, "but she..." I floundered, hunting for what to say that a child might understand.

"Bad," Geir repeated.

"Yup. She puts herself first. I don't trust her, and she's my mother."

"Not trust. Never." Geir nodded solemnly.

"I wondered about that," Bjorn spoke up. "How he sensed Ceridwen before the rest of us."

"Well, they do share blood," I murmured. "Might make it easier."

"Nah. The slam dunk was she talked with him," he

replied, followed by, "Son, your first lesson will be constructing a ward to keep bad people out of your mind."

Geir cocked his head to one side. I was still holding onto his foreleg. Everything he did was so stinking cute, I was having a hard time thinking straight. Bjorn was definitely onto something, though. If Mother had been able to slice right through and engage my son in conversation while Bjorn and I—and the dragons—remained oblivious, we had a problem. A big one, and we had to nip it in the bud. Before something far more evil than Mother approached him.

I let go of Geir's talons and bent close, kissing the top of his head. He lurched over Bjorn's shoulder and grabbed my amulet. "Whoa." I pried his claws away.

He let out a mournful little squawk. "Mine."

Dragons adored gemstones and precious metals. It was hardwired into them. "We'll help you start your own hoard —" I began.

"Bad Grandma told me. That is mine," he howled.

Understanding soured my belly about the time Bjorn halted and turned to face me. "About your jewelry, it started oozing power when you were in labor."

I looked meaningfully at our son, silently telling Bjorn not to upset him further. Tears flowed from our baby and clattered to the floor as gems. I stooped and gathered them, intent on shifting his attention away from the amulet.

"There ye are," Nidhogg shouted from the far end of the passageway.

"Here we are," I agreed as we covered the twenty meters or so between us and the dragon lord.

Nidhogg held out his forelegs and made a chirping

sound. Geir let go of Bjorn and me and bounded to his grandfather, his unhappiness over my amulet forgotten. Thank the goddess he had a short attention span.

"I heard," Nidhogg said without preamble.

"What happened?" I asked, seeking information about how Mother had managed to break free from her prison. I'd ditch the amulet and ring and circlet as soon as I could, but not within plain sight of my son.

"I should have an answer to that question shortly." Nighogg stood aside, and Bjorn and I walked into a cavernous space lit by magic. Long tables were laden mostly with trenchers of various meats. Geir wriggled out of Nidhogg's hold, spread his wings, and landed on the nearest table. Almost before he landed, he sank his snout into a pile of some kind of white-fleshed meat.

As far as he was concerned, we may as well not have been there. He began with the nearest platter. Meanwhile, I grabbed a plate from a nearby stack and walked through the room selecting items to eat. I was beyond hungry. Ravenous was more like it.

A blast of blurry light from Nidhogg told me he'd sealed off the kitchen from the rest of the labyrinth beneath Fire Mountain. "Eat," he said. "Get your strength back."

I'd already settled on a bench and was shoveling food into my mouth nearly as enthusiastically as Geir, although he was more efficient than me. Apparently, dragons didn't need to chew as much as I did. Bjorn sat next to me. He was eating, but he looked worried.

I got it. Fire Mountain was about as insular and safe as locations came. If we couldn't put a couple of days together here without incident, it didn't bode well. Nidhogg was shadowing Geir as he ate his way down the table. Our son was visibly larger than he'd been when he was born.

Big surprise. He'd been eating nonstop.

Nidhogg turned to face us. Not that I'm all that swift reading dragon expressions, but I knew whatever came out of his mouth would be very bad news. "Ysien just reported in. Your mother is back in her cell, but the Morrigan is gone."

Bjorn punched the air with a fist. "They planned this."

"I fear ye're correct," Nidhogg said. "At least, the Morrigan did. This has her signature all over it. She may have paved the way to free Ceridwen, knowing full well 'twas temporary. And then, she took full advantage of the confusion to sashay out of here."

I recalled what I knew about the Morrigan. She'd been banished long before I was born, but she was the Battle Crow and capable of shifting into infinite forms. Shifting aside, she incited battles and was a worse shit-stirrer than Loki ever dreamed of being. It was a wonder the two of them hadn't joined ranks...

"Oh no!" I cried.

"What?" Both Bjorn and Nidhogg stared at me. Geir kept right on eating.

"This can't be accidental. I know it's farfetched, but somehow Loki reached out to her, told her about his plight, and convinced her to help him." The words were no sooner out of my mouth than I heard the ring of absolute truth.

"That's quite a stretch." Bjorn patted my hand as if I'd suddenly grown feeble. It pissed me off.

"Think about it." My voice came out louder than I

meant. "Loki stirs the pot. It's what he lives for. The worse things get, the better he likes it. Well, the Morrigan is the same way. It's why the Celts banished her—something totally unheard of in the pantheon. She's the only one they ever sent away, and it was because of her penchant for setting people against one another and causing trouble."

"She tried to co-opt a young dragon when she was first imprisoned here," Nidhogg rumbled. "If the hatchling hadn't told his mother, the Morrigan may well have gotten away with it. She had the youngster convinced he should free her. The tale he ran to his mother with was that the goddess had fallen into one of Fire Mountain's many chasms and couldn't find her way out."

"What did you do?" I asked.

Smoke plumed from Nidhogg's jaws. "We educated every dragon and sent the Morrigan to Arawn for half the year, where she roasted in perpetual fire. For the time we had her, we buried her even deeper beneath Fire Mountain itself."

"Whatever you did," Bjorn said, "it worked for a long time."

"Aye. Mostly because she gave up trying to outwit us," Nidhogg said. "We never should have put Ceridwen with her. At the time, I thought perhaps the two would comfort each other, and—"

Laughter, harsh and bitter, burst from me. "Sorry," I said around gouts of it. "Mother hated the Morrigan. Didn't you hear when she called her something like a craven bitch before you hauled her here?"

"She said she dinna wish to share the same air," Nidhogg

corrected me. "I thought 'twas manipulation on her part because she dinna wish to be taken anywhere as a captive."

Thoughts crowded into my head, and I raked my hands through my unbound hair. "When was the last time you sent the Morrigan for her stint with Arawn?" I asked Nidhogg.

He understood exactly where I was going with my question. Smoke, ash, and flames spewed from his mouth, bouncing harmlessly off a far wall. "After the Ninth Gate fell, except none of us knew it had been ruptured." He shook his head until his scales rattled. "I have to hand it to her. She tricked us, and 'tisn't easy to fool dragonkind."

"Loki was skulking around the lowest level of Hell," Bjorn broke in. "The Morrigan must have met him there—"

"Aye and hatched the plot that just played out. For once, Ceridwen was conned."

"Yeah, well, I don't feel sorry for her." A quick glance at Geir told me he was still immersed in eating. I sidled to Nidhogg and stripped off my necklace, ring, and circlet. "*Get rid of these,*" I told him in shielded mind speech.

Nidhogg narrowed his whirling eyes, but didn't question me as I feared he might. He took the items. Power flared bright gold with reddish streaks. When it cleared, my jewelry was gone.

Bjorn was on his feet. "Someone has to alert Odin. Now."

"I'll do that," Nidhogg said. "While I'm there, I'll make certain he's up to date on the fate of his work crews and your trip to Cadir's borderworld."

Bjorn nodded. "Dewi told you, huh?"

"Of course. Dragonkind have no secrets from one another," Nidhogg replied.

"What about Mother?" I asked, convinced she had some underhanded plot in mind to wrest Geir from me. Hopefully jettisoning jewels that had once been hers would foil her plans.

"Dewi has that situation well in hand. And we have posted two dragons to keep her confined."

Hel shimmered from empty air at the far end of the kitchen. "I shall go with you," she told Nidhogg.

I waited for him to tell her he didn't require her presence. Instead, he nodded. "Aye, 'tis a good idea."

Geir's head popped up. "Grandma. The good one," he chirped.

"Aye, darling." Hel hustled to him and lifted him into her arms. "Grandma will be back soon. Eat and grow. Surprise me by how much bigger ye are when I return."

He puffed steam. Hel laughed and set him back on the table. I was infinitely grateful he hadn't noticed the missing amulet. Sooner or later, he was bound to. Hopefully, I could find enough shiny pretties to divert him. Should be plenty of those in a dragons' lair.

"We willna be long," Nidhogg said.

Hel trotted to his side as magic burbled around him. Moments later, we had the kitchen to ourselves.

I glanced at my empty plate. I should eat more, but my appetite had fled. "We should be doing something," I muttered.

"We are," Bjorn said. "The sooner you're fully recovered, the sooner we can leave."

"Go where?" Geir asked.

I looked at my son. So young. So vulnerable. So innocent. The innocent part wouldn't last much longer. I didn't want him to go anywhere. I needed him to be safe.

"Wherever we go," Bjorn answered.

I dipped my head and shielded my mind. Our son didn't need an overprotective mother with misguided maternal instincts hovering over him. He needed to learn about his magic.

"About those lessons in crafting a ward," I said. "How about if we begin now?"

Bjorn dropped a hand onto my shoulder and squeezed hard. "Good idea. No time like the present to figure out how his magic will work."

"Where do we begin?" I walked to his side.

"We let him show us how he wields the four elements," Bjorn said, "and then we'll take it from there."

I nodded. "You've helped others learn magic, huh?"

"I have."

Remembering all the years when the only magic I commanded was what I'd taught myself wasn't productive. All it did was piss me off. Before I hunted down Ceridwen and cussed her out for being the worst damned parent ever, I focused on Bjorn and Geir. Our son was on the floor, and Bjorn crouched in front of him.

"Show me earth," Bjorn was saying.

"Want fire." Geir turned his head, and flames burst from his mouth.

"Earth," Bjorn persisted.

"Why? Fire is easy."

"Aye, but spells require a command of all four elements."

Geir's head bounced up and down. "Tell me how."

Bjorn scooped up a ball from the earthen floor and tucked it into Geir's talons. "Earth holds minerals. Gold. Silver. Copper. Titanium. And many others. All dragons love precious minerals. It's how you will persuade earth to come to your call..."

Love for the two of them suffused me with a warm glow. Maybe we'd have a moment to teleport to Midgard so I could show my wonderful son to the witches.

"Daughter!" Ceridwen's unwelcome voice filled my mind. *"Ye must come. They're killing me."*

"Buck up, Mother. You're immortal. And your spying tools are gone. While I'm at it, stay away from my son." I slammed wards around my mind with her name all over them and hoped to hell it would be enough. Neither Bjorn nor Geir looked up, so my guess was they hadn't heard her.

CHAPTER TWELVE, BJORN

Somehow, we cobbled another three weeks together in our cozy room beneath Fire Mountain. At least I believe it was that long. Dragon magic spins a web over everything until prosaic items like the passage of time grow blurry. Rowan and Geir and I returned to the pool every day. It strengthened all of us, but especially Geir. I swear he grew half again as big after each dunking. He'd shed his scales so many times, a small pile of them circled the pool.

Nidhogg and Dewi said to leave the shiny golden bits. They were probably waiting until Geir was done molting to clear up the mess and hide it away where no one could find it. Rather like the cord and placenta, any physical matter could pose a danger to our son, if the wrong person got their hands on it.

His head reached to my chest now, and he was too heavy to lift. He still liked to curl up in my arms, though. Rowan's too. I'd expected him to ask what happened to Rowan's necklace, but he never did. Perhaps with the innate innocence of the very young, he'd known it was evil but had been drawn to it, anyway.

Its absence might have been a relief. It certainly was for me. Kind of like when you don't know until a thing is gone that it wasn't healthy for you. I have to hand it to Ceridwen. She did a masterful job swathing those gems in enough Celtic magic they did feel like they belonged to Rowan. Hell, the jewels had even fooled her.

Sometimes everything made me tired. I wanted to gather up my mate and my child and transport us all to my cottage where I could raise my son, teach him the things that I'd loved as a boy. Except he wasn't a boy. He was a dragon. He might have a human form, but I hadn't seen it except at the moment of his birth.

His aptitude for magic was bottomless. He learned quickly and added his own twists to spells. Many blew up in his face, but he'd laugh and start over. He could craft a credible ward—and he still obeyed when I told him to do something—but I didn't expect compliance for too much longer. Surely, dragons had a phase similar to human children where they refused to do anything.

Nidhogg and Hel had indeed returned quickly, with Odin in tow. After dandling Geir on his knees and coating him with Norse protection spells, he'd growled at me that I was shirking my master sorcerer duties. Nidhogg and he had gotten into it then, and I'd quietly left the room.

Later, I'd asked Nidhogg about whether we should teach Geir to shift, or at least explore whether that was going to be part of his magic. Nidhogg took my question seriously because he'd thought for a while before he said, "Perhaps later. He is stronger and far less vulnerable as a dragon."

"What about Ceridwen and the gems?" I persisted. That episode still bothered me. Rowan and I had talked about it, and I knew her mother was still harassing her.

"Pah." Nidhogg had puffed enough ash I ended up bent over coughing. "That Celtic slut knows how much dragons adore gemstones. She leveraged Geir's hoard-lust and did her damnedest to get to him through the onyx amulet. But she failed. That is the important part."

"Only because Rowan figured it out," I said. Maybe it wasn't a good idea to be so blunt, but I needed Nidhogg cognizant of how close we'd skirted to disaster. Who knew what damage Ceridwen could have done if she'd established a toehold in my son's mind?

I wrenched my thoughts back to today as I trotted through the now-familiar warren of passageways. I'd woken hours ago and left Ro and Geir asleep in our room.

"Hello, mate," rang from behind me.

I swung about and faced Gwydion. He was smiling and garbed in a deep-blue robe sashed in white, staff in hand. Loose for once, his fair hair fell down his chest. Arawn glided next to him, garbed in black. Trousers this time, rather than a robe, were topped by a linen shirt with full sleeves. His dark eyes had regained some of their sparkle. The last time I'd seen him, he looked beleaguered what with all his Ninth Gate problems.

"Got the latches repaired, did you?" I asked and charged forward, hand extended. Both Celts shook it.

"Aye. I did. Have ye added divination to your other skills?"

I shook my head. "You don't appear as...troubled as you did."

Arawn drew his dark brows into a thick line. "Dewi relayed your suspicions about the Morrigan latching onto Loki in my domain. At first, I was furious, defensive, convinced such a thing could never have happened right under my nose."

"But then he paid Bran a visit," Gwydion tossed out.

I waited. Clearly, the Celts didn't require prodding from me. And I was intrigued by what Bran, god of prophecy, had said.

"I'm telling this," Arawn shot a black look at Gwydion.

"Be my guest." Gwydion mock bowed.

Arawn hissed annoyance. "I like to be thorough," he continued. "And so I requested Bran to take a peek into the past to see how my gates were destroyed. As long as he was there, I asked him to determine if the Morrigan and Loki had had any contact."

It wasn't a time to ask questions. If I read his body language correctly, Arawn was uncomfortable enough. His shoulders sat ramrod straight, and a touch of color splashed across his pale skin.

"Without adding unnecessary detail," Arawn went on, "a combination of dragon magic from Cadir and the Celtic world-breaking spell brought my gates down. If I'd retained a gatekeeper, at least someone would have let me know. As it was, months elapsed afore I discovered aught was amiss."

Gwydion sent a pointed look scuttling toward Arawn,

who chopped a hand downward. "Not a word from you. Until ye have a separate realm to keep an eye on, ye've no idea how much time such a task can absorb."

I kept my mouth shut, and my mind shuttered. I was appalled Arawn hadn't so much as bothered to set foot in Hell for however long had passed between the gate-breaking and when he found out about it.

"Bran appeared done, so I left off looking at crystals and tea leaves over his shoulder, but then he called me back." Arawn paused to take a measured breath. "Bran pointed at a third tool. He'd waved his hands over a good sized mirror when I first showed up, but I figured it was for some other purpose. In its surface, I saw the Morrigan and Loki sitting close, heads bent together, thick as thieves."

"What were they saying?" I was done being silent.

Arawn shook his head. "The mirror dinna include audio."

"Still proves they knew each other," Gwydion snarled.

"Agreed." Arawn bit off the word and eyed his companion. "Ye forget, I know the Battle Crow as well as any. She's funneled many a soul to Hell, and I dinna lift a finger to save her from her fate."

"What do you mean?" I asked. "Did you vote on her ouster?"

Gwydion nodded. "Aye, and it had to be unanimous. Had even one Celt cast a dissenting vote, we'd not have exiled her."

"'Twasn't as if we had much of a choice." Arawn's voice held a weary note, as if reliving that part of the past bothered him. "Not if we wanted to maintain our relationship with dragonkind. 'Twas already strained on many fronts, but the Morrigan made sport out of turning dragons against one another."

"She even recruited griffons and Furies and the Harpies to jump into that last brawl," Gwydion muttered. "'Twas the final straw. For us all."

I hadn't heard that tale, but it would keep. "You're here," I pointed out. "Are other Celts with you?"

"Aye. We shall gather tomorrow to cobble plans together," Gwydion told me. "Odin and Thor and a few others from Asgard and Vanaheim are due here as well."

I wasted a few moments battling irritation no one had bothered to tell Rowan or me about what was clearly a cross-pantheon meeting, but I let it go. We were already here, so perhaps our attendance was assumed.

Things would probably proceed quickly once all the players were assembled. Rowan and I had talked about a quick trip to Midgard. She wasn't as worried about the witches now the Celts were back in Inverlochy and helping with the garden, but the bulk of the witches had remained beneath Ben Nevis. So long as they remained within the Celts' ancient stronghold, they'd be safe enough, but they were also cut off from everything.

Rowan had been their eyes and ears. Their go-between to access the world beyond the caves. And she'd been gone for the better part of a month. A very long time as splintered as Midgard was.

"Bjorn?" Gwydion's tone was brisk. I guessed he'd been trying to get my attention for a while.

"Aye. Sorry. I was thinking."

"We heard rumors of an army of dead living on the outer borderworlds," Arawn said.

"We saw one of them," I confirmed. "A Draugar known to Hel. He claimed all the Draugars had escaped and were scattered through the outer borderworlds and the few worlds on the good side of the barrier. Once they answered to Cadir and Loki, but now they're probably piloted by the scoundrels and bastards consigned to the outer borderworlds."

"I'm certain they werena sorry to see Loki and Cadir depart," Gwydion muttered.

"'Tis a prime spot for me to locate those who escaped from behind my Ninth Gate," Arawn said.

"Hel agrees with you," I told him followed by, "Good to see you both. I'm going to run Rowan down, and she and I will teleport to Midgard."

"Ye'll be back in time for the meeting?" Gwydion arched a fair brow.

"That's my plan. Ro's been wanting to show off our son to the witches, and it will give us an opportunity to ensure they're all right."

"The ones in Inverlochy are," Gwydion informed me. "They've been harvesting these past few days. We shall return them, crops and all, to Ben Nevis verra soon."

Relief swept through me. "Rowan will be thrilled. This crop project was her baby, and it will mean the witches have a few months of provisions."

"Mayhap by the time planting season comes next year, Midgard will be a safe place to walk beneath open skies," Arawn said.

"We all hope for that." Gwydion's usual smirk was absent.

After another round of handshaking, I loped toward our room. The door stood open, so I kept right on going to the pool. That and the kitchen were the likeliest options, and Ro would have passed me in the corridor if they'd gone to get a snack. The archway came into sight. I ducked into the calm quiet of the cave holding what was really a small lake. The place carried a sense of peace, of timelessness, that sank into my soul.

Rowan and Geir were swimming, splashing water at each other and laughing uproariously. Neither knew I was here, and I grabbed a moment to watch my love and our child. Tenderness seasoned with love filled me. I'd never imagined I could contain such joy. But with it came worry. We faced unparalleled evil. I was confident Rowan and I could deal with most any threat, but we had Geir to watch over.

If I had my way, I'd leave him here and let the Fire Mountain dragons watch over him. It wasn't perfect, but at least it would keep him out of direct sight of our enemy. Whoever that happened to be. I ground my teeth. Still so much we didn't know. Including exactly who held a grudge against Odin.

I'd had time to think about things, and every door I kicked open led to Odin. Midgard had been convenient, but Yggdrasil's rot suggested the Nine Worlds were the real target. I'd floundered about trying to come up with a way to ask Odin for a list of who he'd pissed off, but I'd finally given up. For one thing, the list had to be long. For another, he probably couldn't remember everyone he'd dealt ill with. As I've said, he's cunning and devious, and his sense of humor has never been a good match for the dirty deeds he's played on others. Don't get me wrong, he's nothing like Loki. Beneath Odin's practical jokes and coarse ways, he has a generous heart.

"Da!" was followed by a shrill trumpet.

I'd been discovered, so I moved deeper into the room and crouched by the edge of the pool. Geir splashed water all over me.

Rowan swam close. Her red hair floated in the water like an exotic breed of anemone. "Probably time for us to get out," she said with a warm smile.

"I ran into Gwydion and Arawn," I told her. "Apparently, there's some big powwow tomorrow."

"I caught wind of something last night," she told me.

"How come you didn't say anything?"

She bent to kiss me and walked to where she'd left the robe she'd mostly lived in since Geir's birth. Her body was back to normal, but her breasts were fuller and her stomach slightly rounded. Those changes would probably be permanent, and they added a sensual allure to her tall figure.

"Probably because I didn't want our vacation to end," she replied. "Living in fairyland has been delightful. Someone else cooks. I don't have to do anything except play with Geir. And you." She grinned naughtily, and I recalled our surreptitious lovemaking the previous night once I'd spelled Geir to a slightly deeper sleep.

My son was still splashing. He sent waves rolling from one end of the lake to the other with magic that sluiced from his outstretched talons. They'd been whitish when he was first born, but they were shading to the ruby color I associated with adult dragons.

I stood and walked to Rowan. "Feel like a quick trip to Midgard?"

She smiled. "I'd love one. I've felt incredibly guilty about the witches."

"Gwydion assures me the Inverlochy batch are fine. Crops are in, and the Celts are ready to move everyone back beneath Ben Nevis."

Her smile broadened. "I am so glad the garden experiment is over. And that it paid off."

I lowered my voice. "Has Ceridwen been bothering you lately?"

"No. That went away shortly after I had Nidhogg dispose of the jewelry. The more I've turned it over, the more I'm certain that little episode where the ring and necklace suckered me into rescuing them from the mineshaft was orchestrated by Mother. She's incredibly powerful, and us sharing blood makes it easier for her to manipulate me."

"Good. One less problem." I nodded briskly.

We had so many facing us, it barely made a dent, but I'd take help from any quarter. I turned to Geir and stretched my hands toward him. Magic floated from me and formed a circle around him. He loved it when I surrounded him with power.

Steam billowed from him as I coaxed him from the water. As soon as his hind legs were firmly planted on the shore, he shook like a mad thing, splattering me even though I stood a good meter away.

"We're going on an adventure," I told my son.

"Where?"

"To visit my family," Rowan told him. "They'll be excited to meet you."

Geir's eyes shaded from copper to silver to green as they spun. Everyone who'd met him had petted and coddled him to the point I was amazed he wasn't more of a handful than he was.

"You must promise to behave and do as we instruct you," Rowan admonished him. "I have a cat who loves me. You mustn't tease him."

Geir stood straighter. "Cats are to eat."

"Not this one," Rowan went on. "He loves me, and he will be very happy to see me. If you allow it, he will love you too."

Geir trundled to where we stood, his brow scrunched in thought. "Who else is there?"

"My family. Men and women who took me in and treated me well after I ran away from Bad Grandma."

"Oooh." A stream of ash puffed from his jaws. "Do they have magic?"

"They're witches," Bjorn told him. "They hold different magic, more earth-based and less powerful than yours."

"Everyone's magic is weaker than mine."

It was an innocent statement, and someday it might be true, but I couldn't let it slide. I bent so our eyes were level. "What have we talked about?"

"Magic isn't everything." He sounded petulant. "But it should be. What else is there?"

I felt about a million years old when I said, "Power is a

gift and a responsibility. If it isn't tempered with wisdom and compassion, it can turn into a scourge. Remember the story of your bad great-grandpa?"

He nodded solemnly. "Loki."

"Aw geez," Rowan muttered. "He's going to think everyone he's related to is a monster."

"Well"—I glanced her way—"some of them are. We don't do Geir any favors if we whitewash the truth."

Magic turned the air around Geir warm with color. Scales clanked to the floor in what must have been his dozenth molt. "I will be good," he told Rowan and me. Spreading his wings, he flew around the cavern experimenting with dips and rolls.

"He flies a lot better than he used to," Rowan commented.

"He does everything better, and it's only going to continue, but eventually we'll run out of time."

She didn't ask what I meant. She understood. There'd come a season to stand and fight. Geir would be there, and whatever skills he'd mastered would have to be enough.

"I need to stop by our room and get my clothes," Rowan told me.

I motioned to Geir, and we followed her out of the cavern. This wouldn't be a long trip, and I wasn't certain when we'd get back to Midgard after today. As soon as Rowan was ready, we walked to the entrance to the caves. A dragon met us there and handed me back the blades I'd had to relinquish to enter. It felt like eons had passed since Geir's birth, but it hadn't been long at all.

Not really. A little less than a month in "real" time.

I built a teleport spell, borrowing from my dragon half so we could use the comfy channels that supplied both light and air.

Geir was so excited he was bouncing up and down when I snared him with my magic, and the cracked red earth of Fire Mountain faded, replaced by a teleport channel. I decided to capitalize on this as a learning experience, so I sketched out how I'd built my spell.

And then I made Geir repeat the steps until he knew them perfectly. He might need to make a run for Fire Mountain, and I'd just ensured he knew how.

Rowan stood next to me, an arm around my waist. "Have I told you lately how much I love you?"

"Probably, but I never tire of hearing it."

She laughed, soft and low. "I love you, Bjorn. You've made me a very happy woman."

"The feeling is mutual, darling."

Geir was muttering the steps I'd just taught him. I listened in to make sure he wasn't skipping any. His next lessons would be in how to fight. Nidhogg, Dewi, Quade, and Zelli had been nagging about that. Once we returned, I'd have to agree to let them drag him to their practice arena—or wherever they honed fighting skills—and kindle the lethal side of his dragon nature.

Would he be old enough? Would all my words about tempering magic with wisdom stick with him? Wielding power could be heady. I'd struggled against its pull when I was very young. At the time, I hadn't understood its magnetism or why its allure was nearly my undoing more than once.

Yeah. Shame on Hel and Nidhogg. If my true parents had been more forthcoming… I stopped myself. What then? Being raised by mortals had probably been good for me because it provided balance. Had I known what I was, I may well have become a terror. Not as bad as Loki, but not too far behind.

"It will be all right," Rowan spoke softly, right against my ear. "It has to be."

I didn't chide her for sharing my thoughts. We were mates; I had nothing to hide. "I hope so," I said, and gripped one of her hands. Our respite in Midgard would be brief, and I was determined to make the most of it.

CHAPTER THIRTEEN, ROWAN

A lot of things worried me, but I put up a good front for my son and Bjorn. I might long for a different set of circumstances, but I'd play the hand I'd been dealt. Just as I'd done through the long years of my life. I'd hedged when Bjorn asked about Mother. I was able to mute her, block her out, but she was still clawing at the edges of my warding.

Sap that I am, I was actually concerned about her. She kept saying someone was killing her, and she did sound weaker, but it might be an act. She was more than capable of that type of manipulation. Cadir loomed large in my thoughts too, though. There'd been a way to kill him, which meant there was probably some secret way to kill any immortal.

Would carving out her heart and feeding it to Fire Mountain do the trick?

I wanted to pay her a visit for two reasons. The first would be to tell her to shape up and behave so the dragons didn't have to waste magic on her. But my second reason was to reassure myself she was all right, and her bellyaching was just one more scheme.

"You're quiet," Bjorn observed. He and Geir had been chatting up a storm as Bjorn taught him the basics of teleporting via the dragons' special method.

"I'm enjoying listening to the two of you."

"Almost there," Geir announced.

I checked the markers flashing by. Written in runes not unlike the ones scribed in Bifrost's walls, they confirmed my son's assessment. "We're lucky," I told him.

"Why?" Scales clanked when he twisted his head to regard me. His baby scales had been softer, and quiet. The newer batches were indistinguishable from those of an adult dragon.

"Before I knew I possessed dragon magic," I told him, "I journeyed to other worlds in a black place. One with no light and no air. The no light part wasn't a problem, but not having air was uncomfortable. Never really got used to it."

He patted the undulating floor we stood upon with a hindfoot. "Only for dragons." Pride threaded through his words.

"Aye," Bjorn said. "Only for dragons."

"When can I see you?" Geir glanced from Bjorn to me.

"You're looking right at us," I joked. I'd understood what he meant.

"Your dragons," he added with a touch of impatience.

Bjorn exchanged a what-do-we-do-now look with me, and I quested about for the simplest answer. Geir might be growing fast, but he was still a baby. "Our dragons live within." I tapped my breastbone. "Neither your father nor I knew we had dragon blood until we were long past grown up."

"Find them," Geir persisted.

"Why is it important?" Bjorn asked.

"So we can fly together."

The corners of my mouth twitched, and I smiled. Yes, my son was still very young. He loved to fly, and, in his dragon mind, families flew together. I rested a hand on his shoulder. "It would be lovely. Your father and I will work on it, but not right now."

I felt Bjorn feed a slight course correction into our travel spell. Light blossomed around us, and we floated downward, not far from the creek that ran near the Ben Nevis stronghold. Geir spread his wings, his intent crystal clear. Him flying off to go exploring hadn't been a problem on Fire Mountain because he'd never been outside.

I got my feet under me and opened my mouth to order him back.

"Nay," Bjorn said. "He's not hurting anything. We can offer him a few moments to stretch his wings. Under Fire Mountain, he never flew more than the length of the main corridor, and it only worked because his wings were small. I doubt he'd be able to finesse that now."

"But it might not be safe, and don't give me the dragons-are-warriors song and dance."

Andraste bounded our way, blonde hair tightly braided and a bow slung across her back along with a lethal-looking broadsword. Garbed in her customary battle leathers, she cut an imposing figure. "Thought I felt dragons," she bellowed and shaded her eyes with a hand. "Och, he's a beauty. How long did he stay human?"

"Only until he was born," I told her, followed by, "What are you doing here?"

"Delivering the witches and the garden's bounty." She put two fingers into her mouth and whistled.

Geir wheeled and flew right toward her.

"How'd you do that?" I asked.

"Youngsters all love Auntie Andraste," she told me with a warmer smile than I'd ever seen on her austere face. She held out her arms. Geir barreled into them, driving both of them to the ground where they rolled about in the dust mock fighting.

Geir chirped and blew steam and bugled. Andraste pivoted from beneath his bulk and flowed to her feet. "He will be a staunch warrior," she pronounced. "He has the right attitude."

She slapped me across the back. "I had my doubts about you, but ye've risen to the challenge. Good work."

I supposed it was as close as she ever came to a compliment. "Uh, thanks. I think."

"Where are you off to now?" Bjorn asked her.

"Why Fire Mountain. Where else? We have the battle of an epoch to plan. I must be part of it."

"You might already know, but the Morrigan escaped," I told her.

A blood-chilling howl burst from Adraste followed by, "Nooooooo. That fucking bitch. What were the dragons thinking to let her go?"

"Fucking bitch," Geir chirped. "Fucking bitch."

It wasn't funny, but I wanted to laugh. Instead, I shook a finger in his face. "Bad words. Pick better ones."

"Oops. Sorry," Andraste muttered. "Havena been around children in a verra long time. So, the Battle Crow is loose, eh? Doesna surprise me. She's drawn to war in the same way as I am, and she wouldna want to miss this one."

"You exiled her once," Bjorn spoke up. "Are the Celts still of one mind about her?"

Andraste shrugged her broad shoulders. Something about the gesture iced my blood, and her words clinched my impression. "Och, mayhap her punishment has lasted long enough. She is a Celt, and none of us are perfect. Well, time for me to be off. See you soon, I'm sure."

Mint, vanilla, and amber burned my nostrils as she summoned a journey spell. I wanted to shake her, remind her the Morrigan hadn't changed. "Wait!" I yelled.

"Aye? Make it snappy, lass."

"The Morrigan and Loki are working together. She met him during the part of her imprisonment where she was supposedly locked behind Arawn's Ninth Gate."

"And ye know this, how?"

"Arawn had Bran scry the past."

The magic that had flared around Andraste retreated; her forehead furrowed in thought, and she nodded slowly. "Och, I can see the attraction. Both of them are born troublemakers. That does cast a different color over her freedom, though. Mayhap 'tisn't such a good idea after all."

Before I could add my own enthusiastic endorsement, she shimmered to nothingness. Geir was still muttering "fucking bitch" under his breath. I squatted in front of him and grabbed one of his forelegs. He curled his talons around my arm in a trusting gesture that caught my heart in a sling.

My lecture might have died unspoken had Bjorn not knelt next to me and said, "There are better ways to express yourself. Bad words always want out, but you can find ones that do a better job."

"Who is this Morrigan?"

"A Celtic goddess. I suppose she's as much your aunt as Andraste, the one who just left."

"Why is she a fuck—" He recovered fast. "Bad. Why is she bad?"

I tightened my grip on him and hoped he'd read my approval. "She never thinks about anyone but herself," I said.

"And she delights in making trouble," Bjorn added. "Come on, let's say hello to the witches, and then we must be gone."

We walked. Geir flew circles above us. I didn't blame him. Walking wasn't the best venue for dragons. As awkward and ungainly as they were on land, they were grace personified in the air.

Tansy and Hilda ran to meet us, and I hugged both women. Bjorn wrapped his arms around us all. "So good to see you," Hilda said.

"I've missed you so much," Tansy tossed out. "So much." She hugged me harder.

A strident meow announced Mort. He took a running jump, caught onto my clothing with his claws, and climbed to my shoulders. Meanwhile, Geir skidded in for a landing, bugling a greeting.

"A tiny dragon," Hilda exclaimed.

"He's precious," Tansy crooned and reached to stroke his scales. He leaned into her touch.

An awkward catch peppered my words when I said, "May I present my—our—son, Geir. He was born about a month ago."

Hilda drew back and stared at Bjorn and me. "But how? I understand he's magical, but that was the quickest pregnancy on record."

"Not amongst magic wielders," Bjorn said and hit the high points about the enchanted pool.

Tansy was still stroking Geir's scales. "You must have a human form," she told him. "May I see it?"

Shock rocked me to my moorings when the scent of hot baked clay rose, along with the prickly feel of dragon power. Moments later, a fair-haired youth with tousled curls stood before me. His eyes were the same ice blue as Bjorn's. If I'd applied human standards, I'd have judged him to be around ten, perhaps twelve. His skin was the same coppery-gold as mine, and he was strongly built for a child with ropy muscles stretching beneath his skin.

Feeling oddly formal, I bowed before I snugged him into my arms and murmured, "Nice to meet you this way too."

He wriggled out of my grasp, his face painted with color. "Good Grandma and Good Grandpa told me not to do this. I wasn't certain I could."

"You mean Hel and Nidhogg."

Geir nodded solemnly. "Dewi too. They all said I was much safer as a dragon."

"You are," Bjorn agreed.

Oblivious to everything, Mort purred like a small locomotive from his perch on my shoulders.

Patrick ran to us, and the round robin of greetings repeated itself. After he'd oohed and ahhed over Geir, he said, "Quickly. Tell me what is happening. All of us are here now, so our forces are no longer split. Is it safe to be out and about, or should we still be remaining within?"

Between Bjorn and me, we told Patrick and Hilda about the army of shades, Cadir, the Morrigan, and Loki.

"That one, the trickster," Patrick hissed. "He won't remain in Jotunheim. For all we know, he's already escaped."

"Odin would have told us," Bjorn said.

"Perhaps he doesn't know." Patrick shrugged and shook his head. "I'm worried for all of you. An army of the dead poses obvious problems. You can't kill them. You can't hurt them. They just keep right on coming at you."

"There are spells—" Bjorn began.

Hilda held up a hand. "Aye, even we know of some, but they take time, and they are far from permanent."

"You should leave the lad here with us," Patrick said. "He will be safe beneath Ben Nevis. Safe as anywhere can be, that is."

Geir had been standing about a meter away talking with Tansy. He tilted his head our way and said. "My place is with my parents. This battle is my first task, the reason I was called from the beyond."

My ears perked up. I wanted to know more about where Geir had been, how he'd heeded a summons, but such questions would have to wait. Talking was coming easier to him, too, probably a product of not filtering everything through his dragon consciousness.

Probably. In truth, I knew less than nothing since I'd never had another form to shift into.

Bjorn ruffled Geir's hair. "Thank Patrick. It was kind of him to offer."

"Thank you." Geir glanced at Bjorn. "Things are... different in this body, but I'm getting used to it."

"Better not get too used to it," Bjorn retorted. "I won't tell the dragons you spent time in your other form. Wouldn't want them to be cross with you."

Geir stretched his arms out and turned in a full circle, rolling his shoulders back. "Feels odd," he pronounced. "Not bad, but odd."

Patrick had asked an important question before we got sidetracked by Geir shifting. I smothered a smile. Maybe my son changing forms wasn't so surprising after all since Tansy, a very attractive young woman, had been the one doing the asking.

"Nothing is any safer than it was," I told Patrick, Hilda, and Tansy. "Be very cautious when you venture beyond the caves. In fact, why are you outside now?"

"Andraste dropped us and the crops off right next to the entrance," Patrick said. "Everybody rushed out to greet us, and they're working on hauling the crops inside. We grew a lot, but it all needs to be processed in some way so it will keep."

"Of course. Bet that canning pot will be busy," Bjorn said.

"And the drying racks," Hilda said. "Never fear, we won't let a single plant go to waste." A soft smile curved her mouth. "The Celts said we were welcome to return when our stocks ran low."

"It was kind of them," I murmured and quit there. By the time the witches ran out of canned and dry goods, either they'd be able to grow food near Ben Nevis, or the world would have blown up around all of us. Back when I'd been living with the witches, I hadn't given a thought to how Earth—Midgard—might be connected to anything other than the mysterious evil pumping ruin through the Breaking site.

I understood a whole lot more now. The stakes were much higher. Loss of the Nine Worlds would reverberate through every universe. It was so unthinkable, it nearly immobilized me.

Pull yourself together. I used my sternest mental voice.

"We should go," I said.

Mort must have understood because his purrs turned to a throaty growl and he jabbed his claws into my back.

"Come tell everyone hello," Patrick urged.

"Won't take more than a few minutes," Tansy chimed in.

Geir had traded turning in a circle for skipping and running as he tested out his new form. I tucked a hand beneath his arm as he barreled past. "Back to dragon you go, child."

"But why? I'm having fun." His gaze lit on Mort. "That's the cat you told me about."

"It is."

Geir's hand shot out. Mort growled.

"Why doesn't he like me?" Geir sounded hurt.

"He doesn't know you. Here." I detached the cat from my shoulders and cradled him in my arms so he'd feel more secure. "Move slowly, and stroke his head. No magic. He doesn't like it."

After a few moments when Mort stiffened in my arms, he allowed Geir's touch. My son smiled. "I like him."

"He will appreciate you once he gets to know you. All animals rely on their sense of smell, and you smell enough like me he will trust you more easily than he might have otherwise."

"I see." Geir bobbed his head.

"You need to shift," Bjorn said, "and then we will bid the other witches hello."

Grumbling like the youngster he was, Geir summoned magic. It flickered and flashed around him until a dragon stood where the child had been. Bjorn turned to Patrick and Hilda. "Any progress talking with some of the humans in the neighborhood about magic?"

A snort pushed past Patrick's lips. "None."

"We did make an effort," Hilda clarified. "A small one. We stopped by the enclave near the lake where Nidhogg killed the goblins that night. Never got past hello. They shot at us."

"Gawk. Thank the goddess you weren't hurt," I said.

"We had the presence of mind to shield ourselves behind one of the standing stones," Patrick told me.

"Aye, but then we had to ward ourselves to get back here," Hilda added.

"You should always be warded when you're beyond the caves," Bjorn warned them. Somehow, when the words came from him, they sounded caring. The same sentence from me would have taken on the flavor of a lecture.

Geir spread his wings. Tansy gazed up at him. "You're beautiful," she cried.

Oh-oh. Before I could intervene, he took to the skies flying this way and that, showing off. Bjorn whistled for Geir to follow us, and we took off at a brisk pace for the caves half a kilometer away. I was surprised Zelli and Quade hadn't shown up, but Fire Mountain was likely a busy place right about now.

Much as the Celts viewed the Norse gods as a step below them, dragons considered both the Celts and the Norse deities inferior. The combination was a pressure cooker, and we'd be lucky to get through the next few days without an explosion or two.

Tansy had been right about greetings not taking long. Being immersed in the witches warmth and good wishes made a thick place form in my throat. Before I dissolved into a puddle of emotion—not good for me or anyone else—I gently extricated myself from several witches who wanted to hug me and run their fingers over Geir's scales.

I still held Mort in my arms. He didn't squawk when I handed him to Tansy. He must have grown used to me being gone, but his stoicism made me feel worse. Like I'd failed him. No matter what I did, there was never enough of me to go around. I felt stretched thin as a dried-up piece of leather on a rack.

It wasn't likely to change anytime soon. I needed to stop feeling sorry for myself and wishing for my old life back. No matter what happened, that life was gone for good.

The bevy of greetings changed to a chorus of "good luck" and "let us know as soon as you can."

I tried to swallow, but it was a losing proposition. So was holding onto the smile that had bloomed when the witches mobbed us with enthusiastic welcomes and compliments about Geir. "You won't need us to determine the outcome of our war with the undead," I told them.

"Aye. You'll figure things out long before we return," Bjorn said.

Patrick stood tall. Raising both hands, he chanted a blessing, one that urged Danu to watch over us and ensure our safe return. I'd take it. And more. Even with all the power of both pantheons and the dragons standing next to me, we were still starting from a one-down position.

"Thank you," I told him once he'd fallen silent. "For everything."

"Rowan. It was a glad day when you joined our coven. You might not be a witch, but you are one of us, and you always will be. You and yours are welcome to bide in our halls."

A tear spilled over, followed by another. They turned to gems before they reached the ground. I stooped to pick them up and walked to Patrick, pressing a ruby and a large yellow diamond into his hands. "Take these to remember me by."

"You will return to us. Believe in yourself, Rowan—and in your magic. 'Tis better than half the battle."

I blinked back more tears, clinging to a ragged edge of control and losing the fight. "If the goddess blesses us, I shall return. And when I do, it will be for more than a few minutes." My voice only shook a little. I was proud of that.

Bjorn wrapped an arm around me. I felt him build a spell and sweep Geir and me into it. Would I ever see my witch family again? They were so dear to me I couldn't stand the thought of never laying eyes on them again.

The Ben Nevis caves should protect them, but only if they didn't play hero and venture outside. Eventually, they were bound to poke their heads out. I had to make certain Midgard was safe by then.

The dragons' travel channel formed around us. Once Bjorn had the spell well in hand, he laced his fingers with mine. "We will repair the damage to the Nine Worlds."

My eyes had moved from swimming in tears to hot, dry, and gritty. "How can you know?"

"I never said it would be easy. We have a long, difficult road ahead. But the Nine Worlds cannot fail. They will not."

Geir chirruped in wordless support.

The struggle between discipline and maternal instinct was ripping me in two. It took all my self-discipline not to divert Bjorn's spell to a distant borderworld. I didn't care where. A spot we could wait out the carnage. Where nothing would touch us if the army of undead marched right over all the magic everyone threw their way.

But I wasn't a coward. Or a quitter. The witches were counting on us. And even though they had no way of knowing, mortals were as well. Absent our efforts, those who'd survived the Breaking were slated for certain destruction.

I wanted a safe haven for my child, but the child in question wanted to fight. I turned to him. "Tell me," I demanded. "Tell me about the beyond. The place you were before you came here."

CHAPTER FOURTEEN, BJORN

I listened to our son, fascinated by his tale. Dragon essence existed in a place beyond time and space, a spot where there were no laws of physics to get in the way. Separate, yet bonded by one shared fabric, music linked them, soothed them.

"Aye," Geir went on. "Sometimes, not often, the music changed, turned into an order. This time, the part of the shared essence that was me understood it was my turn. I was needed."

"Did you know your parents were not full dragons?" Rowan asked.

Geir nodded. "Neither am I. My corner of the shared spirit world never included full-bloods. I was not the only hybrid."

We fell silent, each lost within our respective thoughts. Rowan seemed more settled than she had been. Leaving the witches—again—couldn't have been easy for her. Standing by while our son marched into battle with us was another brain twister. I'd have loved to leave him in the witches' care, but he would never have stayed.

Fool that I was, I'd taught him to teleport as a hedge against being trapped. If I'd insisted he remain with the witches, he'd have waited until we were gone and shaped his own travel spell.

Subtle changes in the feel of my casting alerted me we were nearing Fire Mountain. "Before we go inside," I told Rowan and Geir, "I want to experiment a bit."

"With what?" Rowan tried to sound interested, but I knew her well enough to recognize an anxious note beneath her question.

"We need to see how our magic works when we join it."

"But we already know," she said. "We've fought together enough to recognize how powerful we are together."

I nodded. "Aye, but we haven't included our son."

Her expression developed a stony aspect, but she didn't say anything.

Geir whooped with delight. Clearly, my idea pleased him.

I tucked a hand around Rowan's upper arm. "In a better time and place, I would have left Geir with the witches, and—"

"Noooo," he cried. "I wouldn't have stayed."

"I know," I told him. "It was one of the reasons I didn't insist."

"Why are you so worried?" he asked.

Rowan jerked away from my grip and rounded on him.

"Because we're your parents. Because there are many bad things that would delight in hurting you."

"They can't kill me."

The pride in his young voice made me cringe. Before Rowan could say anything else, I jumped in. "And that is precisely the problem. You can be captured, imprisoned, tortured. And there is a way to kill dragons. It may have been secret once, but now every Celt and Norseman knows about it since they're a relentless bunch of gossips."

"Which means the secret has passed beyond the boundaries of the Nine Worlds. You must not take risks." Rowan picked up the thread of my parental lecture about the time the journey channel spit us out in front of the caves on Fire Mountain. Heat hit me like a wall. Probably that part would never change, but I no longer dissolved into a pool of sweat.

I wasn't totally ready for the transition, so we thumped onto the ground harder than we might have if I'd planned better. A quick scan confirmed all the dragons were inside, unusual because they adored the hot, dry air in this world.

"I don't understand," Geir said. Thank the goddess he wasn't off on a defiant rant. "How can I fight without risk?"

"You can't," I said bluntly. "Rather than beat this to death with words, open your magic to me and let me see what tricks I can weave with it. Your mother and I have worked as a team. Adding your magic will affect how we do things, and I'd prefer to find out how that's going to work now, rather than doing a field test when we're under attack."

"What will we use for targets?" Rowan asked as she

scanned the vista of cracked earth peppered by boulder fields.

"Let's see how the conjoined magic feels first," I said and began plucking and threading strands together. Unlike when it was just Ro and me where our power slotted like two halves of a puzzle, Geir's magic—at least at this stage—was mostly all fire. It kindled fast and burned hot.

"Careful," Rowan warned him. "If you run wide open, you'll exhaust your power."

"It will come back," Geir said cheerfully.

"Not without food and rest, it won't," she told him. "If we're dealing with hordes of the undead bearing down on us, you won't get rest breaks."

Geir dialed back his output, which made integrating it much easier. I finessed a few simple maneuvers. "All right," I told them. "We're going to trade off. I'm passing the reins of our shared magic to Rowan. And then it will be your turn."

"Really? I get to play?" Geir crowed.

Once I'd handed off the spell, I bent my knees a bit and snared Geir with my gaze. "This isn't play. Guiding another's magic is a big responsibility. I want you to feel what it's like to have magic beyond your own to shape."

His excitement shifted to a somber expression, one that didn't belong on any child. My heart hurt for him. Rowan hadn't had a childhood because Ceridwen had been a self-centered bitch. Geir wouldn't have a childhood because he'd come to us in the midst of war.

This wasn't something where we could backpedal afterward—assuming we won—and surround him with toys and games. He'd find them juvenile and uninteresting.

Magic ebbed and flowed from me as Rowan tried different moves.

"This was a good idea," she said at length. "Including Geir is different. It makes us stronger. Keeping him and his magic close makes me feel a little bit better about the whole thing."

"Stop worrying about me," Geir groused.

"I will always worry about you," Rowan told him. "Mothers are like that. Except mine. Your turn. Get ready."

"Bad Grandma."

Rowan nodded. "She started out as a bad sorceress, went on to become a bad goddess, and she was worthless as a mother. If she ever talks with you again, you tell me. Right away."

Geir straightened his shoulders and held his forelegs in front of him. His eyes whirled faster. I followed the course of our magic as Rowan paid it out a bit at a time, stopping at about the halfway mark. Shamelessly, I inserted myself into Geir's mind and watched his progress.

He struggled at first with the infusion of my predominantly earth and water mix and Rowan's earth and air, but it was good for him to learn the other elements. So far, fire was his go-to place, and, while it was powerful, it had drawbacks too. A skilled water-worker could easily annihilate him.

The undead were masters with both water and earth.

"Give him more," I told Rowan.

"Are you certain?"

"Aye. Keep feeding it gradually until he has half again what he's shaping now."

I moved to her side, and both of us monitored our son. If he hadn't had his claws full to the brim, he might have resented us for being overbearing. As things stood, he was so occupied finding ways to deploy what must feel like alien magic, he didn't even notice our presence.

Magic arced from his talons in a barrage of color as excess power bled from him. His jaws were slightly open, emitting smoke and ash as he rose to the challenge we'd presented him with.

I let him run with it until the glowing aura common to all dragons developed tarnished edges, and then I nodded to Rowan to reel things back in.

"You did great," I told Geir.

He turned to me, his movements sluggish. "That was hard."

"Everything worthwhile is." I paused for a moment. "What was the most difficult for you?"

"Water and earth wanted to put out my fire. Balancing them was..." He shook himself until scales clanked against each other before going on. "I'd think I had it, but then it got away from me, and I had to do it all over again."

Rowan smiled. "Yeah. Magic is like that."

A swoosh of wings brought my head snapping around.

Nidhogg's golden bulk was hurtling toward us, and he landed heavily. "Why are you out here?"

I muffled a snort. No hello or how are you or how was Midgard.

"I did the spell," Geir announced, pride shining through his words.

"What spell?" Nidhogg rumbled.

I stood straighter, unsure if the dragon lord would approve of what I'd done, but I didn't report to him. Or to anyone except perhaps Odin, and even that wasn't a certainty. "I wanted us to practice blending our magic," I said.

"Bjorn and I have had ample opportunities to work as a team," Rowan tossed out, "but we hadn't included our son."

Nidhogg shrugged, unimpressed. "Waste of time. He'll be fighting with dragons."

Irritation blasted me. "What do you think Rowan and I are?" I demanded.

His whirling eyes rolled in annoyance. "I've come for Geir. 'Tis high time for him to learn how to fly and fight as a dragon."

Rowan planted herself in front of Nidhogg. "No. If you training him means you're planning to wrest him from my side in whatever is bearing down on us, I forbid it."

Fire roared from Nidhogg. Geir flew between them screeching, "Don't hurt Momma."

Nidhogg bugled a warning, but Geir beat the air with his wings, not giving ground. "I said, you will not hurt Mother."

I was proud of him, but appalled too. Nidhogg was deserving of respect, and Geir had just flipped him off. I moved closer, hands extended. "I'm certain we can talk about this."

"What's there to talk about?" Rowan snarled. "I am not letting him"—she jerked her chin at Nidhogg—"turn our son into some kind of latter-day warrior. I'll never see him again."

"Of course you would." I was still trying for diplomacy.

If we couldn't get along among ourselves, what hope

did we have to present enough of a united front to vanquish the undead and their masters? So wicked they'd been exiled to the outer borderworlds, I could only imagine what the flotsam and jetsam from every world would be like.

Our enemy had to be ruthless, totally without compassion or conscience, but even my most vivid imaginings probably fell short of reality.

"Stand down. All of you," Nidhogg roared.

Geir landed next to Rowan, keeping wary eyes on Nidhogg.

The dragon lord may have been trying for steam, but all he managed was ash and smoke. "I propose a compromise," he said at length.

"What kind of compromise?" Rowan asked.

"Your son is a dragon. He must be taught how to fight as one."

"Why?" I countered. "We were doing all right sharing defensive magic before you got here."

"Because," Nidhogg began, but then apparently changed strategies. "Banking on the chance the two of you may locate your dragon forms at some point," he said smoothly, too smoothly, "I am extending my invitation to include all of you. We will be waiting in the arena."

Rowan opened her mouth. Before she could chuck what was truly an enormous concession back in Nidhogg's snout, I said, "We accept. With humble thanks."

Rowan shot me a you've-lost-your-mind look. I let it wash over me. "Where is the arena?" I asked.

"Has your magic grown so feeble ye canna locate me?"

Nidhogg countered, clearly out of sorts with the turn of events.

"We'll find it," Rowan said. Thank the gods she stopped shy of flapping her hands in dismissal.

"Now. Not an hour from now, but right now," Nidhogg said just before he shimmered to golden streamers as he teleported away.

"You won, Momma," Geir chirped.

"Don't let Nidhogg hear you say that," I cautioned.

"But she did," Geir persisted.

"Yes, well, a good life lesson is never rubbing someone's nose in a fight they lost," Rowan said.

"Shall we find the arena?" I made my tone upbeat and built a spell designed to track Nidhogg. He was my father. We shared blood. When the day came I couldn't locate my own blood, I needed to hang up my spurs.

"What about your blades?" Rowan asked.

I glanced at them. Last time, the dragons had insisted I leave the enchanted steel outside. I decided to let magic be the deciding factor. If it bounced back and slapped me, we'd walk to the cave entrance, and I'd remove the blades. My spell proceeded apace. No boomerang effect. When it was close to its zenith, I motioned Rowan and Geir close.

The transition was fast and seamless. One moment we were standing beneath the harsh beat of Fire Mountain's twin suns. The next we were in an enormous cavern deep beneath the world's surface. Designed much like the old Roman gladiator arenas, this one sported an elliptical field surrounded by raised areas where spectators could squat.

Nidhogg, Dewi, Quade, and Zelli were there. No one

looked particularly welcoming. I was certain Nidhogg had told them what happened. No matter how they felt about him, he was their leader. No dragon would have stood up to him. Not one firmly grounded in his senses. Cadir had forced a confrontation, but he was already well on his way down the rathole of insanity.

Would he have sunk so deep without a good, hard push from Loki?

I'd never know, and it didn't matter. Not really.

Geir stuck close to Rowan and me. "Go ahead," I urged. "It is an honor to have teachers such as these."

"Oh for Christ's fucking sake," Rowan muttered into my mind. *"Lay it on thick, why don't you?"*

I'd have told her to knock it off because the dragons could hear her, but she already knew that. At least no one had said anything about the blades hanging off my body.

Geir extended his wings and sort of floated across the arena to the other dragons. "I am ready," he said.

I motioned to Rowan to join me on the raised seats ringing the arena. I expected her to pass on my suggestion, but she marched across the field until we were positioned roughly halfway between the far end and the spot where the dragons and Geir had taken to the air. When I gazed upward, I couldn't see the upper limits of the cavern, which made it perfect for aerial maneuvers.

I debated my words, but they needed saying. It didn't matter whether I spoke out loud or used telepathy. If the dragons wanted to listen in, they would. "Uh, Rowan. I love you. A lot."

She waved me to silence. "What I did was dumb, but I

was furious, and I've never been any good at modulating my temper. I inherited that from Mother." A muscle along her cheekbone twitched as she clenched her jaw. "I don't like this. At all. But I shouldn't have gotten in Nidhogg's face, either."

"What bothers you the most?"

She looked askance at me. "Planning on a career as a psychotherapist?"

"Just answer the question, Ro."

"Gosh. How can I narrow it to one thing? I didn't get to be pregnant very long. Geir was an infant in my arms for all of maybe fifteen minutes. Since then, he's grown so fast it's worse than watching time-lapse photography. When Tansy urged him to shift, I kind of expected—"

"A toddler?" I cut in.

"Oh hell no. I guess I expected he'd still be a baby. To see him as a kid late in childhood was a shock. He's beautiful, and he'll be a comely man, but where did my baby go?"

"He was never destined to be a baby." The words hurt me to say them. I'd longed for an infant to coddle and hold too, but giving voice to my smashed hopes wouldn't help anyone.

Rowan nodded, the skin around her eyes pinched with sorrow. "I keep telling myself to be grateful for what we have. And how Geir is exactly what he needs to be. What would we have done with a real baby?"

"We'd have left him with the witches, but he would have been so helpless and vulnerable it would have ripped our hearts out. Remember how you felt leaving Ben Nevis today?" I pressed, not wanting to scratch scabs off her heart, but needing her to understand we hadn't had any good choices.

"Yeah. It would have been a million times worse. I'm not sure I could have walked away and left a four-week-old infant, no matter how much I love and trust the witches."

"You wouldn't have had a choice."

"That's what it comes down to, isn't it," she muttered. "We haven't had any choices at all ever since Mother instigated the Breaking spell. Doesn't matter if it wasn't her idea, or if she wasn't working alone. We're stuck with the consequences."

As we'd been talking, the dragons swooshed by shooting fire and smoke and ash. Because he was smaller than the others, Geir was infinitely more maneuverable. His jaws were parted in a smile, and I could tell he was enjoying the hell out of grasping his birthright with his bright-red talons.

"Do you suppose we'll ever discover our dragons?" I asked, changing the subject.

"Would you like that?" She turned her golden eyes on me and added, "You're closer than I am. Your eyes already spin."

"I'm not so sure about being closer," I said. "There have been lots of times when I've sensed your dragon nature pushing for ascendency."

She patted my hand, and the remaining tension whooshed out of her. I felt the energy in the room take a dramatic turn toward Norseland and wasn't surprised when Odin and Thor stalked the length of the arena.

Thor whistled, but the dragons ignored him.

"Nidhogg!" Odin bellowed.

The golden dragon lord flew around Odin's head a couple of times before landing more or less in front of him. "I left the air because I wanted to, not because ye summoned me." He shifted his gaze to Thor. "And certainly not because ye whistled as if I were your dog."

Thor had the grace to incline his head. "Apologies, Dragon. I wasna whistling at you."

"Everyone is assembled," Odin said. "Your presence is needed. None of the dragons will discuss anything without you there."

The scents of rosemary, baked clay, and the sea rolled around me. When they cleared, the Norsemen and the dragon were gone.

Zelli, Quade, and Geir landed near where we sat. When I looked for Dewi, she'd left as well.

"They said I did good," Geir told me.

"Of course you did." A smile softened the harsh cast to Rowan's features.

"Teaching him to blend his power with yours was brilliant," Zelli said.

"Aye," Quade agreed. "It gave him alternatives not open to the rest of us. Impressive ones."

I quirked a brow, wanting to hear more.

"No time right now," Zelli said, "but his ability to call on elements beyond fire will come in verra useful."

"He wields both Norse and Celtic twists." Quade nodded his big head in approval. "They will deepen and grow richer given time."

I got to my feet. Rowan did the same. "When we first

showed up down here, you were furious with us," I said. "I take it you've moved past that?"

The dragons didn't waste time—or insult my intelligence —by denying their earlier ire. "We were angry because of how Nidhogg was disrespected," Quade rumbled.

I'd known as much, but it was good to get these things out in the open.

"Aye," Zelli concurred. "We must pull in the same direction. What we face is grim and enormous and unprecedented. Our enemy would like naught better than for us to lose ourselves in petty infighting."

"I owe Nidhogg an apology," Rowan said. "I'll find time to make it happen after the assembly is over."

"I fear we shall be leaving here verra soon," Zelli told me. "The only purpose of today's gathering is to hash out our strategy, team up, and be gone. Yggdrasil's roots are eroding faster. And the giants are having a horrible time keeping Loki in his prison. Odin and Thor fear he may already have escaped."

Breath whistled through my teeth. "Damn. The Morrigan was loose. If Loki broke free and teamed up with her, the army of shades would have new leadership. Where Cadir hadn't been totally corrupt, the Morrigan had made a full commitment to the dark side of the street.

"Same meeting hall?" I asked.

Quade nodded.

"We should teleport," Rowan said. "It's faster." She held out an arm, and Geir walked near her. Between two blinks her spell moved us to the meeting hall where Nidhogg had presented us to the dragons.

Filled to standing room only, the large chamber felt cramped. Celtic and Norse gods milled about at the front of the room. The blind seers flanked Nidhogg. Ysien stood nearby. Dewi bugled to establish order and instruct everyone to cut the side conversations.

"We go to war," Nidhogg thundered.

Dragon bugles all but drowned him out.

"At least someone is happy about it," I whispered to Rowan and stole a glance at Geir. Dragon to his core, he bounced from one large hind foot to the other. I listened while Dewi and Nidhogg described the constituency of the undead army. Arawn spoke for a few moments about the dead he assumed had signed on with them.

"One unknown," Dewi said, "is who is leading the undead. Our guess is the Morrigan has her oar in this."

"Perhaps she managed to free Loki from our prison," Odin spoke roughly, the words clearly costing him.

One of the blind seers shuffled forward. "We have seen such in our glass," he announced. "Great, slithering darkness led by a crow."

"Did ye see Loki as well?" Odin asked.

"I did, but the timing was unclear." A blonde goddess stepped forward. When light fell on her, I recognized Freya. Seer in her own right, her divinations were rarely wrong.

Odin rounded on her, hand raised as if to strike.

"Not a good idea," Freya snarled.

"Why did ye not tell me?" Odin slowly lowered his arm to his side.

"Better." She tilted her chin at a defiant angle. "As I said, the timing was unclear. I might have viewed a scene from the past."

"'Tis a task we should have addressed together." Bran detached himself from a bank of shadows.

Freya offered the tiniest shrug. "Ye've never offered us the slightest respect."

Odin sliced a hand through the air. "This will stop now." He shoved his face in front of Freya's. "The Celts are our allies."

"Got it," she said, tightlipped.

And there it was. The problem of fighting with those you didn't trust. Freya might have acquiesced, but her surrender had been forced out of her. Those types of capitulations didn't mean crap.

While I'd been stewing over potential problems, Arawn had moved to the front of the assemblage with Hel by his side. "Our strategy to deal with the dead is this," he said.

"We rule the dead," Hel intoned. One of her serpents was wound around her body, up one leg and around her torso.

"Aye, we shall spell them to follow us," Arawn announced.

I wanted to protest it couldn't be that easy or he'd have recaptured his lost souls from behind the Ninth Gate.

"To accomplish that, we must first break the hold others have on them," Hel clarified. "That is the crux."

"Once the dead are out of the way," Nidhogg said, "we must dispatch the Morrigan and Loki."

"How?" a dragon from the back of the room shouted.

"What about the bastards from the outer borderworlds?" another dragon cried.

"Aye, well, our plan is far from complete," Nidhogg admitted. "We must first address the dead. Once that is accomplished, we can deal with the others as they appear."

I didn't like anything about this. There were way too many unknowns, but while I was shuffling doubt like a bad hand of cards, Nidhogg was assigning us to groups. We'd fare better than the poor fuckers Odin had sent to do a cleanup operation, but how much better remained to be seen.

CHAPTER FIFTEEN, ROWAN

"Ready, Momma?" Geir wrapped his talons around my forearm and tugged. He'd grown another several centimeters, and his head was even with mine.

How to answer him? I'd rarely been less ready. I'm not a tactician, and I'd never studied battle strategy like Bjorn had, but even I recognized we were about to launch a fool's mission. One where we were tossing shit at a wall and hoping enough stuck to make a difference.

Was this how all wars were waged?

I looked at my son. Really looked at him and the eagerness stamped all over his dragon features. He was excited, thrilled, exhilarated to be heading off to wage war. I wanted to tell him so many things. How what we faced would mark him, scar him. How he'd never be the same. But how did you impart those things to a child? And did I even want to?

I remembered the first real battles I'd fought—the ones

after I left the Celts and Inverlochy Castle. I'd been so scared my bones had felt liquid, but I'd found a cold, emotionless spot. One where I could shove all my qualms to a distant spot and charge forward. Years later, but well before the Breaking, when I'd been doing my damnedest to blend in with humans, I'd stumbled across a slender book about Zen mindfulness and recognized the technique I'd thought was all my own.

Or portions of it anyway. Most importantly, the ability to live in the moment and not get too far ahead or behind. Behind was pointless. No reason to waste energy on what couldn't be changed. Ahead wasn't much better, particularly when there were a host of options, and my control over which path I trod was limited to circumstances well beyond my control.

"Momma?" Geir's expression sobered, and he unhooked his claws from my arm.

"Yes. I'm ready," I lied my ass off and determined who else was in our group beyond Bjorn, Zelli, and Quade. I'd nearly called them "our dragons" in my mind, but that would be a huge mistake. They didn't answer to us. Gwydion, Bran, and Thor rounded out our small contingent.

The Celts didn't surprise me, but Thor did. Never known for keeping my mouth shut when I should, I looked straight at him. "Are you sure you're supposed to be here?"

The corners of his generous mouth twitched beneath their curtain of red whiskers. "Does my presence offend you?"

Heat rose to my face. I'd just sunk to a new level of rudeness, even for me. "Not at all. I was just...eh, never mind." To mask my discomfiture—as if I could do anything about my cheeks, which were probably bright red—I took a step back and surveyed the other five groups.

Nidhogg, Arawn, and Hel led one. Dewi and Ysien another. Odin a third. Freya and a man who could have been her twin a fourth. I assumed the blond giant was her brother Frey, Norse god of many things including peace, fertility, and crops. For the first time, I noticed a shiny gold torc around Freya's neck fairly bursting with power. Clearly an artifact of some type, it piqued my curiosity. I caught Bjorn's eye and mouthed, "Necklace."

"Aye, it's Brisingamen. Much like the amulet you no longer have, it concentrates her power."

His answer in telepathy told me I'd been wise not to ask her about the item. I felt certain it had always been there, but until now, she'd chosen to keep it hidden.

The two giants I'd met in Jotunheim headed up the last group. It took me a moment to locate their names: Krivar and Brios. Garbed as they'd been the first time I saw them, they wore leather breeches topped by jackets made of furry hides. They'd traded their wooden clogs for knee-high lace-up boots.

Krivar's black hair tumbled around his shoulders, and dark eyes sat beneath thick, hairy brows. A broad, flat forehead, hooked nose, square chin, and blunt beige teeth gave him a doltish appearance, but Bjorn had made certain I knew the giants were far smarter than they looked. By contrast, Brios was quite fair. White hair was skinned back from his forehead and captured in a length of leather. His eyes were an unusual icy blue.

Dragons had been evenly divided among the groups, which meant at least twenty dragons apiece. Except ours. We had two—three if you counted Geir. And yeah, an enormous part of me was still on the verge of snapping him up in a spell and making a run for it. Except I couldn't do that to Bjorn and the dragons. They'd been decent to me. Exiting stage left and leaving Odin and the Celts holding the bag wouldn't bother me at all.

Well, maybe a little bit. Like I said, I've never been a quitter.

Nidhogg trumpeted, and the many side conversations dropped away. Odin joined him and said, "Remain in your groups as you travel. Combine magic to ensure everyone is included. Ye and ye"—he pointed to Frey and the Jotunheim giants—"will position your troops at the barrier holding the outer borderworlds separate from other worlds."

"Kill everything, eh?" Krivar punched the air with an enormous fist.

"Only those intent on fleeing," Nidhogg clarified.

"Aye, spare any who are stupid enough to cross into the outer borderworlds," Odin said. "Those worlds will wither if they remain uninhabited for too long."

"We shall repair the breach," Dewi spoke up. "To ensure those still in the outer borderworlds remain there."

"Aye, and we shall round up the dead and attempt to re-establish dominion over them." Hel nodded Arawn's way. "Nidhogg offered his magic to discover—and destroy—whatever is keeping the shades from accepting our summons."

Tension settled over my shoulders until standing

straight grew hard. Two groups remained. Ours and Odin's. And two malevolent loose ends. The one-two punch of the Morrigan, and possibly Loki, and the unknown numbers of those who'd been exiled to the outer borderworlds.

They were a huge unknown, and one we hadn't granted so much as five minutes of discussion. That was a problem I could address. After a brief internal skirmish about raising my hand—I decided not to—I projected my voice. "I'd like information about the inhabitants of the outer borderworlds who aren't dead yet."

Odin twisted until his single gray eye burned a hole through me. "Why?" he growled.

"I like to be prepared. Do you have any idea how many there are? What percentage of them wield magic? And how many got roped into Loki and Cadir's scheming?"

Odin's severe veneer slid a notch, not much more than that, and he said, "Nay. No idea. No estimates, either."

"Dragon fire will take care of them." A green dragon from Odin's group sounded uber-confident. But such was the nature of dragons.

"Was Cadir the only dragon on the outer borderworlds?" The sound of Bjorn's voice surprised me.

"Aye. He was the only dragon ever forced out of Fire Mountain." Ysien sounded as if he'd bitten through a box of nails.

"Next question." Bjorn was on a roll, but no one had told him to shut up. "Krivar."

The giant mock bowed. "Aye, Master Sorcerer?"

"Has Loki escaped Jotunheim?"

"He was still there at the point when we left," the giant replied.

I'd been listening with my magical senses and heard both truth and hedging in his answer. "There's more," I said flatly, not inclined to play games.

"He is working up to things," Krivar rumbled. "Each attempt brings him closer and closer to breaking his shackles."

"Are the elves not draining his magic?" Thor asked.

"Aye. Daily, but it isna sufficient," Brios said, "and they lack enough innate power to bleed him more frequently."

"All the more reason to hurry," Odin said.

For once, I agreed with the old fucker. But I also wanted time to stand still. If I could freeze-frame this moment, the one before Geir was thrust into the midst of ugliness that could never be erased, I would.

"My contingent will float," Odin went on. "If anyone requires additional muscle, we will pitch in."

"That leaves us," Gwydion said. "I would ken your assignment."

"So ye can argue with it?" Odin tossed back.

"Pfft. So I ken what your expectations are." Gwydion stretched to his full height, impressive for a Celt, but nothing to write home about in a room full of dragons and giants. Maybe getting suckered by Yggdrasil's spell had taken a toll on his arrogance.

"Come on, mate. Get on with things so we can get moving." Gwydion slammed his glowing staff down on the floor.

Heh. Guess I'd been wrong about his run-in with the

One Tree altering anything. Just as full of hubris as ever, he'd clearly blocked out the incident in Bjorn's courtyard.

Thinking about it brought Bjorn's blade collection to mind. They'd been forged for a reason. He had two with him, one short and one long, but what about the others?

Before Odin could answer Gwydion, I spoke up. "This question is for Nidhogg. You told Bjorn he needed an assortment of magic-imbued blades. Will he require the others for our upcoming endeavor?"

The dragon lord's whirling eyes skewered me and then moved to the scabbard and knife sheath belts circling Bjorn's body. He tilted his head back, and I felt a primitive spell build as red- and ochre-shaded air glistened around him. The enchantment grew in strength until a great weight bore down on me. Determined not to let it push me to the ground, I widened my stance and concentrated on moving air in and out of my lungs. No small task.

The old G-force simulators I'd read about years back couldn't have been any more uncomfortable. No one else seemed particularly bothered by Nidhogg's casting, or maybe I didn't notice because I was fighting so hard not to let it get the better of me.

A brilliant flash was followed by the clatter of steel on stones as the remainder of Bjorn's arsenal clattered to the rocky floor.

"Are ye quite done?" Odin asked Nidhogg.

The golden dragon dusted his forelegs together. "Are ye finding fault with my magic? 'Twas an elegant spell. No wasted magic at all. Neat. Clean. Fast—"

"'Twas quicker than sending the Master Sorcerer back to

Vanaheim," Odin admitted sourly and turned his attention to Gwydion. "Ye may like this. Or not. Your group is shy on dragons because your part in our task requires stealth. And a verra small dragon to take on a key job."

"Meeeee," Geir squealed, bouncing from foot to foot.

A fist squeezed around my heart so hard it may have quit beating for a moment or two before it stuttered back into action. "You could have talked with me first," I growled.

Bjorn closed a hand over one of my shoulders. His way of telling me to shut up. Once he was reasonably certain I had a lid on my fury—and my panic—he trotted to where the pile of blades was and sorted them, ending up with a broadsword, a long blade, and two shorter knives.

I waited, mouth dry, heart pounding, to hear my son's fate.

"Because the rest of us are staging a frontal attack," Odin went on after a pause that seemed to last years, "our enemy will not anticipate any of us behind them. Channels run through the broken places in the barrier separating the outer borderworlds from other worlds. I know because I have mapped them. 'Twas what I was engaged in these past few days. The small dragon—"

"My son has a name," I gritted.

"Silence," Odin commanded. Norse magic settled over me like a shroud. It wasn't insurmountable, and I immediately went to work separating its fibers. I needed to listen, too, though. So it slowed my escape. Damn Odin. He hadn't gotten to where he was by being dim-witted.

"The small dragon, *Geir*"—Odin emphasized the name he'd left out—"will enter the northernmost of the channels and follow it to the largest of the outer borderworlds. Those with human forms will be right behind him. "Gwydion. Bran. Bjorn. Rowan. Thor."

"What makes you so certain I will fit?" Thor asked.

"I will hollow out the tunnel and make certain." Geir's clear ringing voice filled me with pride. And dread. I hated enclosed spaces. Ones where you had zero maneuverability and couldn't turn around.

"And us?" Quade inquired in an expressionless tone.

"This is where it gets dicey," Nidhogg stepped in. "Ye willna fit through the channel, so ye must teleport directly to the borderworld. Along with Zelli, of course. Ye will be there when the remainder of your team emerges, and ye will guard their egress onto the borderworld. All of you. Open your minds to me, I shall share the coordinates of the exit point."

I sliced through the remainder of Odin's silencing shroud, vindicated as it fell about me in streamers.

"Not bad." Odin cast an appraising glance my way. "I would have hoped for a few more moments of peace, but—"

"Slight change in plans," I cut in not caring how rude, bitchy, or overbearing he thought me. Before he could tell me to go fuck myself—or worse, encase me in a thicker spell—I plowed ahead. "I will go into the tunnel first. That way if we encounter a forward attack, Geir will not bear the brunt of it."

"But, Momma," Geir began.

"This isn't up for discussion," I told him and meant it.

"Take the blades," Ysien said.

Confused, I looked around to figure out who the hell he

was talking to. Bjorn already resembled a knight errant who'd outfitted himself from a secondhand weapons yard.

"He means you." Bjorn handed me a slender longsword and a dirk. About the same length as the one I always wore, but much beefier, it sported a serrated blade that looked damned lethal.

A woman can never have too many knives, so I found ways to fasten them to my body. Both had scabbards—and belts. The two of them felt clunky, but there wasn't a way to consolidate their straps.

When I looked up, Odin was staring at me. "No more arguments?"

"Not sure about arguments." Gwydion's tone was smooth and threaded with the same do-it-my-way castings I remembered from my childhood. After being caught up in a similarly imbued spell once, I'd given him a very wide berth. Perhaps he'd left me alone after that incident too. I'd thrown all the magic I commanded at him in my struggle to break free. And won. In retrospect, maybe a half- or quarter-dose of my power would have been enough.

We'd never talked about it, but I was certain my ability had shocked him. Once I'd made good on my escape, I'd left him standing gape-jawed in one of Inverlochy's many basements.

Just another charming memory from my miserable childhood. I swallowed my distrust and antipathy for all things Celtic, reminding myself those days were long gone. I wasn't a puny kid anymore. And I'd probably always underestimated my abilities—because no one believed in me until I took up with the witches.

Thinking about them made me sad. And determined. We had to shut the breach, corral the shades, and take out their unprincipled overseers: the living who'd been thrown to the dogs on the outer borderworlds. I didn't truly believe we could do much about the Morrigan or Loki, but maybe I was selling all of us down the river on that one.

As long as the Morrigan was free and Loki was, well, himself, there'd be no true respite. For any of us.

Gwydion had begun talking again. "Perhaps Bran and I could travel astride the dragons and be part of the forward guard to maintain the integrity of everyone else's entrance onto the borderworld."

Bjorn didn't wait for Odin's pronouncement. He spun to face Gwydion, swords clanking together with his sudden movement. "No. Not just no, but hell no. My son will be in that tunnel. And my wife. What if we run into trouble?"

"I will be there too," Thor said softly, adding, "What kind of cowards are you?" Though his question held the same easygoing tone, it must have stung. I gloried in the expression on Gwydion's smug face. Bran was harder to read, and I had no idea if he'd even known what Gwydion was about to suggest.

"And then there is the small matter of dragon-riding," Zelli said. "I dinna offer ye leave to sit astride me."

"Nor I," Quade boomed.

Gwydion shrugged. "Fine. 'Twas a bad idea." He was doing his best to save face, but I went for the jugular.

"None of us like enclosed spaces," I said sweetly.

"Ye're scarcely trained as a warrior," he tossed my way.

"And just think how good a job you might have done if

you'd given a shit," I shot back. "You had access to me throughout my childhood, my formative years—"

"Enough," Nidhogg roared. "Ye are not helping anything."

If the shoe fits... I unclenched my fists and sucked it up. "I'm sorry," I told Gwydion.

He shook his head. "Nay, lass. I had that coming. And probably more. Not sure what got into me." His expression hardened, and he hissed, "Ceridwen. Somehow that poor excuse for a Celt inveigled her way into my head."

"Told you sleeping with her was a bad idea," Bran said sourly.

"Christ! Did she miss anyone?" I asked, and then remembered Geir. "You didn't hear that," I told him.

"Didn't hear what? That Bad Grandma was a serial slut?" My son grinned at me.

"Where did you hear that expression?" Bjorn sounded indignant.

"From your mind." Geir's reply was all innocence. Bjorn winced, so I guessed he'd been caught dead to rights. Had the world been a simpler place, I'd have rebuked my son for using his magic to invade another's privacy. Balanced against what we faced, Geir tapping Bjorn's thoughts was less than trivial.

Odin turned away. "We leave in thirty minutes in the following order. Frey's and Krivar's groups will leave first. Dewi's group next."

"Then my group," Nidhogg rumbled. "With Hel and Arawn."

"Correct," Odin said. "Last groups to leave will be Thor's and mine."

I was raw, and rage far too near the surface. I barely, but only barely, managed to not query him about why our group wasn't labeled Rowan's or Bjorn's.

I don't remember leaving the dragons' cavernous meeting room, but Bjorn herded Geir and me down the maze of corridors to the room we'd been staying in. Once we were inside, he shut the door and sealed it with magic. I had a feeling what was coming, and I wasn't far off.

"I love both of you," Bjorn said, "and there's not time to sugarcoat what I have to say. Geir."

Our son focused his gaze on Bjorn. "Aye, Da."

Bjorn switched to Old Norse, which told me how frantic he was to get his meaning across. "Ye will follow directions from your mum and me. No questions asked. There willna be time for questions, nor answers. Do ye understand?"

"Aye, but—"

Bjorn grabbed Geir's foreleg. "No buts. If anything happens to Rowan or me, do what Gwydion and Bran and Thor tell you."

"What if they say different things?"

My throat developed a knot halfway down. Geir had asked a very good question, one worthy of a much more experienced dragon.

A corner of Bjorn's mouth twisted downward. "Pick the one that seems wisest to you."

Geir bobbed his head solemnly. The seriousness of what we were running into headlong might finally be sinking in.

Bjorn turned to me. I held my hands up, palms facing outward. "I promise."

"What exactly are ye promising?"

"To bury my antipathy for the Celts and for Odin. To view us as a team, one that's only as strong as its weakest link." I blew out a breath. "That weak link will not be me."

"Good woman." Bjorn transferred his hand from Geir's foreleg to my shoulder.

Somehow, we ended up in each other's arms with our son sandwiched in between. "Do ye sense Ceridwen?" Bjorn asked me.

I shook my head. "When Gwydion said she was messing with his thoughts, it came out of left field and caught me off guard."

"I can feel her," Geir said. "Not often, but sometimes just at the very edges of things."

"Has she spoken with you?" Bjorn's tone could have etched glass.

"Nay. I promised to tell you if she did. And I would instruct her to go away. I'm no longer a baby for her to take advantage of."

I blinked hard and fast to keep tears from spilling over. No more surreptitious crying for me. Not when my tears turned to rubies and sapphires and diamonds. "We should leave," I managed around the lump in my throat.

Instead of letting go, I hugged them harder, murmuring, "I love you guys so much."

And then, the old Rowan showed up, the kickass bitch one. Finally. Thank all the bloody fucking saints. I'd missed her fire and her attitude. I untangled myself from my men, and said, "We've got this."

Breath hissed from between Bjorn's teeth. "We must win. What choice do we have?" He dismantled his privacy spell, and the three of us marched up the hall. For all my petty grievances, we had a damned strong team. I liked the sound of it, so I set "damned strong team" to play over and over as a backdrop to whatever thoughts might crop up. Less optimistic ones that could sabotage my best efforts.

This would be over one day, and Bjorn and I and Geir could attempt to build a halfway normal life for ourselves. I bit back a grimace. Who the fuck was I kidding? We'd never be the white-picket-fence, two-cars-in-the-garage type family. But maybe, just maybe if all the stars lined up right, we wouldn't spend the next few centuries engaged in active warfare.

We emerged outside the caves to Odin clucking, "Time to move." Gwydion, Bran, and Thor were already in place. The anger Odin wore like a shield had cracked, and, for once, compassion rose to the fore. Good. He should be worried. If the Nine Worlds failed, the carnage would take a huge chunk of him along with it.

Bjorn constructed a dragon journey spell, and it swept us into its maw. Bran's nostrils twitched as he scented the baked-clay scent of Bjorn's spell. "Intriguing," he murmured. "The dragon power adds far more than fire to the mix."

I sucked air into my lungs, blew it out, and did it several more times. "This is the calm before things get interesting," I muttered. "Let's do our best to savor it."

"I want the storm," Geir said.

I wondered if he was making a joke, but after I glanced at my son, I understood full well he'd meant every word.

"Good lad." Gwydion nodded approvingly. I could have strangled him. Instead, I gritted my teeth and looked away. My son was part of this—no matter how much I wished things were otherwise. And I refused to burden him with my doubts.

I should kiss Gwydion's toes. He was treating Geir as an equal, something he'd never done for me. The insight was sobering, and I focused on the shitstorm we were walking into.

CHAPTER SIXTEEN, BJORN

I would have given anything if I'd been able to leave Rowan and Geir with the witches, or even the Celts at Inverlochy. I finally, finally had a family. My job was to protect them, not to toss them square into the center of a maelstrom. I rolled my mental eyes and shielded my thoughts. I hadn't been paying the slightest attention when Geir plucked my assessment of Ceridwen from the forefront of my consciousness.

He needed to know the truth about Rowan's mother, but some of the details could have been glossed over. I'd been grateful he hadn't asked for an explanation about what "serial slut" actually meant. Hopefully, he'd lumped everything together under his bad grandmother rubric.

Love for him and Rowan seared me to my soul and beyond. I'd never expected to find love in my life. None of the women who'd crossed my path ever touched more than my body—and very few got that far. Rowan had been different from the moment I laid eyes on her. Might have been as simple as her dragon nature singing to my own, but I believe it ran deeper than that.

For all my years dealing with various and sundry problems—magical and otherwise—I'd come across many requests from clients wanting potions to make someone fall in love with them. I'd never asked how they knew with absolute certainty the object of their affections was the one for them. Even if I had, I doubt they'd have had any better answer than I do about Rowan.

She touched me in ways I'll never fully absorb. Shining brighter than any star, she drew me like a lodestone. If that was love, I had it bad, but I wouldn't change a thing.

Geir fascinated me. While I hoped that someday I'd father a different type of child—one who actually needed parents—Geir's burgeoning ability and intuitive grasp of magic blew me away. I checked the trajectory of my travel spell and made a course correction.

"We're doing fine," Thor said in his deep voice. He and the Celts had been so quiet, I'd almost forgotten they were there.

"Odin said the northernmost channel, right?" I sought confirmation.

"Yeah." Rowan nodded tightly. "Good of him to act as a scout."

"He performs many noble deeds." Thor bobbed his shaggy head. "But he likes it best if no one notices. Tarnishes his image as a total bastard."

Gwydion and Bran chuckled.

My eyes widened. If Rowan was saying anything

positive about Odin—and she just had—a new woman had ridden into town. "It was decent of him," I murmured.

She must have heard the caution in my voice because she shot me a pointed look and asked, "What?"

"Eh. Thor's comment about being a badass aside, Odin lives for shit like that. I bet he brought a few shades from the Hunt with him to speed things along."

Rowan made a face. "I'm surprised they didn't jump ship."

"Ha! I'm not. The dead who comprise the Hunt have it better than their departed comrades. Why do you think there's such staunch competition for who gets to be a Rider?"

"I wasn't aware there was," she replied.

"Remember the Draugar we ran into?" I asked.

"Of course, I do. He blamed Hel because his petition to join the Hunt had been denied, but I didn't think the positions were coveted. I simply figured Bjarke was looking for a route out of Hel."

"If the dead weren't already, well, dead, they'd murder one another to ride with Odin," Thor said and laughed at his own joke.

"Hel is two places, isn't it?" Geir spoke up.

"Aye," I told him. "In the Nine Worlds, it's part of Niflheim. Hel rules over the dead who didn't die victorious deaths. She is strict, but fair. I'm certain she took the Draugars' escape hard."

"On the other hand," Gwydion cut in, "Hell also floats around Midgard. That version has nine levels and is ruled by Arawn, Celtic god of the dead. He's always hidden his worst charges behind the Ninth Gate."

"What's that?" Geir asked. "And why is everything nines?"

One easy question, the other far more difficult. I offered my son kudos for asking.

"The Midgard Hell has nine levels," Bran went on. "You pass through gates to get to each one. The important thing here is Arawn's gatekeeper left a long while back. He didn't pay it much heed, and someone broke the locks to the Ninth Gate."

"They all escaped and went where we're going," Geir said.

"Aye, lad," Gwydion agreed. "But the more important part is we believe Arawn's slipshod attitude toward needed repairs allowed the Morrigan and Loki to join forces."

"Loki is Bad Great-Grandpa. Who is Morrigan?" Geir asked. I was proud of his curiosity, but chagrined we were related to so many unsavory characters.

"The Morrigan is a Celtic goddess," Bran began. "She is one of the original—if not the original—Celtic deity. Her primary form is a huge crow. Because of that, she is known as the Battle Crow."

"She can shapeshift to whatever she wishes to be," Gwydion added. "Her magic is so powerful it occasionally surprises even me."

"Is she worse than Bad Grandma?" Geir furled his brows.

"Aye. If ye're meaning Ceridwen, much worse," Gwydion confirmed.

"Why didn't Arawn fix the latches?" Geir looked from Gwydion to Bran.

Bran shrugged. "Time is...different when ye live forever. 'Tis simple to fault Arawn, point blame his way, but he was conducting his affairs as he always has. If a decade passed between his trips to Hell, 'tis how he has always done things. How was he to know he needed to change his methods?"

Rowan bristled. "There's the Celtic hubris I remember. No matter how crappy or beyond the pale one of you stepped—" She broke off abruptly. "Sorry. I promised myself I wouldn't go there. Momentary lapse."

"Arawn canna change what has passed," Gwydion said.

"Aye, flogging him with it serves no useful purpose," Bran added.

A quick pass through Rowan's mind yielded exasperation. The Celts had done plenty of flogging for no useful purpose where she was concerned. Instead of giving into frustration, she nodded and muttered, "I'm not sure about the whole nine-thing."

"Nor am I," I told my son. "Odd numbers hold the power of transformation, though. Even numbers have balanced energy. Odd are constantly in search of change."

"I hadn't heard that," Rowan murmured, "but it makes sense."

I checked my spell again. "We're nearly there," I said and gripped Rowan's hand. She slid her fingers in with mine. "I propose a slight alteration."

"What?" she growled.

"I will go first," I told her, adding, "It's not negotiable."

"We are amenable to that," Gwydion said.

"I must be last," Thor tossed out. "The channel should be large enough by then to allow my passage. "I would offer to go first, but speed is our friend. If I have to hollow out the opening to accommodate my girth, it might take twice as long."

His comment reinforced my belief that Odin had sent his undead minions to scout the various channels. "We will emerge in the place between worlds," I reminded everyone. "No air."

"The tunnels hold air. 'Tis stale at the entry point, but gets progressively thicker," Thor told us.

My casting crumpled around us, the transition not as elegant as I would have liked. Where my journey spell held muted light as well as air, we'd been plunged into a murky gloom. While I could still think—before hypoxia got the better of me—I sent magic in a northerly arc hunting for a break in the airless void.

There's something unnerving about the place between worlds. Maybe the absence of landmarks. I located a spot where my power didn't have the same feel bouncing back at me and called, "*This way.*" Telepathy trumped talking when breathing was a struggle.

Rowan and Geir pulled ahead of me, easy to keep track of because both glowed with a soft inner illumination. Rowan's blue-white and Geir's golden. He was holding his own. I'd wondered how the rapid shift to no air would impact him.

Gwydion and Bran passed me on my other side in a cloud of mint and vanilla that felt out of place here. A couple more meters and I reached the spot I hoped would yield entry to the channel. Were Quade and Zelli in place yet? How long was this conduit, anyway?

I should have asked Odin, but perhaps he'd imparted that information to Thor. *"Do you know how many meters the passageway is?"* I asked Thor, who swam through the void next to me.

"Nay. Ye were correct shades did the spade work, and they've mostly lost their sense of things such as distance. This is one of the longer channels, but in better repair than the others."

"Over here," Rowan called a bit breathlessly.

Impressed, I hurried to where she hovered in the dim recesses of infinite blackness. *"How'd you find it so fast?"* I asked her.

"Cadir. How else? This is the spot he chewed his way to freedom, and the feel of my own blood is all over it."

"Bad Grandpa?" Geir piped up.

I grimaced. It was dark, so he probably didn't notice, but my son had identified a passel of less-than-illustrious relatives. I started to tell him not to let it bother him, but words were cheap. In the end, Cadir had demonstrated a saving grace or two. Best to focus on them—but afterward.

"No reason to wait," I told everyone.

"I'm behind Da," Geir told Rowan.

She didn't argue, obviously recognizing the safest spot for our son was right between us. I kindled a mage light and examined the hole in the ether. Shreds of matter hung from it. How long had it taken Cadir to tunnel his way past the outer borderworlds?

I was pretty certain he'd done all this on his own since I had a hard time envisioning Loki getting his hands quite this dirty. As in, I couldn't imagine the trickster setting foot on an outer borderworld or dealing with the discomfort of not being able to breathe. Loki was a dick, but he liked his creature comforts.

On that cheery note, I pushed forward. One thing bothered me. If a full-sized dragon like Cadir had made his way through this space, why was Odin so insistent Quade and Zelli wouldn't fit?

Damn it, anyway. Why do I always come up with the good questions too late in the game to ask them? I redirected my mage light so it illuminated the way ahead. So far, Thor's prediction about stale air hadn't materialized, but I kept moving. It was harder than I'd anticipated mostly because I was fighting against a dense groundswell.

I led us deeper into a rounded enclosure studded with what might have been calcium projections sticking out of the walls at odd angles. Whatever they were, they were sharp. More like coral than calcium. After fifty meters, the way narrowed until it became claustrophobic.

Turning around wasn't an option, even if the rest of us hadn't been strung out behind me. One thing was certain, there would have been no way for Cadir to fit through here unless he'd sliced through the passage with magic. I examined the walls for cut spots that had healed over, but didn't find any.

My magical senses vibrated. Whatever we were passing through was living, sentient. The walls changed from black to more gray, and I recognized the squiggly things I'd seen around Yggdrasil's root system. At the time, I hadn't believed there was any connection between the outer borderworlds and whatever was floating in the void near the One Tree, but maybe I'd been wrong about that.

It was impossible to tell from inside.

"Getting tight," Rowan called from behind me.

I got the message and swung magic in an arc to push the walls farther apart. *"How's everyone managing?"* I continued using telepathy, not at all sure the walls wouldn't swallow my words.

A collection of grunts was followed by Thor who asked, *"Can ye move a wee bit faster?"*

Something about the tone of his question caught my attention. Had he sensed something amiss? Presumably he and I carried at least half the same magical ability, so I switched things up and extended my antennae farther, hunting threats.

Nothing specific came to me, but I battled a growing sense of unease. Keeping the walls from moving together required a constant infusion of power. They were changing in consistency. The spiny protuberances had almost vanished. Thank all the gods. I'd have had to cut each one off individually at this point, or we'd have had no way to move past them.

Where the walls had been dirt like, now they were more spongy. I experimented with pushing against them, hands splayed, and they moved aside sufficiently to allow me to pass. At some point, air had returned. Not a lot, but enough.

"How is Geir managing?" I asked Rowan.

"I'm fine," he answered. "The walls don't like me."

"What does that mean?" I demanded.

"They appear to not like touching him," Rowan confirmed.

The channel took a hard right turn followed by a hard left. I tried sending out directional vectors to determine how far we were from the outer borderworld where this passage originated, but came up dry. Time passed, so much time keeping my guard up became a challenge.

To deal with growing inertia that alarmed me, I set up a round robin of different magical approaches. One pushed the walls out a bit. The next scanned for threats. The third kept my mage light from foundering. The outward pressure had increased until I felt like I was swimming through thick mud. I could breathe, however. That last part helped.

"How much farther?" Geir asked.

"Probably not much." I aimed for an upbeat note. Not having any fucking idea where we were was taking a toll on me. Had the other groups arrived on the borderworld by now? How was their frontal offensive going?

They basically had two tasks. Rounding up the shades and closing the fissures that had allowed two-way travel. Dealing with the Morrigan, and possibly Loki, felt far less critical. Neither of them were going anywhere. My mind was wandering. I went back to my threefold magical round robin.

Push. Scan. Light.

Despite my efforts, my light was definitely weaker than it had been. I did a quick once-over to check my magical reservoir, not surprised to find it depleting far quicker than I'd assumed it would. I had no idea how long we'd been in the tunnel, but if a similar span clicked by, I'd be down to bedrock. Not an appealing proposition. If the hairs prickling the back of my neck were any indication, threats were closing on us with a whole lot more stealth than the walls.

"Report. One at a time starting at the back," I said.

"Move faster." Thor's tone was terse as he essentially repeated what he'd said earlier. This time, he added, *"I'm closing the passageway once I'm through."*

My eyebrows shot up. Not that turning around had been an option, except perhaps with a tightly executed somersault, but Thor had apparently sensed danger behind us and wasn't taking any chances.

"Good call," Gwydion said, followed by, *"Bran and I are surviving, but my staff suggests we have...company."*

"Okay from my position," Rowan said.

"Me too." Geir sounded tired. I didn't blame him. Lethargy dogged me, coming from far more than fighting for every meter of progress.

I've never been overly reactive. Good thing, or the endless bleakness with soft, spongy walls pressing in from top, bottom, and sides would have been a deal breaker. A ragged laugh forced past my throat. More like a bad joke. Deal breaker suggested I had a choice in the matter, and I didn't.

Pull it together, fast, an inner voice ordered. It was very much like something my adoptive father might have said, and it steadied me. An idea bloomed, and I projected my mind voice in front of me this time. *"Quade?"*

"Aye. What is taking you so long?"

Men are supposed to be stoic, but a relieved whistle pushed past my lips.

"What?" Geir asked.

"We must be near the end. I can communicate with Quade."

"Smart," Rowan called. "I never even thought about raising Zelli."

"Well?" Quade was back sounding every bit like his imperious self.

"Close quarters and a brisk headwind that's done nothing but grow worse," I replied.

"Keep coming," he told me.

Seemed curious. What choice did I have?

"What do you know that I don't?" I pressed.

He repeated himself. This time, he added, *"Hurry."*

I narrowed my focus to the undulating walls. I was still using my hands to push off and keep the spongy material as separated as possible. At first, I'd thought I was hallucinating about it getting harder to push the sides apart, but the struggle was real.

Breath came faster, and my heart pounded against my chest. Heedless of my dwindling magic supply, I added power to the mix to make it possible to continue forward.

"What's wrong?" Thor asked softly into my mind. I recognized Norse shielded telepathy and understood he didn't wish to alarm the others.

"Something doesn't want us to get through." The words had no sooner left my thoughts than I read incontrovertible truth in them. It rattled me, but I shunted everything except progress to a distant back burner. One of the first tenets of magic is you have to believe what you're doing will work.

"Visualize and make it happen," I muttered out loud to give myself momentum.

"No shit," Thor hissed back. *"Ye're using Norse magic. Switch it up to dragon. Should solve one problem."*

I cursed myself fifty times over for being an idiot. Geir had told me the walls weren't bothering him. Why hadn't I put two and two together? Probably because employing my less familiar side was far from automatic. I took a few deep breaths, centering myself as I searched for Nidhogg's contribution to my character.

As if it had been hovering in the wings, eagerly awaiting its turn on stage, dragon magic roared from me. The unwieldy tunnel jumped back a meter, and I sailed through with everyone else behind me.

"More like it," Quade bellowed so close he nearly deafened me.

I took a shot at the calculations that had always carried me through, but my current rate of eating up magic was unprecedented. For once, I'd have to trust to fate there'd be enough to guide us to the other end. The next time I felt for Quade's solid presence, my magic pinged back cleanly.

"Almost out," I yelled. I had very little magic left and didn't want to waste it on telepathy.

"Yay!" Geir crowed from behind me.

Pride for him filled me to overflowing. He hadn't complained. Not once. A patch of brightness hovered ahead, contrast to the gray undulating channel. It took longer than I expected to reach it. I was still working hard, breath rasping as I forced my lungs to pump faster.

The sense of urgency I'd been fighting almost since we

entered the channel had grown exponentially. "Get ready," I cried. Probably a wasted warning. Everyone else's magical hackles must be at full mast, right along with mine.

Finally, finally, when I was running on fumes, the brightness crashed over me. I spun as fast as I could and grabbed Geir, tossing him to what I hoped was safety. Dragons bugled behind me. I held the gateway, a portal that made it a personal mission to crush the daylights out of me, while Rowan, Gwydion, and Bran hurried through.

"Thor!" I bellowed.

"Coming. I'm shutting it down behind me."

His enormous body crashed through about the time my arms refused to hold anything beefier than a matchstick. Shockwaves from an explosion tossed me three meters in the air. Pain seared my eardrums. I had the presence of mind to weave air to cushion my fall. Even with that, I hit hard enough to squish breath from my lungs, but at least I didn't break anything.

Before I could take stock of who was where, a blast of familiar magic flung me into the air and onto Quade's back. "Ready yourself. We must fight." He punctuated his words with a warning bugle that should have chilled any enemy.

"Where is Geir?" Frantic to locate my son, I whipped my head in every direction until I saw him flying next to Zelli and Rowan. Questions battered me. We'd had a close call with the tunnel that probably would have been a hell of a lot closer if Thor hadn't had the presence of mind to seal it behind us. His quick thinking meant our enemy couldn't sneak up from behind.

"Annihilate them!" a deep voice thundered. When I

looked at the ground below, it burst upward and hordes of shades flowed from every opening. They held the burnt ochre gleam characteristic of the dead, and flowed under and through each other.

"What the hell?" I shouted. "Arawn and Hel were supposed to take care of them." And then, I shut up. Talk about rhetorical commentary. Me saying the enemy arrayed below us shouldn't be there was like telling an extra sun it had no place in the skies.

A line of creatures so ungodly beautiful they had to be vampires sashayed out of nowhere, urging their army of shades forward.

Gwydion, Bran, and Thor formed a circle and lit it with magic. It held the shades at bay, but it wouldn't last forever. Grinning and laughing, the vampires hustled forward, their bare feet gliding over broken ground.

"Find your dragon," Quade ordered.

"What do you mean?"

"We're short dragons," he said in a tone that suggested I'd turned simple. "The three on the ground are done for—unless they teleport out of here."

A downward glance told me the Celts and Thor had passed the point of no return. They'd never free up enough magic—or time—to teleport. They were immortal, but there were many things worse than death. Being captured by vampires was one of them. If I somehow figured out how to shapeshift, it would provide two dragons. Quade and me.

Geir was too small to ride.

This was a battle that had to be fought from the air, not the ground. Weariness rattled my bones, but I dug deep. If there was a dragon in there—and there damned well had to be—I'd find the son of a bitch.

Big words, but believing in results is over half the battle.

"No time for pep talks," Quade commented acidly.

"Shut up and let me think."

He could have tossed me off his back and told me to pound sand. He didn't. Closing my eyes, I channeled the nascent power that lived within me.

CHAPTER SEVENTEEN, ROWAN

I'd rarely been as glad to leave anywhere as I would be to get out of that goddamned tunnel. About the only bright spot was my son dead ahead of me. The walls recoiled from his touch. Once he made that discovery, he baited them and laughed softly when they beat a retreat. I didn't connect the dots until Bjorn channeled dragon magic, and the walls drew back as if he'd slathered poison on them.

Whatever encased us was alive. I'd understood that from the beginning. Once I recognized how dragon magic was abhorrent to it, I sprinkled some of my own about. With similar results. A grunt from Gwydion told me he appreciated the extra space.

I sensed Cadir—my father—all through the channel. He'd clearly traversed this pathway, and his dragon magic had forged a track large enough to accommodate him. Lacking dragon enchantment, Odin had assumed the dragons would never fit. Apparently, he hadn't thought about Cadir's escape. Or perhaps, he'd assumed Father had help from Loki.

Or had left by some other route.

I'd sensed Cadir all over the chewed-up bits at the opening to the channel, but blood calls to its own. I felt torn about him. On the one side of things, I was infinitely grateful not to have had a second critical parent, but he had a hell of a lot more warmth than Ceridwen. She'd never loved anyone except herself. Cadir had genuinely loved her, and, in his own twisted way, he'd wanted to love me.

That's the thing with ancient beings. They got stuck in how things were when they came into the world. When he'd told me I could keep his rooms on Fire Mountain tidy, he wasn't necessarily being a chauvinistic bastard. I ground my teeth. Why was I making excuses for him?

None of it mattered, anyway. He was dead. I still hadn't quite come to terms with there being a way to kill something I'd been certain was immortal. Did it mean there was a way to do away with me? Or the other Celts?

If so, who knew about it? Clearly, the dragons had harbored their secret forever. If I asked Gwydion point-blank whether the Celts had a similar fatal weakness, would he answer? Meanwhile, a bright spot flickered ahead of me. Partially blocked by Bjorn's body, it came and went, but we had to be close to an exit point.

We'd been inside this passageway for a whole lot longer than I'd expected, but the transition beyond its spongy borders was so sudden, it flummoxed me. One minute Bjorn jerked Geir through a rip in the gray walls. The next, he grabbed me. I'd barely shot through the gap when Zelli's power snagged me and threw me onto her back. Panicky, I scraped my gaze this way and that until I zeroed in on my son, flying as if he didn't have a care in the world.

The tight place in my chest that was making breathing a bitch released its hold on my heart. Bjorn looked as if he were holding the gateway open. Gwydion stumbled through, followed by Bran.

Where was Thor? I'm not sure which came first, but an explosion rocked the world beneath us. Bjorn shot into the air from the spot where he'd been holding the portal open, followed by Thor's beefy form. This was one of the scruffy borderworlds. Dead trees. Dead bushes. Not so much as an insect or a bird to break the monotony. I bet there wasn't any water, but there had been at one time or another. Otherwise there wouldn't have been dead vegetation.

Bjorn barely hit the ground before Quade snapped him up. Thor scrambled to his feet and joined the Celts.

"What's happening?" I cried.

"Ye barely escaped." Zelli didn't mask the censure in her voice. "Quade and I were trying to see if there was a way we could hurry things up from our end, but we couldna find one. The dead are restless. As are their masters."

On the heels of her words, the ground exploded. Shades poured through multiple rents flowing into and through one another. Geir shrieked a challenge and painted them with fire.

"Save your magic," I shouted.

My son flew close, whirling eyes focused intently on the

dead who reconstituted themselves from the dregs of his flames. "They can't die?" he chirped.

"Already dead," I told him.

"Aye," Zelli added, "'tis a problem. But there are ways of enticing them to leave."

Speaking of which. *"What do you suppose happened to Hel and Arawn?"* I switched to telepathy.

"Doona know," Zelli said.

Thor and the Celts had formed a magical barrier around themselves and faced outward, keeping an eye on the shades tossing themselves against their protective shield.

Movement caught the corners of my eyes, and I spun my head around in time to see half a dozen vampires gliding our way. All men, their hair was long and lovely in a variety of colors. Their bare-to-the-hips bodies could have been studies in artistry. They may as well have been naked because skintight breeches left nothing to the imagination.

Why were they so gorgeous? Surely, they hadn't all been centerfolds for *Playgirl* before they died. Something about the transition to vampire must carry a hunk-gene with it.

"They're different," Geir observed.

"Aye, but they're dead too. Just in a different way," Zelli told him.

The saber strapped to my body hummed in anticipation. It knew there were ways to kill vampires. Plenty of them, but all required up-close-and-personal attention. Beheading was my personal favorite. There was something satisfying about the crunch of vertebrae as a blade separated head from body. The older ones didn't bleed at all. They just sank into a heap of rotten bones.

Thor pulled his hammer from where it hung across his back. Mjollnir was fearsome to look at, but had it been forged with enough silver to kill a vampire? I knew less than nothing about Norse-crafted weapons, but I would have laid bets my saber was attuned to vamp destruction. No other reason for it to be so excited.

The vampires were closing on Gwydion, Bran, and Thor. The dead had formed a tight circle around them as well. Gwydion's staff blazed red, and he hurled power at the advancing vampires.

Zelli bugled her outrage and sent a broad swathe of fire at the vampires. Their clothing and hair ignited instantly, and their perfect, golden skin blistered. I've never understood what makes them different from other shades, but they are. Dragonfire wouldn't kill them, but it could make them damned uncomfortable.

"I can do that too," Geir crowed and aimed his own ribbon of fire at their feet. Howls of pain met his efforts. Encouraged, he delivered more fire.

Off to one side, Quade tossed additional flames into the mix. When the dragons were done, the vampires would be bald and naked with huge burned spots. Skin would slough off, hair would grow in, and they'd be back to their old stunning selves. In addition to their other unsavory traits, vamps had incredible powers of rejuvenation. Probably because they weren't exactly healing what was already dead. More like slapping the illusion they projected back together.

For the millionth time, I damned the Celts to Hell and back. They could have taken a spare moment or two to educate me. The saber vibrated against my thigh again. A downward glance showed vampires stomping about screeching in pain. I'd never get a better opportunity.

"I'm going down there," I told Zelli.

"Nay. Ye're not."

"I am. Beheading them is the only way. Or a silver stake through the heart, and I'm shy on silver stakes just now."

It wasn't up for discussion. I turned my mind voice Geir's way. *"Momma is going down there. You will remain in the air next to Zelli. Do you understand?"*

"I want to go with you," he wailed.

"Remember the discussion we had before we left? The one where Da told you to do what you were told, no matter what?"

Geir nodded, but his eyes spun so fast I could barely follow them. Nothing more to say, so I wrapped myself in wards and unsheathed my blade. Its song filled my mind and my heart with the feel of Bjorn's magic and battle lust. I welcomed its strength.

Picking a spot below, I leveraged power and jumped to it, blade swinging and ready. The first vampire was a piece of cake. I'd positioned myself perfectly, and the blade was a flawless companion.

I hefted the sword and swung, putting my weight behind the movement. Being tall helped, but the metal snagged on something, and I had to saw my way through gristle and bone. By the time the head rolled free, I was panting for breath. Worse, the other five vamps had closed on me. The stench of burned rotten flesh was cloying, thick in my nostrils. So extreme, I gagged as I struggled to breathe.

Dragon fire rained down on the vampires, but they were close enough to me to limit its damage. Smart fuckers.

They'd done that on purpose. My blade glowed red, anxious for its next victim. Music rose around me. It took a second, but I understood my blade was singing, urging me on.

One of the vamps made a grab for my arm, but my ward stymied him. I needed space to swing the blade, something I no longer had. I stabbed at bare, burned feet to get them to move, but the vampires laughed in my face.

Damn. They smelled worse than the one Ceridwen had adopted for a pet. Roadkill mixed with decayed garbage.

A wrenching, tearing noise blasted me, but I couldn't look away from the vampires. I was badly outnumbered, and all they had to do was break through my shielding and bite me. The lore suggested they'd have to drain me and entice me to drink from them to turn me, but sometimes the lore was wrong.

What if a single bite would do the trick? And I'd spend the rest of my immortal days as one of the undead? A shudder ran down my back; I redirected my thoughts fast. What the fuck had the horrendous noise been? I shoved the point of my blade through more feet, but my slender margin was shrinking. No way to draw back and try a frontal approach with the tip of my sword through a heart.

I drew my short blade, but it wasn't glowing like the long one. Clearly, it had been forged to deal with something other than vampires. I couldn't see through the circle around me. Zelli would take care of Geir. She was more protective than I was. How were Bjorn and Quade doing? What about Gwydion and his group?

Gah. What was wrong with me? I should be fighting, not worrying about everyone else. I sheathed the knife and gripped the hilt of the longsword with both hands, willing its magic to flow into me. Something was sapping my will, and my money was on the vampires.

They must have a way to immobilize their victims, or they'd starve to death. Not many people would willingly tilt their necks and expose their jugulars for the undead to feast from. My throat was dry; my stomach twisted in a painful knot. Proximity to all those vampires was doing a number on me.

I had to find a way out before I couldn't. A mocking voice in the very bottom of my mind suggested I should have made a run for it after I killed the first vampire. It didn't sound anything like me at all.

Had a vampire managed to slither past my wards and into my head?

The specter of mind control terrified me. I'd thought I was out of adrenaline, but its bitter taste coated my tongue, and my heart jumped to triple-time rhythm. I upped the ante on stabbing feet. As I whirled in a circle, going from foot to foot, the ring of vampires moved back a tiny bit.

Was it enough?

I eyed the length of metal. Did I have enough space to swing it upward? Maybe cut off a dick or someone's balls? I had to keep my hands on the hilt. The blade was razor-sharp, and I couldn't risk cutting myself. The scent of my blood would drive the vampires to worse than they were already doing.

Right now, they were toying with me, but it could get worse. Much worse. I'd watched a seethe tear into a group of Fae long before the world broke. The Fae had won, but it hadn't been pretty. They'd sustained losses, and I had no idea what they'd done with their newly undead Fae companions.

I drew my sword arm back; my elbow ran into a vampire. The feel of him even with clothing between us shaded my vision to gray, almost as if I viewed the world through undead eyes. I tried again, careful not to brush against my warding.

Damn it. Not enough room. I stabbed more feet. Black blood oozed onto the ground. The ripping noise battered me again. What the unholy fuck was it? And then one of the vampires flew through the air. I didn't question how or why. I had the space I needed, and I hefted my blade and cleaved through another vampire neck. This one went easier for some reason. Maybe because terror was driving me.

"Two down. Four to go," I shouted to give myself courage and let these undead creeps know I wasn't in a backing down mood. I was in this to the death. Theirs, not mine.

From above me, I heard Geir crowing with delight.

Another swing. Another head hit the dirt. This must have been a younger vamp because blood sheeted from his severed vessels. It stank worse than he did.

The remaining three vampires backed away from me. I skinned my lips back from my teeth and screeched, "Oh no you don't."

A dragon I didn't recognize, blue-black and shiny, picked up another vampire and threw him down on the ground hard enough I heard bones break. Great. We had more dragons. Odin must be here somewhere. He'd said his team was floating.

I'm not picky about how I kill the undead—or anything evil. I sliced through the neck of the one splayed across the ground. He dissolved into dust before my eyes.

When I looked up, on the hunt for my next victim, the remaining two vampires were nowhere to be seen. Gwydion pelted toward me and wrapped me in a huge hug while shades milled this way and that. "Excellent sword work." Gwydion pounded my back.

I started to say no thanks to him. Instead, I muttered, "Thanks. Where's Odin?"

Bran and Thor joined us, wading through a river of shades. They were an annoyance, but they couldn't hurt anything. Not without direction. Mindless, they were ripe for the plucking. It gave me an idea.

"Odin's not here," Thor told me. "Why would you think he was?"

The blue-black dragon stomped vampire remains with his big hind feet before lumbering forward. Something seemed familiar about him, but I was almost certain I hadn't seen him in Fire Mountain. For one thing, his scales were iridescent. Black, rimmed by turquoise, they reflected all the colors of the rainbow.

"Rowan. It's me," was followed by a bucketload of steam.

I fell back a pace and looked at Bjorn. In his dragon form. "How?" I sputtered, followed rapidly by, "I want to shift too," and then, "Damn my eyes. You're beautiful."

His eyes, the same brilliant blue as when he was human, spun faster.

Quade landed next to me, crushing at least twenty shades. Zelli and Geir joined us on the ground. Geir ran nimbly to Bjorn, excitement streaming from him. "You're like me, Da. Like me."

Bjorn bent and scooped our son into his forelegs. The combination of gold against iridescent black was striking and stirring. My throat thickened, and my heart was glad for them.

I felt left out, but I could live with it.

Ghosts ran at us, but we brushed them aside.

"I told Bjorn he had to find his dragon form," Quade rumbled. "At the time, I wasn't thinking about silver being lethal to vampires. I believed our best chance was in the air."

"Of course." Zelli's eyes whirled faster. "Any dragon would draw that conclusion."

"Bjorn required better reasons than I could give him to locate his dragon form," Quade went on. "Apparently, seeing you surrounded by vampires provided the impetus he needed."

Bjorn set Geir down and nodded. "It did. You might not have noticed," he said to me, "but their fangs were out. They were intent on getting them into you any way they could."

"Would one bite have done it?" I asked and closed my teeth over my lower lip hard enough to hurt.

"Yes," Bjorn told me, and then he rounded on Gwydion and Bran. "You should be ashamed. You taught her nothing."

Gwydion shocked the crap out of me by bowing. "Ye are correct, Master Sorcerer and now dragon shifter. We should have done more, and I am humiliated by our shortcomings."

"Me as well," Bran was quick to chime in.

"Kinsmen!" rang from behind me. I kicked a few ghosts aside and came face to face with a Celt I'd never met before.

Black hair flowed to midback, and she was garbed in beige hunting leathers, much like Andraste preferred. Her eyes were dark and intense beneath stark black brows.

A sour taste coated my tongue. "The Morrigan, I presume."

She sneered at me. "Ye're Ceridwen's get. With that dragon lover of hers. I warned her, but she dinna listen. Stupid bitch."

"Ye're more trouble than ye're worth." Barely leashed fury rode beneath Bran's words.

"Hard to keep a good woman down," she purred.

"Ye're neither good nor a woman," Gwydion snapped and stomped until he stood eye to eye with her. The air around the Morrigan developed a liquid aspect, and she morphed into the biggest, blackest crow I'd ever seen. Her head reached Gwydion's chest, and she clacked her sharp beak in his face. Unlike her human form, her eyes took on an amber hue. Lidless, they bored into Gwydion, and he shook his staff at her. Bran loped over to join the fray.

Hopefully, they'd keep her busy for a while. As in not focused on me.

Thor stared at the Battle Crow and muttered curses in Old Norse.

The idea that had formed in my mind developed wings, but I needed to let the others know what I was about. The Morrigan would pick up anything threaded with Celtic enchantment. Was I capable of sorting out my dragon magic? I'd done it in the tunnel.

To be on the safe side, I vaulted onto Bjorn's back, hoping to communicate privately with him. Once he knew, he could tell the others. His scales were warm and welcoming beneath me. I resisted an urge to wrap my arms around his neck and never let go.

Warm laughter burbled through my mind. "You can ride me anytime, darling."

I covered my thoughts with laughter of my own as I sketched out what I wanted to do. The stink of vampire intensified. More were heading our way. If we were going to move, we had to do it now before someone else stepped in and took over piloting the dead.

Ribald laughter pounded into my brain like an icepick. I didn't even have to look to know Loki had joined us. A low, guttural growl rattled from Geir, followed by a shrieking bugle.

"Look what I found." Loki capered about, my son suspended between his hands.

Bjorn painted the trickster's feet with fire. It didn't faze him. Next, he blasted him square in the side. Nothing so much as smoldered.

"Teleport!" I shrieked at Geir.

He writhed in Loki's big hands. "Can't. He has my magic."

Quade and Zelli tag-teamed the problem, moving behind Loki. Quade knocked him to the ground. Zelli reached for Geir, but her claws bit through empty air.

"Nooooooo," tore out of me followed by something that sounded like an animal in mortal pain. I blinked and looked once more, but Loki was gone and Geir along with him.

How could it have happened so bloody fast? The answer hit me between the eyes. Blood ties were the strongest. Loki knew damned good and well Hel was Geir's grandmother. He'd cast a familial teleport spell and snapped Geir up. Probably the only reason he hadn't netted Bjorn too was because his dragon side was in ascendency.

I sheathed my blade and summoned tracking magic. I'd get even later. Right now, finding Geir before his trail faded —or Loki disguised it—was the most important task I'd ever faced in my life.

CHAPTER EIGHTEEN, BJORN

Magic poured from me as I put a tracking spell together. Rowan's plan to marshal the dead to do our bidding was inspired, but nothing mattered if we didn't get out son back. Ro's power slammed into me, joining my burgeoning spell.

"Chasing Loki won't work," Thor told me flatly.

"Why not?" I puffed ash and smoke. My transition to dragon had been a crapshoot. I'd tried and failed, tried and failed, tried and gotten stuck between forms before I finally punched through. Like all enchantments, there was a trick to this one.

"Loki just dealt what he believes is a mortal blow to our side by abducting the dragon princeling. We could spend years tracking him and never find him. He's a master at covering his movements. While we're following one dead end after another, he'll take over the world, complete the destruction of Da's domain."

"Odin hasn't told us everything." It was obvious, but I wanted to make certain Thor understood I wasn't harboring illusions.

"Why should he?" Thor countered. "By that token, neither have I."

I kept right on building my spell. Leaving my son to Loki was not going to happen. Not if I could help it. I added in a marker that would alert me to Geir's unique energy—assuming we got close enough to him to activate it.

"I can help you find him," the Morrigan said sweetly. A sidelong glance told me she wasn't a crow any longer.

"Aye. Ye bargain for your freedom," Gwydion said sourly.

"Och, ye always were a smart one." She patted the side of his face until he slapped her hand away.

"Bjorn!" Rowan screeched. I didn't have to look to know vampires were near. Their stink gave them away.

"Do it," I yelled.

Compulsion flowed from Rowan, thick as clotted cream. She followed her magic to the ground and kept it rolling. The dead flocked to her call, forming nice, neat rows as they faced off against a whole lot more vamps than we'd just dispatched. I didn't waste time counting them. What did it matter if there were twenty or fifty?

It bothered me so many were hiding on the outer borderworlds though. Had they always been here, or was this a new development?

"Brilliant," Gwydion cried in Rowan's direction.

He, Bran, and Thor wove their power in with Rowan's

until a veritable army of shades stood ready to take on the vampires.

"Ooooh. Fun," the Morrigan purred. Clearly, she'd picked a side, and it wasn't aligning herself with Loki. I didn't trust her, but we had something she wanted: not being hunted for the rest of her days. It might be enough to keep her in line.

For now.

Worry for my son ate at me like a buzz saw grinding away at my equanimity from within. I started a tracking spell again. No matter what Thor said, I couldn't remain here.

A burst of Celtic power glistened around the Morrigan. Violet sparks arced from her outstretched hands. The shades shambled forward, impressive because of their sheer mass. If I hadn't been so distraught about Geir, I'd have laughed at the confused expressions on the vampires' faces. They summoned magic. I felt their pathetic efforts, but the dead were already taken.

By us.

Vamps dealt in mind control, in sex-and-blood rituals. Other magics were beyond their ability. Their superhuman strength was derived courtesy of the vampire transformation. Nothing magical about that part of their skill.

I'd never fully understood the mechanism of commanding shades, but they seemed to have a tiny little vulnerable area in their decaying brains. Whoever had possession of that place could control them. The part I didn't know was if the hundreds of dead flowing toward the line of vampires would have any impact at all. The shades surged forward, screeching a battle cry. The vamps didn't even break stride. Either they weren't worried, or this situation had never come up before.

About the time the two lines of undead met head-on, a robust blast of Norse power was followed by Odin, a passel of dragons, Hel, Nidhogg, and Arawn.

I bugled. Odin raised his shaggy eyebrows, clearly recognizing me at once.

"Where in the fuck have you been?" Rowan shouted.

"Busy," Nidhogg said succinctly.

"Yeah, well, Loki has your grandson."

Outraged roars from Hel and Nidhogg made my ears ache.

"When?" Odin spat out the word, all rough edges, but he looked rattled by the news.

"A few moments ago," Rowan said. "Bjorn started to build a tracking spell, but Thor told him it was pointless."

Odin opened his mouth and bellowed his fury to the skies.

Meanwhile, Arawn had draped what looked for all the world like steel mesh over all the dead—shades and vampires alike. They added their howls of rage to the mix. The flash of fangs told me the vampire segment of the horde had sunk to their most primitive reaction. Bite anything in their path. They only looked human. None of their humanity remained once they'd been turned.

"Hel!" Arawn boomed to make himself heard over the din.

She twirled to face him, her face a mask of naked wrath. "Take them where ye will," she shouted back. "I must hunt for my grandson."

"I canna do this by myself."

Judging from the set to Arawn's shoulders, the admission cost him. Much like the Norse gods, the Celts were a proud lot.

"Aid him," Odin ordered.

"But Geir," she protested.

"I will go after him. Find me once ye've secreted the dead where they canna bother anyone again."

"It takes time—a lot of time—to lock vampires away." The tight angle of Hel's jaw told me she was on the verge of rebellion.

"Och, ye're a rare bunch of ninnies," the Morrigan squawked. Part goddess, part Battle Crow, she was in the midst of a shift. Winging skyward almost before her wings were done forming, she cawed furiously. A tawny mist puffed from her beak. The dingy fog spread and formed a bunch of vectors. Each zeroed in on a vampire.

I had no idea what the Morrigan was up to until the first arrow bit through Arawn's netting and augered into a vampire's chest. A shocked expression wiped out his arrogant grin, and he crumpled to the ground, leaving a pile of cracked bones. More arrows buried themselves in vampires, courtesy of the Morrigan and her magical intervention. It was a neat trick. Maybe I could figure out what she'd done.

Rowan ran to me and vaulted to my back. "Gwydion took over my portion of the casting. They don't need me anymore. Build that spell, and let's find our son."

"I will command that effort," Odin materialized right next to me, flanked by Thor.

A flash of red wings and a vivid bugle announced Dewi and more dragons. "We did it," she shouted. "I sent the giants and their contingent of dragons home. Frey and Freya too. All the gateways are shut. The remaining shades are all right here." Her jovial expression faded. "What happened?"

Before anyone could tell her, a high, keening wail rose from her throat. "Our dragon princeling is gone."

It was the second time in a few minutes someone had referred to my son as a prince. I'd have to find out what the hell they meant. After we got him back. Odin wasn't the only one playing his cards close to his vest. The blind seers hadn't revealed everything, either.

An intense blend of Celtic and Norse magic buffeted me. When it cleared, Hel, Arawn, and the mass of undead were gone. Minus the vampires. Somehow, the Morrigan had culled them out of the herd with the finesse of a cattle rustler. Most of the vamps had reverted to dust or bones. The few remaining ones were trying to crawl away, but more of that lethal mist rolled from the Crow. Apparently, the poison darts had homing devices built into them.

Light blazed around the Morrigan, and she shifted back, dusting her hands together. "Ought to do it." She sounded pleased. "What's left? Och, the princeling. We shall find him, and then I'll return to my rightful spot."

"Where might that be?" Bran asked acidly.

"Why, with you and my other loving kinsmen," she returned with a cheery smile.

If my son's existence hadn't hung in the offing, I'd have been impressed by her nerve. She had all the audacity of a crooked politician. One who posited their version of the truth so frequently, everyone else doubted theirs.

"Ye're not coming," Odin said flatly.

She settled her hands on her hips. "And why not?"

"Ye took up with Loki. For all I know, the two of you are still working together," Odin told her.

"Aye, the topic is closed," Thor thundered. His foul mood echoed around him until lightning lit the borderworld's skies.

The Morrigan shrugged. "Fine. Have it your way. Loki and I did spend time together. A lot of time." She paused, the sexual insinuation obvious. "Nothing like both being outcasts to bind us together. Regardless, I played him for my benefit, and I can find him. Fool that he is, he still trusts me. Men are such dimwits when it comes to their dicks."

"I want her to help," Rowan said.

The Morrigan's timeless face split into a broad smile. "More sense than that mother of yours. I like you already."

"Don't waste your time," Rowan growled. "I don't like you, but I'd enter into a pact with Satan himself if it would return my son to me."

"Our son," I reminded her in a flood of fiery ash.

"Oh for Christ fucking sake, Bjorn. This is not a time to split hairs. We need to find Geir. And we should have left half an hour ago."

A tremor in Rowan's voice told me how close she was to losing it. I wasn't far from a breaking point myself. Something about the dragon's form intensified every emotion until I wanted to rip my scales off. I'd probably get used to it after a while, but I felt raw, abraded.

Zelli and Quade had been huddled with Dewi, Nidhogg, and Ysien. The other dragons had left quietly, so quietly I hadn't noticed they were gone until now.

"We will do this," Odin said. "Bjorn, find your human body. Ye will ride Quade. Rowan will ride Zelli. Thor will take Ysien, and I will be astride Nidhogg."

"I will carry Bran and Gwydion," Dewi said, followed by, "'Tis a one-time proposition, boys. Doona grow used to it."

"Wouldna dream of it," Gwydion muttered.

"What about me?" the Morrigan asked in such a saccharine tone it made my skin crawl.

"Ye have wings," Odin growled. "Use them."

It seemed like a good time to visualize my human form and tumble into it. Much smoother than my first transition, one moment I was dragon, the next I stood shakily on the ground with Rowan next to me. Miraculously, my clothing survived both changeovers. I'd always assumed shifters had to remove their garments, so they didn't end up in a pile of rags, but perhaps dragon shifters were a law unto themselves.

Before I really got my legs under me, Quade scooped me to his back. His magic soothed my sore places to a point, but I wouldn't be whole again until Geir was back safely.

Worry for my son scoured me to bedrock. If Loki harmed him, I wouldn't rest until the trickster was staked out on rocks, suffering the tortures of the damned forever. Being drawn and quartered would work. Or keelhauled. So long as it was endless.

"We will find Geir," Quade told me.

I didn't know what to say to him. The dragon was trying to be kind, supportive, but I needed results, not words.

Odin's spell rose around us, thick with the scents of the sea. Norse magic has always felt like coming home to me, but today it had the opposite effect. Did I want to have anything to do with a pantheon where the gods played cruel tricks on one another?

Stole children to make a point?

"Not like that." The Morrigan's shrill retort broke into the pit my thoughts had become. "Ye want to find him right off, not muck about leaving a trail a mile wide."

"What is in this for you?" Odin narrowed his one eye at her.

I readied a truth net, but Rowan beat me to it. The Morrigan laughed in her face as silvery webbing covered her from head to toe. "Ye try spreading yourself betwixt Fire Mountain and the Ninth Circle of Hell. I've burned for centuries, wasted those same centuries. I am done being punished. Do ye hear me? Done." Her voice rose to a howl. "My magic is strong. Ye may as well use it."

"Ye may be done with being exiled, but are ye done with Loki?" Odin asked.

The Morrigan rolled her dark eyes. "Och. More than done. He was amusing at first, but he's an oaf in bed, and a self-absorbed boor. I used him, and he was so arrogant, he never guessed. I'm surprised ye allow him in Asgard."

Odin didn't dignify her comment with a response.

"She told the truth," Rowan said. "Insofar as I could tell."

"Fuck all of you," the Morrigan shouted. "Ye netted me in a truth casting. Of course I fucking told the truth. I'm sick of being locked up. Do I want to help find the little bastard? Hell no, but I will because unlike the rest of you, I can keep my eyes on the prize. Now, let's get out of here before Loki is well and truly gone."

She lifted her hands and began to chant. Power jumped to her command. In truth, I was shocked by how strong she was. Her magic was pure Celtic—it created a shimmering violet aura around her imposing form. She was more powerful than any Celt I'd ever come across. And then I remembered what Bran had said about her being one of the original Celts.

The more I thought about it, the more certain I was it had to be the source of her extraordinary power.

Quade was uncharacteristically quiet, but his solid presence meant the world to me. I knew my son couldn't hear me, but I sent love his way. Told him we were going to find him and to hang on.

"He's not a human youngster," Quade said. "Dragons have resources, even at verra young ages."

"Regardless of his race, he is my child," I told Quade. "I know Loki, and I wouldn't trust a cockroach to his care."

Quade spread his wings. We flew through a gash the Morrigan had opened in the still air of the borderworld. Five dragons and their riders—and a crow. Among us, we commanded a shit ton of power, but would it be enough?

"Loki is many things," Quade spoke into my mind, *"but he respects blood ties to a point. Doona forget Geir is his great-grandchild."*

The reminder made things worse. Did Loki have a sinister ulterior motive? Like raising Geir to follow after him?

His own children—a wolf, a serpent, and Hel—had spurned him.

Nah. Loki didn't have a single nurturing bone in his entire body. He demanded absolute devotion from his followers, and Geir would spit in his face. Having a docile dragon at his beck and call might hold appeal, but Geir would never play the part.

My hands had been fisted so tightly, they cramped. I unbent my fingers. Loki's reasoning didn't matter. I didn't care why he'd shanghaied my son. All that mattered was getting him back. Once he was safe, I could plot my revenge.

And revenge there would be.

Before I understood what I was, I'd stepped back a pace, been deferential to the gods even when I thought they were full of crap. No more. We flew through a void, but it was different from the place between worlds. Just as dark, but with air to cushion the beat of Quade's wings.

"Where are we?" I asked.

"Not sure." Something tense, uncomfortable sat beneath his words. He didn't trust where we flew. Neither did I. What if the Morrigan was leading the lot of us into some trap she'd designed with Loki ahead of time. I could see them plotting, but I was losing my objectivity, getting sidetracked in conspiracy theories.

The Morrigan had told the truth about being done with Loki. And about being willing to trade anything for her freedom. Not that she hadn't broken loose, but she clearly didn't fancy being hunted, concealing herself in hidey holes to avoid discovery, forever.

Yeah. Immortality had some big downsides. No matter

how far you ran, other immortals would dog your trail until you turned around, tossed your hands in the air, and surrendered.

"This obviously isn't a dragon journey tunnel, neither is it the way I used to move from Vanaheim to the borderworlds," I persisted.

"Either the Celts have their own methods of traveling, or this place is unique to the Morrigan." Quade had switched to shielded mind speech in the dragons' language.

"Bran suggested she's like Dewi. Is she?"

"What do ye mean?" Quade replied.

"Does she predate the other Celtic gods?"

"I doona know her history. If Bran said as much, 'tis probably true."

Bands of light broke the blackness of our surroundings. I sought a pattern, but couldn't find one. Red washed over us. Then blue. Then yellowish-white. And then we flew through darkness again. The sharp bite of magic raised the small hairs on the back of my neck, and I sent power arcing outward seeking information. Rowan's magic laced with mine. Together, we hunted the length and breadth of the Morrigan's flight path.

Every flare of color showed her winged form forging ahead. She flew about the same speed as the dragons with her smaller wings, but considerably lighter bulk. "Ready yourselves," the Crow squawked.

"For what?" Dewi asked. "I know you, Sister. All too well."

After a spate of pissed-off caws, the Morrigan said, "That's all the thanks I get? This was a shortcut, but 'tis steeped in Celtic magic. *My* magic. We shall cross beyond its protection. The change can be jarring."

"As in, best brace myself," Quade rumbled. "That one is a mistress of understatement."

I wondered how he knew the Morrigan. Someday, once we had our son back, I could catch up on dragon history and how it intersected with the Celtic gods.

The blackness lit in a kaleidoscopic blend of shades so bright, I hooded my eyes. Rowan was still linked to me. I felt emotions sliding through her. Much like me she tripped from fury to panic to terror to hope. We had to do a better job hanging onto hope, she and I. It was too easy to sink into blind fury, which wasn't useful since we'd need a combination of subtlety and skill to outfox Loki.

Coming in like a sledgehammer was what he was expecting, and it was the wrong approach. The marker I'd set before we left the borderworld went off like a rocket. It meant Geir was close enough to sense.

"Ro. He's close."

"How do you know?" Her tone blazed with love and hope.

Before I could answer, a tsunami of an airwave struck Quade broadside. It nearly unbalanced me, and I ended up lying across his back before I righted myself. All five dragons trumpeted and tossed fire this way and that.

"No fire!" I shouted as the next disturbance swatted me across the back hard enough to drive air from my lungs.

"Be strong and fast. This willna remain open long," the Morrigan screeched and ripped an opening in wherever we were with her beak. Rather than a tearing noise, the sound of rocks grinding against one another poured through me.

Grunting and cursing, Quade soared past the gap. In the process, he caught a wingtip and nearly catapulted us into a spin. Zelli and Rowan emerged next. Apparently, Zelli had been paying attention because she timed the beat of her wings to avoid the jagged edges around the odd place we'd come through.

Alfheim spread below us, green and lush with its sun at midheaven. I recognized the feel of the place, but what an odd spot for Loki to choose. No love lost between him and the elves. None at all.

"Hurry!" I shouted. The hole was, indeed, closing, growing tighter with each passing minute.

Dewi blasted through next, slower than usual because of her two-passenger burden. "Morrigan!" she screeched.

The Battle Crow circled lazily before flying back toward Dewi. "Aye, Sister?"

"Help me. Two dragons remain."

"Och. Odin can figure things out."

"He canna, and ye know it. Ye led us through the earliest Celtic paths, the ones we trod when we moved from our mother world. They are closed to all but us."

"Really? I must have forgotten."

"Will ye assist me or no?" Dewi snarled a challenge. Fire blasted from her open mouth.

"All right. All right. No need to get testy. Ye always did have a problem with that temper of yours." Still clacking her beak disapprovingly, the crow sent a languid bit of power toward the vertical slit. It was tight enough, a man would have had trouble crawling through.

Peals of thunder rocked me. Lightning forked through the hole and latched onto the Morrigan's sliver of magic. The edges of the gap drew wider, not appreciating being burned by lightning. Nidhogg was no one's fool. Neither was Ysien. Dragon fire followed Thor's lightning.

Seemed to do the trick. The breach flapped to both sides, and the last two dragons rushed past its borders. Odin's face was contorted in fury. "If I ever get my hands on your black-feathered hide," he shouted, "ye'll be worse than sorry."

"Och. Words. Words. Words." The Morrigan cawed laughter.

The beacon that was my son burned far brighter here. "Let's go," I urged.

Rowan and Zelli were already beating a trail northward. Everyone else would figure it out once they were through with their dick-waving contest. We caught up with Rowan and flew quick and sure.

"When we get there," I told Ro, "let me handle this."

She twisted to face me, hair flowing behind her in the slipstream. "I don't think so."

"I know Loki. You don't."

Her striking features were set in stony lines. "I don't give a flying fuck. We will do whatever we have to down there. I'm not about to let you or anyone else muzzle me. Got it?"

Anger rose, hot and heady. "He has all the cards," I gritted out. "He has our son. We will do whatever we have to, including making ridiculous promises we have no intention of keeping, to achieve our ends."

For a moment, I expected her to launch herself off Zelli's back, land in my lap, and start throwing punches. Her face crumpled, and I wanted to wrap my arms around her, reassure her we'd figure this out. But I wouldn't lie to the woman who meant everything to me.

Nothing was a given dealing with Loki. He was batshit crazy, and everything depended on me being able to read him right.

Rowan sat straighter and mumbled, "Sorry."

My heart hurt for her, but we had to be strong. The land soared up to meet us, and the dragons touched down. Rowan joined me on the ground, and we hurried forward. Geir was close. Just beyond a band of cliffs I was certain held caves.

Usually, the elves rushed to meet me. They had a second sense about my arrivals. Not today. The spot we'd come out on Alfheim was deserted.

The Morrigan skidded in for a landing just ahead of us, shifting as she flew. When her feet touched the ground, she was back in goddess gear. "Loki, darling," she crooned. "We have company."

CHAPTER NINETEEN, ROWAN

"What the fuck?" I shrieked at the Morrigan. Truth spell or no, the bitch had sold us out.

She dug her fingers into my upper arm and hissed, *"Enough out of you, Missy. Play along,"* into my mind.

I wrenched out of her grasp.

A spot in front of the cliffs where I'd sensed my son's presence turned shiny with Norse magic. Loki pranced out of a gateway that slammed shut behind him. He opened his arms, and the Morrigan ran lightly into them.

Bjorn wrapped an arm around my shoulders, but I was spun too tightly for the subtle magic required for private conversation. Zelli and Quade closed from behind us.

The Morrigan wriggled out of Loki's embrace. "I did my part," she purred. "Where is the princeling?"

"Safe." Loki grinned. He mock-bowed so low his multi-hued hair—mostly red, but with bits of black, silver, and green—touched the ground. Tall and large-boned as befitted his giant heritage, he was clean-shaven with eyes the shade of curdled cream. A red cape had been tossed over his shoulders. Tight leather pants sat beneath it, and his chest was bare. As were his feet.

Odin and Thor closed on their kinsman. "Release the dragon," Odin thundered.

Loki laughed in his face. "Make me."

No one was paying any attention to me or Bjorn. I knew exactly where Geir was. I felt him, thought I heard him wailing for me, but it may have been my imagination. He wasn't the wailing type. I leaned close to Bjorn and put my mouth right next to his ear. "I'm going to teleport in there."

"Not without me," Bjorn whispered back.

I shook my head. "I might get away without notice, but power from two will attract attention."

"Then I'll go."

Before I could draw arguments about why it had to be me, Bjorn shimmered to nothingness. I had to hand it to him. His spell was simple and stylish. Made sense. We were on a Norse world, and it was his go-to magic. No one so much as glanced our way—except Quade who nosed me in the back. Maybe a warning to hold my ground.

Yeah. I've never been much of a direction follower. Or a team player. I gave it a few more moments. By then, Odin, Thor, and Loki were fully engaged in a shouting match. The Morrigan had moved off to one side, nearer Dewi, Gwydion, and Bran than the Norse trio. Was it her subtle way of telling us she was playing the role of a double agent?

I caught up with myself. Trusting the Morrigan was a big mistake. And even though the other Celts were at least saying the right words, I didn't exactly have faith in them, either. When the chips are down, people's true colors bleed through. For some reason, it made me feel slightly better about the Morrigan. She'd been honest when she said she was looking out for number one. And her body language hadn't been all that effusive when she'd let Loki embrace her.

Where was Bjorn? Why hadn't he teleported back out here with our son?

The next nudge in my back came from Zelli. The barest brush of her in my mind told me we were going to follow Bjorn. He'd escaped notice. No way the two of us would, but I didn't care.

Dragon magic with its baked clay and herbal scents swept me into its maw, and the lush thicket we'd been standing within ceded to cool darkness. I kindled my mage light and ran toward where Bjorn's and Geir's energy pulsed like stars.

I didn't figure we'd have a lot of time before Loki followed us, but maybe Odin would pull a rabbit out of a hat and restrain him. Bjorn's light glowed soft blue. He sat with his back against a wall, our son gathered against him.

"Geir! Baby, my baby!" I closed the remaining distance between us, but my son didn't stir. Something grabbed my heart in a viselike grip. "What's wrong with him?" I managed around a throat that was too thick to breathe through, let alone form words.

"Not sure." Bjorn's voice was even. "He lives."

Zelli placed her snout against Geir's body, breathing him in. "Not poison," she said briskly. "He's caught in enchantment."

Magic jetted from me as I did my own assessment. I felt the edges of the spell, but they were obtuse, tangled. I couldn't sort out where it began or where it ended. "Can we chop into the middle of it and just pull it aside?" I asked.

Bjorn shook his head. "Too risky. These things should be dismantled by the one who cast them, otherwise..."

"Otherwise, what?" My voice was far too shrill. I fell to my knees and wrapped my arms around my comatose child.

"We could damage his mind," Zelli said.

"What happens if we take him back to Fire Mountain?" I was grasping at straws, but there had to be a way to defeat Loki's casting, absent his cooperation.

"Won't work, either," Bjorn said in Old Norse. "Why do ye think I dinna leave with him. The working has its roots here, in Alfheim. We canna move him without stretching the spell. As it stretches, it will press against Geir, suffocating him. He willna die, but he will suffer."

I stroked his golden scales, mollified by the beat of his heart and the warmth within his body. I inhaled, blew it out, and did it again. "Okay. So we can't start at the midpoint of the spell, and we can't move Geir away from Alfheim."

"Correct," Zelli and Bjorn said with one voice.

"What can we do?" At least now I understood why Loki hadn't hightailed it in here after us. He assumed we'd be helpless in the face of his devious magic-craft.

"If we can reach Geir," Zelli spoke slowly, "he can cut his own way free."

"I tried." Bjorn sounded forlorn. "He's moved beyond my call."

"Aye. He is in a type of stasis. 'Tis where dragons go

when they doona wish to deal with something horrible." Zelli's words were stark, and they made me want to kill Loki.

"If Geir went to ground on his own," I said, battling hope that jabbed me in the vicinity of my soul, "he can find his way back."

"If he knew we were here, it would help," Zelli muttered and puffed steam over Geir. No so much as a scale fluttered.

She kept steam flowing until it felt like a sauna in the cave. I reached into my son's mind over and over again. Cajoling, shouting, urging him to find himself. Reassuring him we were here.

Nothing I did made a difference.

After a few minutes, I recognized we needed more than repeating what wasn't getting through to him. Geir had been so excited to see Bjorn in his dragon form. Maybe, just maybe, if I found mine, the magic from my transformation would reach wherever he wandered. I tucked Bjorn's arms more firmly around our son and rocked back on my heels.

"What are you doing?" he asked.

"You know me too well," I said and got my feet under me. "I'm going to shift. You managed it, so I should be able to as well."

"Might be just the thing." Zelli cast hopeful, whirling eyes my way. "It will take especially strong magic your first time. Perhaps it will reach Geir."

"Pointers?" I asked Bjorn.

"Don't try too hard." He made a face. "Visualize a dragon and fall into it."

"Any dragon? How will I know what color I am?" I made

a grab for the clearheaded place I valued. The one where magic simply flowed to me with very little energy output.

Zelli wrapped her talons around my shoulder. I felt a shot of dragon magic shudder through me. When it cleared, she said, "Ye're red, like Dewi but with red-gold wings."

I nodded and drew back a few paces, breathing to center myself. My thoughts were all over the map. Worry for my son superseded everything, but I couldn't go there. Maybe if I was a dragon, there'd be some magical channel I could tap into to reach him. I shook my head. Nope. Bjorn had already tried that. Except he was in his human form, not his dragon.

"Quiet!" My inner voice was stern. Bjorn's power flowed into me, and I grasped it like a lifeline. Nothing the two of us couldn't do together. I readied myself as best I could. I didn't want to fuck around making one mistake after another as I grappled with shift magic, something new for me.

I held an image of a red dragon with lighter-colored wings in my mind and pushed my consciousness into it.

Nothing.

Changing things up some. More fire. Less earth. I tried once more. Bjorn was in my magical center making adjustments. He'd been where I was, and I trusted him implicitly.

In my mind's eye, I walked into a floating void. It tugged at me, tore at me, reshaped me. Bones altered, skin stretched, scales grew. Every sense was ten times more acute, but victory was a long way beyond me. I'd be a dragon once the alterations quit rippling through me, but the whole reason I'd done this was for my son.

"Momma?" Geir's voice rushed into me. "What are you doing here?"

The vacuum—more of a dark place with undulating edges—expanded. In the light from my scales, I saw my son crawling toward me. It was hard forcing my unfamiliar body to do anything, but I lumbered toward him and then fell on my belly and wrapped my forelegs around him.

I understood plenty about astral travel. I'd done it enough to recognize the part of my son in my arms was a projection. Apparently, he had access to far more than I did when my astral portion separated from my body. For one thing, he could speak.

"I'm here to help you find your way back," I told him. "Da is waiting. And Zelli. You must return to your body."

"Bad place." He shuddered in my forelegs. "Bad man."

"Yes to both," I agreed, "but you must do what's hard. You must come back so we can take you home."

"Take me now."

I hesitated. How much truth could he stand? But there wasn't any way around it. I had to tell him everything. "I can't take you anywhere without the rest of you. The bad man cast a spell. He trapped you in it. We can't unravel it, but you can. To do that, you have to find your way back to your body."

I shifted my bulk and cradled him against my chest. No matter how desperately I wanted to do everything for him, the next move was his. I couldn't force him to return to a place that had scared him so badly, he'd made a run for it.

"I understand," he said in a surprisingly steady voice and gripped my foreleg in one of his. "You'll be with me, right?"

"Every step of the way. I love you, heart of mine."

"Love you too," he chirped, sounding more like himself. The projection I held in my arms dispersed.

Dragon magic, rich and heady, coursed through me. I directed it to return me to Geir, Bjorn, and Zelli, but my power was different. Raised to the nth degree and damn near uncontrollable. When rocks rained down from above, I reeled my spell in several notches until everyone swam into focus.

The place where Geir had found me was obviously a kind of parallel universe, connected with this one, yet not wholly overlaying it.

Geir stood between Bjorn and Zelli, listening as they instructed him on how to defeat the spell that bound him from within.

Bjorn broke off long enough to say, "Here's your momma. I told you she'd be right behind you."

Zelli dropped a foreleg onto my shoulder. "Nice work, Dragon Heir, but I'll miss having you on my back."

"Who says I'm done riding?" I countered and focused on Geir.

His whirling eyes were closed, and dragon enchantment swirled around him. I employed the same psychic vision I accessed in my other form and illuminated the warp and weft of Loki's spell. Damn. Maybe Bjorn had been able to see it far better than I, but it was impressive.

Just as perverted and twisted as the one who'd cast it, it wove under and over and through Geir's magical center. A couple of passes would have had the same effect, but Loki had just kept going. At least a dozen rounds of corruption snaked through my son. No wonder the poor kid ran away. Anyone would have.

Just looking at the casting made me feel dirty, and fury rocked me to my clumsy hind feet. "Ye're disturbing his concentration." Zelli tightened her hold on my shoulder.

I tossed a damper over my ire. It was harder than I expected. I've always been quick to blow up, but something about the dragon being in ascendency exacerbated that part of things. Bjorn's power shone brightly within me. He'd never withdrawn, and I glommed onto his levelheaded presence. I might not need his magic right this moment, but I needed him.

Admitting it to myself was empowering in an odd sort of way. Me, who'd never needed anyone, had finally taken an unvarnished look at my solitary existence and found it lacking.

I've never been patient. I suppose it goes along with a tendency to lash out first and ask questions later, but standing by watching as Geir solved his problem, biting through one strand at a time with magic, was hard.

"Can we help?" I asked.

"He doesn't need our help," Bjorn said, pride shining through his words.

He didn't, but I wanted things to go faster. "What happens once he's free?" I murmured.

"I will take him to Fire Mountain," Zelli said. "Immediately. He will be safe there."

I didn't like the idea of being separated from my son again, but I recognized the wisdom in her suggestion. I wasn't done with Loki—or the Celts. And I didn't want my son subjected to the scene I was about to unleash. He'd been scarred enough by today's events.

"I will go with you," Bjorn told Zelli and exchanged a pointed glance with me. I read him well enough. He was telling me to let everything go and accompany them.

I shook my head. "I'll be along soon enough, but I'm not done here."

Geir was nearing the end of Loki's convoluted casting. He had Bjorn's temperament. Instead of rushing, and maybe making a mistake, he continued as he had been. Even. Methodical. Love for him nearly flattened me. Admiration too.

"There." Geir opened his eyes and shook himself until his scales rattled. "I did it. I'm free."

Steam puffed from me. I was surprised by how reflexive it was. I felt the beginnings of Zelli's teleport spell and said, "Zelli and Da are taking you to Fire Mountain."

"Where will you be?" He gripped me with his bright-red talons.

"I will be there soon. First, there are a few things I need to say to the bad man who did this to you."

Geir puffed out his chest. "Take me. I want to tell him off too."

Bjorn walked in front of our son and shook his head. "Not a good idea. He snared you once, which means he knows the feel of your unguarded places."

"I'd do better defending myself," Geir insisted. "I know how he does things too."

I blew out a breath. This one contained a column of fiery ash. I turned my head to the side to avoid hitting anyone.

Crap. Every exhalation was a shocker, and all this was brand new.

"My place is with you," Geir said.

My insides melted, but he was right. I nudged Zelli and shook my head. "We are a family, and we will do this together."

"Ye're coming to Fire Mountain?" She raised a scaled brow in disbelief.

"Eventually. First, we're going outside. If Loki is still there, I plan to give him a dose of his own medicine."

"We are stronger than him when we join our magic," Bjorn reminded me. "Not cannier, but stronger."

He turned to Geir. "Are you certain?"

Our son nodded solemnly. "He hurt me. I get to tell him what a bad man he is."

"Whatever you say won't change Loki," I cautioned my son. "He's been running roughshod over everything in his path his whole life."

"It will change me," Geir replied.

Everything was harder to control in my dragon body, including my emotions. Tears formed and fell as a collection of gems worthy of a king's ransom. Bjorn scooped them into his pockets and grinned rakishly. "We can fight over who gets what later."

Magic swelled around us, cutting through me, and we emerged close to the spot we'd left. Not much had changed. The dragons had formed a circle around Loki, and the pleasant day had disintegrated into a roaring electrical storm, courtesy of Thor's anger.

The only one to notice us at first was Quade. With a

delighted bugle, he scooped Geir into his forelegs and swung him high. Geir squealed, and I began to hope Loki's perfidy wouldn't scar him for life.

Pushing between Dewi and Nidhogg, I planted my bulk in front of Loki. His odd, cream-shaded eyes narrowed. "Och, so ye found your dragon's form, eh? I told Cadir 'twas bound to happen sooner or—"

"Silence." Fire blasted from me, along with a rain of ashy smoke. Pleasing as it would have been to douse the trickster in dragon fire, I had a feeling it wouldn't touch him.

A quick shot of power returned me to my familiar body, clothes and all. I crossed my arms beneath my breasts. "You will never touch my son again."

Geir had taken to the air. He shot fire at Loki's head shrieking, "Never. Bad man. Bad bad man."

Loki laughed. "I've been called far worse, child. Good on you for finding your way back."

Bjorn stood next to me. I felt his power coil within me like a serpent on the hunt and went with his lead. Together, we crafted a net of dragon, Norse, and Celtic magic while Loki capered and joked, ignoring ash raining on his head from Geir still flying above him.

Our child would be a force to be reckoned with. Undeterred by Loki ignoring him, he kept right on telling the trickster what a bag of shit he was. Somehow, Geir intuited what Bjorn and I were doing, and threaded his power in with ours as our netting grew large enough to hopefully contain the trickster.

Like ours, yet not, our son's magic acted as a linchpin.

When we got around to kindling the snare, it just might do the trick.

Odin, Thor, and the Morrigan maintained a steady stream of arguments. Our trap was nearly set when an infusion of Norse magic nearly knocked me off my feet. Odin reached within me as easily as if I'd been an open paper sack. He wrenched the mixed magical weave from Bjorn and me and tossed it neatly over Loki.

Satisfied howls flew from Geir, right along with a shot of power from his outstretched talons. The net blazed bright red before it turned a blinding white.

The trickster laughed harder—until his efforts to defeat the thing failed. Norse power rose around him until the air burned blue-white with it, but our enchantment clung to him like a limpet.

I'd been right about Geir's contribution providing the edge we needed to do the job.

"Many thanks." Odin bowed in our direction. "I do believe that will hold him."

"What are you going to do with him?" I shouted.

"Not for you to know," Thor told me.

He mounted Ysien. Odin vaulted astride Nidhogg, and the Norse dragon picked up the trickster in his forelegs. "Behave," he snarled, "or ye'll get a face full of fire."

Geir flapped to a landing in front of Bjorn and me. "Punish him," he shouted after the retreating Norse gods.

"Never fear, princeling," Odin called over a shoulder. "We plan to."

There it was again. Princeling. What the hell was that all about? I was too tired to get into it with anyone, and I didn't want to lay anything more over my son's shoulders. Not today. He'd had enough. We all had.

"Let's go home," Bjorn suggested. "Fire Mountain first, and then Midgard."

"Not Vanaheim?" I quirked a weary brow.

"We'll get there too, but after we've reassured the witches all is well."

A rush of love so profound it brought more tears—and more gems—to my eyes seared me.

Gwydion and Bran hurried over. "We will welcome you in Inverlochy whenever ye choose to visit."

I looked around. "Where's the Morrigan?"

Dewi joined us and laughed, but without much mirth. "Och, that one. As soon as ye emerged with Geir, she bid us a not-so-fond farewell. Ye'll see her at Inverlochy. She did her part, and a bargain is a bargain."

"I hope to hell they don't let Loki off so easily," Bjorn sputtered.

"Odin has plans for him," Gwydion said.

"What plans?" Geir piped up.

"Ye'd approve, young dragon." Bran patted his scaled shoulder. "Hel, Fenrir and Jormungand will ensure Loki doesna escape as the three of them work to repair the damage to Yggdrasil's roots. The One Tree will assist them."

"Who are they?" Geir asked. "I know Hel. She's my good grandma. But the other two. Fenrir and Jor-something."

"Loki's other children," I told him. "They hate him as much as you do."

A burst of brilliance morphed into Hel. I blew out a weary breath. I'd had just about as much extended family time as I could take for one day. Maybe Ceridwen had done me a favor by being absent.

"Och. Ye're safe!" Hel raced to Geir and wound her arms around him.

"Good Grandma," he purred.

"Aye, child. Good Grandma." She pushed back and examined him with magic and her eyes. "None the worse for wear, I see."

"Ye've been pressed into duty," Gwydion informed her.

She rolled her dark eyes. "Nay. Doona tell me. Whatever it is will keep till Odin runs me down. Since I know something is afoot, I may avoid him for a while. Meantime, I have a passel of new dead to attend to. Doona expect to see Arawn any time soon. He has a fuller plate than me. Wait a bit," she told Geir—and I suppose me and Bjorn—"and then come visit me in Niflheim."

"I will," Geir said.

"Good boy." Hel kissed his forehead and then vanished as quickly as she'd materialized.

Quade built a journey spell. I remember it settling around us and Geir wrapping his forelegs around me, but the rest of the trip faded to black. Guess shifting took more out of me than I knew.

Or maybe I was just plain done in all the way to my bones. Bjorn and I had accomplished a miracle—with a lot of help from our allies. Most importantly, we had our son back. The outer borderworld problem was fixed. All that remained was hunting down residual evil in the Nine Worlds and killing it off. A big job, but doable now the portals were sealed again.

Before we left Fire Mountain, I'd make certain the dragons spent more time working on defensive magic with Geir. Bjorn and I could benefit from a tutorial too. Neither of us knew jack shit about being dragons.

The thought rocked me, reminded me I could shift. I tried to tap into a sense of wonder, but all I felt was numb. The miracle of everything would mean a lot more once I'd slept for a few hours.

CHAPTER TWENTY, BJORN

Two Weeks Later

Power crackled in the dragons' training arena, turning the air blue with a static charge. Rowan and Geir were practicing aerial strafing runs under Nidhogg and Ysien's watchful eyes. I watched through my dragon's eyesight, which was quite unlike how I viewed the world in my other body. Colors reflected differently, and I was far more sensitive to movement in a vertical plane.

I'd had my turn at battle strategy and was picking up pointers I'd missed in the heat of things when I was in the air. The wonder of my dragon form hadn't quite percolated through all the layers of my heart and soul. But I was getting there. For some reason, I'd assumed shifters had dual personalities, but it didn't hold true for the three of us. We were the same "person," regardless of whether we had wings and scales or not.

We were nearly ready to leave Fire Mountain. For several reasons.

The most important was we had a lot to do back in the Nine Worlds. While the dragons paid lip service to us having responsibilities outside their domain, they were doing their damnedest to ensure we remained. It had more to do with Geir than Rowan—er, Runa—and me, but our hosts had been closemouthed when I'd asked why they'd referred to our son as a prince.

Nidhogg clapped his forelegs together, talons clanking like chains. "Ye've done well."

My mate and son swooped around the oblong arena, playing with each other. Geir had been enthralled by our dragon forms, and we'd indulged him by shifting often. He was still growing fast and was about half Ysien's size.

Nidhogg and Ysien glided to where I stood. It was a dragon maneuver where they extended their wings for balance and lift, but were still mostly walking. "There will be a special meeting in the council room," Ysien told me.

"You expect us to be there?" I furled my scaled brows.

"Aye. Why else would we tell you about it?"

To avoid blowing ash in his face, I summoned shift magic. I'd never warmed to Ysien. His patronizing attitude still made me want to punch him. The punching equivalent for a dragon was raining ash and smoke over whatever was closest. I still had difficulty controlling what emerged from my mouth, and I didn't want to anger him.

Like all of us, Ysien was who he was, spines and all. Nidhogg relied on him, and he was intensely loyal to dragonkind. After dealing with Loki, I'd lowered my standards and been more accepting of Ysien and a few others who rubbed me the wrong way. At least, I was trying. They might be highhanded and annoying, but dealing with them was trivial compared with Loki or Ceridwen or Cadir.

My body finished rearranging itself. Shifting came easy after my initial batch of failures. I nodded at the blue dragon. "Thank you for including us."

"Ye're quite welcome," Nidhogg inclined his head in return. "Consider leaving Geir with us while ye check on the Nine Worlds." I opened my mouth, but he was quick to add, "Consider it. There are many advantages."

"I'm certain there are," I replied. "Runa and I have talked it over. Our place is in the Nine Worlds. We will visit here, of course, but our homes are in Midgard and Vanaheim."

"Yours, perhaps." Ysien spewed ash off to one side. "But Geir belongs here. In Fire Mountain."

I looked dead at both dragons. "Nay. His place is with his mother and me. What time is this special meeting?"

"Now." Nidhogg did not sound pleased, and I'd become skilled at reading him.

"We will be there," I said, grateful when both he and Ysien teleported out of the arena.

I motioned to Runa and Geir—no reason not to use her dragon name here in Fire Mountain. It made the dragons happy and didn't put her at risk. My mate and son floated down next to me. Runa shifted, and it gave me an idea.

"Geir. How about if you shift?"

"Why?" He tossed his head back.

I drew a power circle around the three of us and draped

it in warding. It wouldn't keep Nidhogg from eavesdropping, but it would make him work harder. "There is a special council meeting," I told my family.

"When?" Runa raised a russet brow.

"Right now. The dragons will make another pitch for Geir to remain with them."

"I'm going with you," Geir said. "I don't care what they want."

"You will hold your tongue at this meeting," I said. "And it would help if you wore your human form. They think of you as one of them. You are, but you have another face, and this would be a good time to show it."

"We'll need something for him to wear." Runa narrowed her eyes. "A quick stop by our room should yield trousers and a shirt. Bet he'll fit into your stuff."

"He might," I said and focused on Geir. "What about it?"

The air around him glistened with his particular blend of power. It was similar to what Runa and I achieved with our mingled magics. When the light cleared, he was human. At least in form. His blond hair hit him midback, and he might have been a youth in his late teenaged years. Well-shaped muscles spanned his lanky frame.

He shook himself from head to toe. "Feels weird," he muttered.

"Of course it does," Runa told him. "Just like being dragons feels odd to your da and me. While we're about it, I'm not especially warming to hearing myself called Runa. It might be my 'true name,' but I get this big, fat disconnect when someone calls me by it."

"Once we return to the Nine Worlds, you can be whomever you'd like," I said. "Come on. We should hurry."

Courtesy of a couple of fast teleport spells, we were walking into the dragons' council chambers a scant handful of minutes later. My breeches and shirt more or less fit Geir. At least, he wasn't buck naked. I hesitated beneath the arched entry as I searched for an unobtrusive spot where we could stand.

"Walk to the front," Nidhogg boomed.

Damn. My instincts had been spot on. This "special" meeting was aimed at Geir. The dragons were determined to hold him here, but I was equally determined to leave. Fire Mountain might be the ancestral home of my dragon side, yet it wasn't the home I sought. Nor was it where I wished my son to grow up.

I placed Geir between Runa and me. We joined hands and walked the length of the ridiculously large chamber that was jampacked with dragons. Steam puffed from hundreds of jaws until the mist hovered so thickly I could barely see a few meters ahead.

When we finally reached the dais, I guided us off to one side.

"Your place is here." Nidhogg pointed to an open spot between himself and Dewi. The other elders stood behind them.

"We're good where we are, thanks." Runa smiled brightly.

I half expected to see Odin or Hel, but everyone in the room besides us were dragons.

"I said—" Nidhogg began.

Dewi motioned him to silence. "As they will," she told him, punctuated by a blast of telepathy that bypassed me.

The twin blind seers shuffled forward. "We will share a vision," one said.

Amid a chorus of bugles, the second one raised his forelegs. Unlike the other dragons whose talons were red, his were milky just like his eyes. "Quiet. And then I shall begin."

I shielded my thoughts. The roomful of dragons reminded me of a bunch of children settling in to listen to a bedtime story. Eager and focused, they stopped talking among themselves.

"Deep within our beginnings, while we gloried in the wonder of being dragons, our elders cautioned us we could command still greater magic. Most of us dinna believe such was true. After all, dragons are the most powerful magical beings in all worlds."

Bugles and trumpets raced through the chamber. The blind seer waited, his jaws lolling in a satisfied smile. Once the crowd quieted, the other seer picked up the tale. "Over eons, we lost sight we could be more than we are until the Breaking. It opened our eyes not just to treachery within the Nine Worlds, but to Cadir's half-dragon spawn and her...potential."

"Thanks for keeping me in the dark so long," Runa mumbled, obviously not caring the dragons would hear.

The seer nearest us turned his sightless gaze our way. "Remember when I answered one of your questions? Told you that ye command the full spectrum of power. All four elements. All four seasons. All the strength of both the

Norse and Celtic pantheons. With dragon magic to season the mix."

I nodded. Runa did too.

The seer angled his head to one side. "Your son holds every magical element that I listed within him. He is the future of dragonkind. He embodies our greater magic, our potential."

Whoops and bugles rose to a deafening pitch.

I caught Runa's gaze out of the corner of one eye and saw her shake her head. I agreed. I'd fight to the death to avoid the dragons transforming Geir into a symbol for some new breed of wyrm.

Prince, my ass. They'd turn him into a stud horse.

A green female hustled from the far side of the room. I smelled pheromones long before she reached us and stepped in front of my son. "Just once," she smiled enticingly. "What harm could it do?"

Calls of, "I want him too," reached me.

Geir had shrunk back against Runa, but he straightened and strode purposefully to the empty spot between Nidhogg and Dewi, giving the hussy dragon a wide breach. I shooed her away. She might have approached us, but I was banking on her not spreading her misplaced lust any nearer Nidhogg, Dewi, or the elder council arrayed behind them.

"Quiet!" Nidhogg thundered. "Our prince would speak with us."

I watched Geir's face, hunting for clues. Had them labeling him "prince" stoked his young ego? Would he fall into line, accept the dragons' plans for him? Was I being selfish by wanting him to remain with us? Runa gripped my hand. "Believe in him," she said near my ear.

Geir stood straight and clasped his hands behind him. "Thank you for giving us a chamber and food. Thank all of you who fought to secure the outer borderworlds." He scrunched his eyes closed for a moment.

When he opened them, he went on, "While I appreciate the, um, honor you've offered me, I am not your prince. I shall remain with my parents."

"For now, perhaps." Nidhogg's tone was silk and compulsion. "But surely, once ye've had time to realize how much ye miss Fire Mountain, ye'll return to us."

"I have no idea what my future holds," Geir said in clear, ringing tones. "I am still very young. It will take a long time for me to figure things out. To be honest, being responsible for anyone's future except my own doesn't sound very appealing."

Pride for my son swelled through me. He'd had very little in the way of direction from Runa and me, but he had good instincts. Before the dragons could engage him with further inducements, he hurried back to my side.

"Good time to leave," Runa murmured.

"Never been better," Geir agreed.

Caught between wanting to be gone ten minutes ago and a need to at least pay lip service to the manners cherished by dragonkind, I said, "Get a spell going. I'll be ready soon."

Moving midway between where I'd been standing and the dais, I bowed. "I second my son's thanks for your hospitality, but we have overstayed our welcome. We shall stop by and visit from time to time, but we have much work ahead of us. The Nine Worlds will not knit back together without help. And I am still their Master Sorcerer."

I stood tall and waited. Would Nidhogg order me to remain? I didn't think he had that level of authority, but neither did I want to end up in the position of being insubordinate.

Better not to burn bridges.

Nidhogg—my father—snared me in his hypnotic gaze. I stared back, waiting, but I wouldn't wait forever. Perhaps he knew as much because he finally nodded. "I will see you in the Nine Worlds. Ye and your mate and my grandson."

"I will look forward to it."

"Ye canna let them leave," one of the seers protested.

"We are not their jailers," Dewi said in a pointed tone, followed by, "and I shall see you when ye stop by Inverlochy Castle."

It was good enough for me. I made my way to the magic bubbling around my mate and my son. As soon as I got near enough, it whisked us into a dragon journey spell. "Nice work," I said once we were headed toward Midgard.

"Some things about commanding dragon magic are quite useful." Runa grinned.

"Did I do the right thing?" Geir looked from his mother to me.

I started to say yes. Instead I turned his question back at him. "Did you do what felt right to you? What was in your heart?"

"I did," Geir replied.

"Then it was the right thing," Runa reassured him.

"I don't know where I fit," Geir went on. "I'm not like them, but I'm not like you, either."

I wrapped an arm around his shoulders. "You'll figure it out."

"We all pass through a sticky spot like that," Runa told him. "For me, it lasted until I found the witches and they taught me whoever I was was all right."

"How old were you?" Geir trained his eyes on his mother.

"Way older than you," she retorted.

Speaking of witches, I sensed the markers in her journey spell. "Headed for Ben Nevis, are we?"

"Is that all right?" She furled her brows.

"More than all right," I replied. "After two weeks of dragons, I'm not ready to face the Celts or Odin and Asgard quite yet." I wasn't exactly keen to pick up the reins of my sorcery practice, either. I'd do it, but a break would be welcome.

"Know what you mean." Runa's generous mouth split into a smile. "They always want something. With the witches, we can just be ourselves."

"Ourselves," Geir echoed.

We chatted of this and that as we crossed the distance between Fire Mountain and the Nine Worlds. This and that being various applications of magic and what might work best in a particular situation. Not a usual conversation in most families, but a necessary one in ours.

"How long do you think it will take to clear out the rest of the goblins and trolls and whatever else got stuck in the Nine Worlds?" Runa asked.

"No idea. It will take as long as it does," I told her. Privately, I figured decades would pass before we finished our cleanup work. If we ever did. Evil was ubiquitous. Eradicating it beyond a certain point wasn't practical. And then there was the niggling issue of the Morrigan, Ceridwen, and Loki. I figured the shrouding we'd fashioned would hold the trickster for a while, but not forever.

I doubted Odin would have the stomach to keep him locked away when the shroud's magic faded.

"Did the Morrigan kill all the vampires?" Geir asked.

"Probably not," Runa told him. "Plenty of vamps on Midgard."

"I figured out what she did," our son announced. "Easier than cutting off their heads."

"You can teach us." Runa rested a hand on his shoulder.

I patted the collection of enchanted steel hanging off my body. I'd be glad to tuck the blades away in a cupboard in my cottage on Vanaheim. At least the longsword Runa carried had come in handy.

"Almost there," she said.

Sure enough, a portal formed, and we tumbled onto the familiar packed-dirt courtyard in front of the Ben Nevis cave system. From long habit, I scanned the area for threats but didn't find any.

Runa's nostrils twitched, and she inhaled. "Home. It smells like home."

"It smells earthy and welcoming, like Midgard," I said. The dry, hot air on Fire Mountain wasn't nearly as annoying as it had been my first trip there, but its sameness had grown old. The climate on the dragons' world never changed. I shrugged. I appreciated my dragon-nature, but it would never displace the rest of me.

Welcoming shouts reached me, following by pounding feet. Tansy burst from the caves first, followed by Patrick and Hilda. "Ro! You're back," she cried. Mort shot between their flying feet and launched himself into Runa's arms, yowling like a mad thing.

When I looked at Geir, he was smiling. Perhaps he felt the rightness of being here too. Or maybe he was smiling at Tansy since she'd latched a hand around his arm and was chattering a mile a minute.

"Tell us everything," Patrick said once he left off wringing first my hand and then Runa's.

"Rowan! We've missed you," Hilda squealed and hugged her tight, squishing the cat between them.

"I've missed you too, and it's so good to be Rowan again. Just plain Rowan." My mate's golden eyes shone with joy.

The other witches piled into the courtyard. "I'm guessing it's safe enough to be out here," Leif said gruffly.

"It is," I told him. "We sealed the breach. It's the beginning of healing for the Nine Worlds."

Patrick drew his gray brows together. "Aye. Beginning nails it. We have a long road ahead, and Earth will never totally recover."

"It won't be the same," I agreed, "but the humans will be able to start rebuilding. After a time, we'll be rid of most of the evil that's been stalking Midgard."

"Most," Hilda said, "but not all. We had trolls and goblins before the Breaking."

"Aye, but a manageable number," Leif said. "The other

things, the puffed-up bats and snakes and other weirdnesses, they're gone. Right?"

"They will be," I said. "Sealing the holes in the barrier keeping the outer borderworlds separate might mean they'll wither naturally."

"Say more about that," Patrick urged.

"If they required an infusion of energy from their home world, it's been cut off," I clarified.

Mort had switched from yowls to purring. He was curled around Rowan's neck in his preferred spot. Tansy and Geir were still talking. She'd be good for him, teach him more about his human side than Rowan and I put together could.

The courtyard had filled with witches. Everyone wanted to touch us, hug us, offer thanks for the work we'd done to patch up Earth's broken places. For the first time in a long time, I allowed myself to relax. We'd earned this respite. All of us.

After a while, we followed the witches inside to their common room for a meal and mead. We being Rowan, Geir, me, and Mort. I threaded an arm around Rowan. "You look happy."

"I am. If I had my druthers, we'd never leave here, but it's not practical."

Pulling her off to one side, I let the witches flow around us and waved Geir and Tansy to go ahead and find seats in the common room.

"Enjoy today," I told Rowan. "None of the rest of it is going anywhere, and worrying about what lies ahead will only drag you down."

A corner of her mouth twitched into half a smile. "Have I told you lately how much I love you?"

"Yes, but I never tire of hearing it."

"I love you, Bjorn Nighthorse. The goddess was smiling on me when I stopped being bitchy long enough to let you into my life."

Instead of answering, I closed my mouth over hers and kissed her soundly. We'd find our way to the common room eventually. Later, much later, we'd locate an empty chamber for Geir. I had plans for my mate once we finally had some alone time.

She broke away from our kiss. "Plans, eh? I like the sound of that."

"Wench. You're spying on my thoughts again."

"Guilty as charged." She batted her eyes my way and smiled.

"You'll like the reality even better. When my plans move from thought to execution."

"Promise?" She laughed, rich, warm, seductive.

I laughed too. "Stop it. The witches are making a special meal for us. If you keep that up, I'll back you against a wall, build a ward around us, and ravish you."

She pressed the rounded peaks of her breasts into my chest. "You're tempting me. Food takes a while. We could be done before it is."

What can I say? I'm a man. We're weak, and sharing a room with our son in Fire Mountain had a definite dampening effect on anything amorous. Rowan grabbed my arm and practically dragged me to the far side of a doorway I hadn't noticed. A dusty pallet lay on the floor. I'm surprised I had the presence of mind to spell the door shut before I gathered her into my arms, made a few clothing adjustments, and sank my length inside the wonders of her body.

You've reached the end of the Dragon Heir series. Thanks so much for reading through to the end. Please take a few moments and leave a review for *Dragon's Heir*. They mean so much to authors. Doesn't have to be fancy. A few lines will do it. Thanks in advance!

If you enjoyed this dystopian fantasy, you might like my Dragon Lore books. A sample from *To Love a Highland Dragon*, second of that series follows. Why not the first, you might ask. At one point it was the first book of Dragon Lore, but then I wrote a prequel titled, *Highland Secrets*. All the books in that series can be read as standalones, and I believe they'll delight you and provide hours of reading enjoyment.

BOOK DESCRIPTION, TO LOVE A HIGHLAND DRAGON

A dragon shifter stirs and wakens in a cave beneath Inverness, deep in the Scottish Highlands. The cave's the same and his hoard intact, yet something's badly amiss. Determined to set whatever's gone wrong to rights, Lachlan Moncrieffe ventures above ground—and wishes he hadn't. His castle's gone, replaced by ungainly row houses. Men aren't wearing plaids, and women scarcely wear anything at all, particularly the woman who accosts him with unseemly banter. What manner of wench is she to dress so provocatively?

In Inverness for a year on a psychiatry fellowship, Dr. Maggie Hibbins watches an oddly dressed man pick his way out of a heather and gorse thicket. Even though it runs counter to her better judgment, she teases him about his strange attire. He looks so lost—and so unbelievably, knock-out gorgeous—she takes a chance and stands him a meal.

Lachlan's shock when he picks up a local newspaper at a pub is so palpable, Maggie jumps in with both feet.

She knew something was off, but the hard-to-accept truth bashes gaping holes in her equilibrium. He looks odd, sounds odd, acts odd because he's a refugee from another era. Her half-baked seduction scheme takes a hike, but her carefully constructed life is still about to change forever. Born of powerful witches, Maggie runs headlong into the myth and magic that are her birthright.

TO LOVE A HIGHLAND DRAGON, CHAPTER ONE

Kheladin listened to the rush of blood as his multi-chambered heart pumped. After eons of nothingness, the unexpected sound surprised him. A cool, sandy floor pressed against his scaled haunches. One whirling eye flickered open, followed by the other.

Where am I?

He peered at his surroundings and blew out a sigh, followed by steam, smoke, and fire.

Thanks be to Dewi—Kheladin invoked the blood-red Celtic dragon goddess—*I'm still in my cave. It smelled right, but I wasna certain.*

He rotated his serpent's head atop his long, sinuous neck. Vertebrae cracked. Kheladin lowered his head and scanned the place he and Lachlan, his human bondmate, had barricaded themselves into. It might've only been days ago, but somehow, it didn't seem like days, or even months or a few years. His body felt rusty, as if he hadn't used it in centuries.

How long did I sleep?

He shook his head. Copper scales flew everywhere, clanking against a pile littered around him. More than anything, the glittery heap reinforced his belief he'd been asleep for a very long time. Dragons shed their scales annually. From the amount circling his body, he'd gone through hundreds of molt cycles. But how? The last thing he remembered was retreating to his cave far beneath Lachlan's castle and working with the mage to construct strong wards.

Had the black wyvern grown powerful enough to force his magic into the very heart of Kheladin's fortress?

If that's true—if we really were his prisoner, why'd I finally waken? Is Lachlan still within me?

Stop! I have to take things one at a time.

He returned his gaze to the nooks and crannies of his spacious cave. He'd have to take inventory, but it appeared his treasure hadn't been disturbed. Kheladin blew a plume of steam upward, followed by an experimental gout of fire. The black wyvern, his sworn enemy since before the Crusades, may have bested him, but he hadn't gotten his slimy talons on any of Kheladin's gold or jewels.

He shook out his back feet and shuffled to the pool at one end of the cave where he dipped his snout and drank deeply. The water didn't taste right. It wasn't poisoned, but it held an undercurrent of metals that had never been there before. Kheladin rolled the liquid around in his mouth. He didn't recognize much of what he tasted, but he was thirsty and it seemed safe enough, so he drank some more.

The flavors aren't familiar because I've been asleep for so long. Aye, that must be it. Part of his mind recoiled; he suspected he was deluding himself.

"We're awake." Lachlan's voice hummed in the dragon's mind.

"Aye, that we are."

"How long did we sleep?"

"I doona know." Water streamed down the dragon's snout and neck. He knew what would come next, and he didn't have to wait long.

"Let's shift. We think better in my body." Lachlan urged Kheladin to cede ascendency.

"I doona agree." Kheladin pushed back. *"I was figuring things out afore ye woke."*

"Aye, I'm certain ye were, but..." But what? *"Och aye, my brain is thick and fuzzy, as if I havena used it for a verra long time."*

"Mine feels the same."

The bond allowed only one form at a time. Since they were in Kheladin's body, he had the upper hand. Lachlan wasn't strong enough to force a shift without his help. There'd been a time when he could have but not now.

Was it safe to venture above ground?

Kheladin recalled the last day he'd seen the sun. After a vicious battle in the great room of Lachlan's castle, they'd retreated to his cave and taken their dragon form as a final resort. Rhukon, the black wyvern, pretended he wanted peace. He'd come with an envoy that turned out to be a retinue of heavily armed men.

Both he and Lachlan expected Rhukon to follow them underground. Kheladin's last thought, before nothingness descended, was disbelief because their enemy hadn't pursued them.

Humph. He did *come after us but with magic. Magic strong enough to penetrate our wards.*

"Aye, and I was thinking the same thing," Lachlan sniped in a vexed tone.

"We trusted him," Kheladin snarled. *"More the fools we were. We should've known."* Despite drinking, his throat was still raw. He sucked more water down and fought rising anger at himself for being gullible. Even if Lachlan hadn't known better, he should've. His stomach cramped from hunger.

Kheladin debated the wisdom of making his way through the warren of tunnels leading to the surface in dragon form. There were always far more humans than dragons. Mayhap it would be wiser to accede to Lachlan's wishes before they crept from their underground lair to rejoin the world of men.

"Grand idea." Lachlan's response was instantaneous, as was his first stab at shifting.

It took half a dozen attempts. Kheladin was far weaker than he imagined and Lachlan so feeble he was almost an impediment. Finally, once a shower of scales cleared, Lachlan's emaciated body stood barefoot and naked in the cave.

Lacking the sharp night vision he enjoyed as a dragon,

because his magic was so diminished, Lachlan kindled a mage light and glanced down at himself. Ribs pressed against his flesh, and a full beard extended halfway down his chest. Turning his head to both sides, he saw shoulder blades so sharp he was surprised they didn't puncture his skin. Tawny hair fell in tangles past his waist. The only thing he couldn't see was his eyes. Absent a glass, he was certain they were the same crystal-clear emerald color they'd always been.

He stumbled across the cave to a chest where he kept clothing. Dragons didn't need such silly accoutrements; humans did. He sucked in a harsh breath. The wooden chest was falling to ruin. He tilted the lid against a wall, but it canted to one side. Many of his clothes had moldered into unusable rags, but items toward the bottom fared better. He found a cream-colored linen shirt with long, flowing sleeves, a black and green plaid embroidered with the insignia of his house—a dragon in flight—and soft, deerskin boots that laced to his knees.

He slid the shirt over his head and wrapped the plaid around himself, taking care to wind the tartan so its telltale insignia was hidden in its folds. Who knew if the black wyvern—or his agents—lurked near the mouth of the cave? Lachlan bent to lace his boots. A crimson cloak with only a few moth holes completed his outfit. He finger-combed his hair and smoothed his unruly beard.

"Good God, but I must look a fright," he muttered. "Mayhap I can sneak into the castle and set things aright afore anyone sees me. Surely my kinsmen will be glad the master of the house has finally returned."

Lachlan worked on bolstering a confidence he was far

from feeling. He'd nearly made it to the end of the cave, where a rock-strewn path led upward, when he doubled back to get a sword and scabbard—just in case things weren't as sanguine as he hoped. He located a thigh sheath and a short dagger as well, fumbling to attach them beneath his kilt. Underway once again, he hadn't made it very far along the upward-sloping tunnel that ended at a well-hidden opening not far from the postern gate of his castle, when he ran into rocks littering the way.

He worked his way around progressively larger boulders until he came to a huge one that totally blocked the passageway. Lachlan stared at it in disbelief. When had that happened? In all the time he'd been using these paths, they'd never been blocked by rock fall. If he weren't so weak, summoning magic to shove the rock over enough to allow him to pass wouldn't be a problem. As it was, simply walking uphill proved a challenge.

He pinched the bridge of his nose between a grimy thumb and forefinger. His mage light weakened.

If I can't even keep a light going, how in the goddess's name will I be able to move that rock?

Lachlan hunkered next to the boulder and let his light die while he ran possibilities through his head. His stomach growled and clenched in hunger. Had he come through however much time had passed to cower like a dog in his own cave?

"No, by God." He slammed a fist against the boulder, and it went right on through. The air sizzled. Magic. The rock was illusion. Not real.

Counter spell. I need a counter spell.

Mayhap not.

He stood and took a deep breath before walking into the huge rock. The air did more than sizzle. It flamed. If he'd been human, it would've burned him to ashes, but dragons were impervious to fire, as were dragon shifters. Lachlan waltzed through the rock, cursing Rhukon as he went. Five more boulders blocked his tunnel, each more charged with magic than the last.

Finally, sweating and cursing, he rounded the last curve, and the air ahead grew brighter. He wanted to throw himself on the ground and screech his triumph.

Not a good idea.

"Let me out. Ye have no idea what we'll find."

Kheladin's voice in his mind was welcome but the idea wasn't. *"Ye're right. Because we have no idea what's out there, we stay in my skin until we're certain. We can hide in this form far more easily than we can in yours."*

"Since when did we take to hiding?" The dragon sounded outraged.

"Our magic is weak." Lachlan adopted a placating tone. *"'Tis prudent to be cautious until it fully recovers."*

"No dragon would ever say such a thing." Deep, fiery frustration rolled off Kheladin.

Steam belched from Lachlan's mouth. *"Stop that,"* he hissed, but his mind voice was all but obliterated by wry dragon laughter.

"Why? I find it amusing ye think an eight foot tall dragon with elegant copper scales and handsome, green eyes would be difficult to sequester." Kheladin paused a beat. *"And*

infuriating we need to conceal ourselves at all. Need I remind you we're warriors?"

"Of course we're warriors," Lachlan said affably, sidestepping the issue of hiding. He didn't want to risk being goaded into something unwise. Kheladin chuckled and pushed more steam through Lachlan's mouth, punctuated by a few flames.

Lost in a sudden rush of memories, Lachlan slowed his pace. As a mage, he would've lived hundreds of years, but bonded to a dragon, he'd live forever. In preparation, he'd studied long years with Aether, a wizard and dragon shifter himself. Along the way, Lachlan forsook much—a wife and bairns, for starters, for what woman would put up with a husband so rarely at home?—to bond with a dragon, forming their partnership. Once Lachlan's magic was finally strong enough, there'd been the niggling problem of locating that special dragon willing to join its life with his.

Because the bond conferred immortality on both the dragon and their human partner, dragons were notoriously picky. After all, dragon and mage would be welded through eternity. The magic could be undone, but the price was high. Mages were stripped of power, and their dragon mates lost much of theirs too, as the bond unraveled. Rumor suggested that mages who became dragon-less risked madness—an additional stumbling block and strong incentive to choose wisely.

Lachlan hunted for over a hundred years before finding Kheladin. The pairing was instantaneous on both sides. He'd just settled in with his dragon, and was about to chase down a wife to grace his castle, when the black wyvern attacked.

Rhukon had approached Kheladin long before Lachlan did, but the dragon rejected the bond, spawning long-standing animosity. That Rhukon finally acquired a dragon of his own hadn't lessened his ill will one whit.

"What are ye waiting for?" Kheladin sounded testy. *"Daydreaming is a worthless pursuit. My grandmother is two thousand years old, and she moves faster than you."*

Lachlan snorted. He didn't bother to explain there wasn't much point in jumping right into Rhukon's arms through the opening in the gorse and thistle bushes growing at the mouth of the cave. An unusual whirring filled the air, like the noisiest beehive he'd ever heard. His heart sped up, but the sound receded.

"What in the nine hells was that?" he muttered and made his way closer to the world outside Kheladin's cave.

Lachlan shoved some overgrown bushes out of the way and peered through. What he saw was so unbelievable, he squeezed his eyes shut tight before opening them and looking again. Unfortunately, nothing had changed. Worse, an ungainly, shiny cylinder roared past, making the same whirring noise he'd puzzled over moments before. He fell backward into the cave, breath harsh in his throat, and landed on his rump.

Lachlan shook his head and balled his hands into fists. Frustration and disbelief battered him, making him wonder if he'd died only to waken in Hell. Not only was the postern gate no longer there, neither was his castle. A long, unattractive row of attached structures stood in its stead.

"Holy godhead. What do we do now?"

"Go out there and hunt down something to eat," the dragon growled.

Lachlan gritted his teeth until his jaw ached. Kheladin had a good point. It was hard to think on an empty stomach.

"Here I was worried about Rhukon. At least I understood him. I fear whatever lies in wait for us will require all our skill."

"Ye were never a coward. 'Tis why I allowed the bond. Get moving."

The dragon's words settled him. Ashamed of his indecisiveness, Lachlan got to his feet. He brushed dirt off his plaid and worked his way through bushes hiding the cave's entrance. As he untangled stickers from the finely spun wool of his cloak and his plaid, he gawked at a very different world from the one he'd left. There wasn't a field—or an animal—in sight. Roadways paved with something other than dirt and stones were punctuated by structures so numerous, they made him dizzy. The hideous incursion onto his lands stretched in every direction.

Lachlan curled his hands into fists again. He'd find out what had happened, by God. When he did, he'd make whoever erected all those abominations take them down.

An occasional person walked by in the distance. They shocked him even more than the buildings and roads. For starters, the males weren't wearing plaids, so there was no way to tell their clan. Females were immodestly covered. Many sported bare legs and breeks so tight he saw the separation between their ass cheeks. Lachlan's groin stirred, his cock hardening. Were the lassies no longer engaging in modesty or subterfuge and simply asking to be fucked? Or was this some new garb that befit a new era?

He detached the last thorn, finally clear of the thicket of sticker bushes. Where could he find a market with vendors? Did market day still exist in this strange environment?

"Holy crap! A kilt, and an old-fashioned one at that. Tad bit early in the day for a costume ball, isn't it?" A rich female voice laced with amusement sounded behind him.

Lachlan spun with his hands raised to call magic. He stopped dead once his gaze settled on a lass nearly as tall as himself, which meant she was close to six feet. She turned so she faced him squarely. Bare legs emerged from torn fabric that stopped just south of her female parts. Full breasts strained against scraps of material attached to strings tied around her neck and back. Her feet were encased in a few straps of leather. Long, blonde hair eddied around her, the color of sheaves of summer wheat.

His cock jumped to attention. He itched to make a grab for her breasts or her ass. She had an amazing ass: round and high and tight. What was expected of him? The lass was dressed in such a way as to invite him to simply tear what passed for breeks aside and enter her. Had the world changed so drastically that women provoked men into public sex? He glanced about, half expecting to see couples having it off with one another willy-nilly.

"Well," she urged. "Cat got your tongue?" She placed her hands on her hips. The motion stretched the tiny bits of flowered fabric that barely covered her nipples still further.

Lachlan bowed formally. He straightened and waited for her to hold out a hand for him to kiss. "I'm Lachlan

Moncrieffe, Laird of Clan Moncrieffe, my lady. 'Tis a pleasure to—"

She erupted into laughter—and didn't hold out her hand. "I'm Maggie," she managed between gouts of mirth. "What are you? A throwback to medieval times? You can drop the Sir Galahad routine."

Lachlan felt his face heat. "I fear I doona understand the cause of your merriment...my lady."

Maggie rolled midnight blue eyes. "Oh, brother. Did you escape from a mental hospital? Nah, you'd be in pajamas then, not those fancy duds." She dropped her hands to her sides and started to walk past him.

"No. Wait. Please, wait." Lachlan cringed at the whining tone in his voice. The dragon was correct that the Moncrieffe was a proud house. They bowed to no one.

She eyed him askance. "What?"

"I'm a stranger in this town." He winced at the lie. Once upon a time, he'd been master of these lands. Apparently that time had long since passed. "I'm footsore and hungry. Where might I find victuals and ale?"

Her eyes widened. Finely arched blonde brows drew together over a straight nose dotted by a few freckles. "Victuals and ale," she repeated disbelievingly.

"Aye. Food and drink, in the common vernacular."

"Oh, I understood you well enough," Maggie murmured. "Your words, anyway. Your accent's a bit off."

His stomach growled again, embarrassingly loud.

"Guess you weren't kidding about being hungry." She eyed him appraisingly. "Do you have any money?"

Money. Too late he thought of the piles of gold coins and

priceless gems lying on the floor of Kheladin's cave. In the world he'd left, his word was as good as his gold. He opened his mouth, but she waved him to silence. "I'll stand you for a pint and some fish and chips. You can treat me next time."

He heard her mutter, "Yeah right," under her breath as she curled a hand around his arm and tugged. "Come on. I have a couple hours, and then I've got to go to work. I'm due in at three today."

Lachlan trotted along next to her. She let go of him like he was a viper when he tried to close a hand over the one she'd laid so casually on his person. He cleared his throat and wondered what he could safely ask that wouldn't give his secrets away. He could scarcely believe this alien landscape was Scotland, but if he asked what country they were in, or what year it was, she'd think him mad.

Had the black wyvern used some diabolical dark magic to transport Kheladin's cave to another locale? Probably not. Even Rhukon wasn't that powerful.

"In here." She pointed to a door beneath a flashing sigil.

He gawked at it. One minute it was red, the next blue, the next green, illuminating the word *Open*. What manner of magic was this?

"Don't tell me you have temporal lobe epilepsy." She stared at him. "It's only a neon sign. It doesn't bite. Move through the door. There's food on the other side," she added slyly.

Feeling like a rube, Lachlan searched for a latch. When he didn't find one, he pushed his shoulder against the door. It opened, and he held it with a hand so Maggie could enter first. "After you, my lady," he murmured.

"Stop that." She directed the words toward his ear as she went past. "No more *my ladies*. Got it?"

"Aye. Got it." He followed her into a low ceilinged room lined with wooden planks. It was the first thing that looked familiar. Parts of it, anyway. Men—kilt-less men—sat at the bar, hefting glasses and chatting. The tables were empty.

"What'll it be, Mags?" a man with a towel tied around his waist called from behind the bar.

"Couple of pints and two of today's special. Come to think of it..." She eyed Lachlan so intently it made him squirm. "Make that three of the special."

"May I inquire what the special is?" Lachlan asked, thinking he might want to order something different.

Maggie waved a hand at a black board suspended over the bar. "It's right there. If you can't read it—"

"Of course, I can read." He resented the inference he might be uneducated but swallowed back harsh words.

"Excellent. Then move."

She shoved her body into his in a distressingly familiar way for such a communal location. Not that he wouldn't have enjoyed the contact if they were alone, and he were free to take advantage of it.

"All the way to the back," she hissed into his ear. "That way if you slip up, no one will hear."

He bristled. Lachlan Moncrieffe did *not* sit in the back of any establishment. He was always given a choice table near the center of things. He opened his mouth to protest but thought better of it.

She scooped an armful of flattened scrolls off the bar before following him to the back of the room. Once there, she dumped them on the table between them. He wanted to ask what they were but decided he should pretend to know. He turned the top sheaf of papers toward him and scanned the close-spaced print. Many of the words were unfamiliar, but what leapt off the page was *The Inverness Courier* and presumably the current date: June 10, 2012.

His heart thudded in his ears, deafening him with the roar of rushing blood, as he stared at the date.

It had been 1683 when Rhukon chivied him into the dragon's cave. Three hundred twenty-nine years ago, give or take a month or two. At least he was still in Inverness—for all the good it did him.

"You look as if you just saw a ghost." Maggie spoke quietly.

"Nay. I'm quite fine. Thank you for inquiring...my, er..." Lachlan shut up. Anything he said was bound to be wrong.

"Good." She nodded approvingly. "You're learning." The bartender slapped two mugs of ale on the scarred wooden table.

"On your tab, Mags?" he asked.

She nodded. "Except you owe me so much, you'll never catch up."

Still shell-shocked by the realization hundreds of years had slipped past while he and Kheladin slept, Lachlan took a sip of what turned out to be weak ale. It wasn't half bad but could've stood an infusion of bitters. Because it was easier than thinking about his problems, he puzzled over what Maggie meant about the barkeep *owing her so much he'd never catch up*. Why would the barkeep owe her? His nostrils flared. She must work for the establishment—

probably as a damsel of ill repute from the looks of her. Mayhap, she hadn't been paid her share of whatever she earned in quite some time.

Protectiveness flared deep inside him. Maggie shouldn't have to earn her way lying on her back. He'd see to it she had a more seemly position.

Aye, once I find my way around this bizarre new world.

Money wouldn't be a problem, but changing three-hundred-year-old gold coins into today's tender might prove challenging. Surely banks existed that could accomplish something like that.

One thing at a time.

"So." She skewered him with her blue gaze—Norse eyes if he'd ever seen a set—and took a sip from her mug. "What did you see in the newspaper that upset you so much?"

"Nothing." He tried for an offhand tone.

"Bullshit," she said succinctly. "I'm a doctor. A psychiatrist. I read people's faces quite well, and you look as if you're perilously close to going into shock."

Keep right on reading. Click here for buy links from all vendors including e-book, paperback, and audio.

ABOUT THE AUTHOR

Ann Gimpel is a USA Today bestselling author. A lifelong aficionado of the unusual, she began writing speculative fiction a few years ago. Since then her short fiction has appeared in many webzines and anthologies. Her longer books run the gamut from urban fantasy to paranormal romance. Once upon a time, she nurtured clients. Now she nurtures dark, gritty fantasy stories that push hard against reality. When she's not writing, she's in the backcountry getting down and dirty with her camera. She's published over 70 books to date, with several more planned for 2019 and beyond. A husband, grown children, grandchildren, and wolf hybrids round out her family.

Keep up with her at www.anngimpel.com or http://anngimpel.blogspot.com

If you enjoyed what you read, get in line for special offers and pre-release special reads. Newsletter Signup!

ALSO BY ANN GIMPEL

SERIES

Alphas in the Wild

Hello Darkness

Alpine Attraction

A Run for Her Money

Fire Moon

Bitter Harvest

Deceived

Twisted

Abandoned

Betrayed

Redeemed

Coven Enforcers

Blood and Magic

Blood and Sorcery

Blood and Illusion

Demon Assassins

Witch's Bounty

Witch's Bane

Witches Rule

Dragon Heir (Summer and fall, 2019)

Dragon's Call

Dragon's Blood

Dragon's Heir

Dragon Lore

Highland Secrets

To Love a Highland Dragon

Dragon Maid

Dragon's Dare

Dragon Fury

Earth Reclaimed

Earth's Requiem

Earth's Blood

Earth's Hope

Elemental Witch

Timespell

Time's Curse

Time's Hostage

GenTech Rebellion

Winning Glory

Honor Bound

Claiming Charity

Loving Hope

Keeping Faith

Ice Dragon

Feral Ice

Cursed Ice

Primal Ice

Rubicon International

Garen

Lars

Soul Dance

Tarnished Beginnings

Tarnished Legacy

Tarnished Prophecy

Tarnished Journey

Soul Storm

Dark Prophecy

Dark Pursuit

Dark Promise

Underground Heat

Roman's Gold

Wolf Born

Blood Bond

Wolf Clan Shifters

Alice's Alphas

Megan's Mates

Sophie's Shifters

Wylde Magick

Gemstone

Lion's Lair

Unbalanced

STANDALONE BOOKS

Branded, That Old Black Magic Romance (paranormal romance)

Edge of Night (short story collection, paranormal and horror)

Grit is a 4-Letter Word (nonfiction)

Heart's Flame (post-apocalyptic romance)

Icy Passage (science fiction romance)

Marked by Fortune (post-apocalyptic coming of age story)

Melis's Gambit (historical paranormal romance)

Midnight Magic (paranormal romance)

Red Dawn (post-apocalyptic paranormal romance)

Shadow Play (historical paranormal romance)

Shadows in Time (Highland time travel romance)

Since We Fell (contemporary romance)

Warin's War (paranormal romance)

www.ingramcontent.com/pod-product-compliance
Lightning Source LLC
Chambersburg PA
CBHW051007180726
48291CB00006B/2010

* 9 7 8 1 9 4 8 8 7 1 5 6 3 *